MW00324576

THE WINGED CHILD

HENRY MITCHELL

Copyright © 2021 by Henry Mitchell

All rights reserved. No part of this publication may be reproduced, distributed, or transmitted in any form or by any means, including photocopying, recording, or other electronic or mechanical methods, without the prior written permission of the publisher, except in the case of brief quotations embodied in critical reviews and certain other noncommercial uses provided by copyright law.

ISBN: paperback 978-1-7353926-3-9
Ebook 978-1-956183-91-7

Library of Congress Control Number: 2021943021

Any references to historical events, real people or real places are used factiously. Names, characters, and places are products of the author's imagination.

Cover Design by Diana TC, triumphcovers.com
Edited by Jean Lowd

First Printing Edition 2021

Published by Creative James Media

For Rosemary, who taught me how

PROLOGUE

Wendl woke from the dream, heart pounding, chest heaving, gasping for breath. His throat hurt, felt tight, as if a scream were caught in it. He lay still on his cot, allowing his body to settle, inviting his mind to return to him. He thought the dream might slip away into the night, but instead it rose up clear in his mind, every detail as sharp and vivid as if he'd lived it awake.

He dreamed he was walking. He'd been walking for a long time. His lantern flickered out hours before. Crickets rattled the dark around him. Gravel crunched under his sandals. Now and again as he walked, his foot caught against something that sounded like a wooden timber. From far away among unseen trees, a call and response between a pair of owls. If it was night, it was moonless, and when Wendl looked up, he saw no stars. The pervasive unlight narrowed his world down to himself.

It did not occur to Wendl in his dream that he should be afraid. He didn't even feel lost, alone in his dense dark, although if there had been anyone there to ask, he couldn't have told them his destination. He held his staff in front of him, like a pendulum, the lower end just a few inches above the ground, and swung it back and forth, like someone blind, for in the pitch blackness, he was precisely that. When the tip rang against something metal to his right, he veered slightly left, and when his stick encountered a similar obstacle on his left, he bore right. Wendl went on this way for some indeterminate time until the ground under him gradually began pulsing, like an echo of his own footfalls. Then he stopped, awaiting revelation.

The vibration swelled and gathered into an audible rumble. The darkness ahead paled into a gray fog, swallowing up the railbed where Wendl stood. The rails either side of him gleamed in the rising light, and the rumble gathered and grew into a deafening roar like the voice of a dragon. Wendl turned to behold the blinding and terrible eye bearing down upon him. He might have taken it for a dragon, but there were no dragons yet among the Fallen. It was only a train, and Wendl was standing in its way.

No time left to scream or run or even pray. Wendl closed his eyes and felt the monstrous steel thing shred his being awake again. It was a dream. He would not say it was only a dream, for Wendl knew the meaning of it. He opened his eyes and stared through the opening that served as window and door to his austere cell. No surprise to see the dense fog beyond, not quite black, but faintly luminescent, whether by its own light or from the moon filtering through from above, he couldn't tell. But the message was clear. Somewhere on the other side of the Separation, his way had opened.

Wendl dressed as quickly as he could in the cast-off clothes he had retrieved from the Fallen on previous incursions. He slung his bag, already packed and ready, across his shoulder, took his staff from beside the door on his way out. As he walked, the fog closed behind him, swallowing door and wall. As soon as he felt unseen by all eyes within the abbey, Wendl turned on edge, narrowing, flattening, opening a bright hairline crack against the gray, and folded himself into it.

As the fog thinned and lifted, Wendl saw that he was still walking along the railway, just as he had in his dream. The rails, crusted with rust, didn't gleam as the sun crested the ridge behind him. Ahead, several trees lay fallen across the tracks. Lifeless and leafless, they had obviously blocked the way for seasons past. No train had run these rails in a long time. He walked on, listening to the morning gather into birdsong and rustle. Somewhere out of sight beyond the next bend, a truck toiled, growling and groaning up a mountain highway. Far away, beyond the wooded ridge to his left, a chainsaw snarled and sputtered. Some forestworker needed to sharpen a saw chain, Wendl thought.

The track straightened, leveled as he went. The woods, steep and close upon either side, parted, revealing the village of Drovers Gap, just as he recalled it. A highway ran for a quarter-mile parallel to the railroad before it lifted on a bridge across the tracks and disappeared behind the slope of a ridge. An uneven rank of aging brick buildings straggled along the far side of the highway. Most of the structures seemed in good repair and occupied. Vehicles were parked in front and even early in the day, people wandered in and out. It was a town that had seen better days perhaps, but worse days, too. Not a town sick or dying, but a community down its years repeatedly reinventing itself, accommodating its shifting place in the world.

Wendl tasted the air, drank in the light, happily satisfied

that he was arriving more-or-less on the scene and the moment he had intended. All he needed to do now was wait and follow. He stopped, adjusted himself, and when he considered he looked and smelled appropriately disenfranchised, left the abandoned railroad, waited for a break in the light traffic, then crossed the highway to join the Fallen.

I

TIME AFTER TIME

Here comes the friendly evening dark,
not spark of sun nor shard of moon
can linger long enough to stay it
rising up to claim and cover us,
erasing all mistakes and every blame;
Now we lay us down to sleep,
our souls are not our own to keep,
be our dreaming ill or sweet,
we trust God's night to hide us
until we're seen anew by morning light.

CHAPTER ONE

Millicent McTeer kept her eyes shut. She felt the sun's heat on her face but lay still, pretending to herself that she still slept. Bleeding through her closed lids, the red glow of a new day flickered slightly as a breeze danced the curtains in the open bedroom window. The familiar close warmth of pillows and quilts eventually persuaded her that the outer world was still intact and passably safe for habitation. She raised a hand to shade her face and opened her eyes.

Barnaby Bear, missing one button eye, a tuft of his insides protruding through the resultant head wound, lay cradled in her arms. Breakfast smells wafted up from the kitchen on the floor below. The cleaning staff bustled and bumped in the hall outside her door. Millicent tried to recall the dream that woke her, or was it a memory, of flying somewhere. She watched dust motes dancing in the sunlight streaming through her window and pouring thick and gold like new honey across her bed. Through the window, a glimpse of pale green leaves and a snatch of birdsong. It was morning and it was Saturday and it was spring and it was her eighth birthday.

Finally convinced she was real, Millicent sighed, pushed back the covers and climbed out of bed. She stood for a moment rubbing sleep from her eyes, listening to the murmur of all the lives in Hillhaven's other rooms. She gazed at the child in her mirror and thought it was a fine thing to be eight years old and know how to fly.

Cora would be in any minute now to herd her into her bath. Then she would be dressed in clothes not entirely of her own choosing and sent down to her breakfast. After that, she would have until the afternoon to get ready for her party.

About to go down to her birthday extravaganza that afternoon, she saw several of her friends already gathered at the foot of the stairs, like fans waiting for a television star, it occurred to her. No grownups hovered in sight. She was still full of thoughts of being airborne, convinced in her head that her flight the night before was something beyond a dream. A mad, irresistible impulse seized her like a hawk takes her prey. Millicent beamed down at the upturned expectant faces, answered the chorus of Happy birthday's with a shouted, "Watch," and launched herself into the void. Her trajectory was not quite as she planned, and in an instant she discovered that landing is much more precarious an endeavor than flight.

Everything hurt after that. Everything but her right arm, which had gone numb and lay twisted at an unnatural angle from her shoulder and would not respond to her command to straighten. A cloud of faces, configured to varying degrees of curiosity and concern, peered down at her. A little girl was crying somewhere. Millicent's mother, Amelia, knelt over her, put her face close and lay a hand lightly on her chest and whispered, "Don't move, Angel. You'll be all right."

From farther away, a woman's voice, maybe Cora's, said, "I've called EMS."

Later, in the hospital Emergency Room, when Amelia asked her why she'd done such a thing, Millicent lied, "I don't know."

She knew in her heart, though, there had been a time when she had wings. She couldn't recall exactly when or where, but she could recollect the experience of it, when she had been as real as the air, able to will herself upward and beyond, held to her place in the world by grace rather than gravity. She thought it might have been when she was a baby, before she got weighed down with words and wants. Maybe it had even been before she was born or in a time yet to come. But in her secret mind Millicent determined that what she had done once, she could do again. She would just have to re-learn the skills she forgot as she had grown more and more human and less and less herself.

That night in her bed, tucked beneath her quilts, her cast elevated on a pillow beside her, Millicent chased sleep but could not catch it. Her arm only ached a little, but the air was restless, stirred by spirits she often sensed but never quite saw, until tonight. She felt somebody watching her. A cool benevolent presence, not familiar but not a stranger, either. Millicent opened her eyes to discover, standing beside her bed, her great-grandmother Alice, the first McTeer to know Hillhaven as home. She recognized the old woman immediately from photographs prominent on several walls within the inn.

"Aren't you dead?" Millicent asked the gentle shade.

I've been dead a long time, child, and for a little while, I've been as lively as you.

She heard the ancient voice somewhere inside her chest. It made not a ripple in the quiet air, so when Millicent responded, she only thought the words, *but that was a long time ago, not now.*

Alice, wavery and transparent as a curtain fluttering in a breeze, still managed a smile. *Now is where the real is, little one. Real never goes away. Once and forever are the same place.*

This didn't quite make sense to Millicent, but she thought that in time she might understand what the ghost had told her.

Her father took Millicent to have her cast removed. On the way home in their car, which was a year older than herself, she sat staring at her pale limb. "I thought there'd be feathers," she whispered while they waited for a traffic signal to release them.

Joshua McTeer laughed, reached over and patted her shoulder before the car began moving again. "To preserve your mother's peace of mind, let's not talk about flying for a while. Best keep your wings folded out of sight until they're big enough to carry you."

"Do you have wings, Dad?"

"Sure I do. Runs in the family."

"So, why don't you ever fly?"

Joshua shot her a convincingly wistful glance. "Grownups aren't allowed to fly in this country, Angel.

Otherwise, on special occasions, like birthdays, I just might."

"That would be showing off," said Millicent, affecting her mother's stern expression.

"I suppose it would, but that didn't stop you trying, did it?"

Millicent couldn't summon a proper retort, stared intently at the road ahead.

Joshua rescued her from silence. "Anyway, grownups can't fly, except on airplanes. It's the law."

"Then, I don't want to grow up," declared Millicent. "Ever."

"I truly hope you don't," said her father, watching the truck in front of them turn without flashing a signal. "I hope that when you become a woman grown and strong, you are still my little girl inside."

Millicent found no more words to say over the next two blocks until they turned onto McTeer Street. Ahead, she could see Hillhaven, the inn that had been run by their family ever since her great-grandmother Alice inherited it from her employer and life-long friend, who had no family of her own to whom she could pass it on.

"Will you always be my dad?" Millicent asked, gazing up at her father, who kept his eyes on his road.

"I'll always be your dad, Angel," he said. "Ever and ever amen."

That sounded to her like an impossible promise. "Even when you are dead and gone?" she asked, using a phrase she'd overheard from one of the guests at the inn.

"Nobody's ever dead and gone, Angel," Joshua said as if he really believed it. "We just change when the time comes. Our wings grow back and we fly away."

"Like butterflies?"

Joshua nodded. "Oh, lighter than that."

"But if you fly away, I won't be able to see you." Millicent protested, on the verge of tears.

Joshua smiled the sad, sweet smile that had made Amelia Montford his wife. "When you need to see me, you will."

The teacher, Miss Inez Hester, waxed enthusiastic about President Ronald Horne and his administration's America for Americans initiatives, a subject not included in their textbooks and not of vital interest to most of her young pupils. "Whose parents have texted Representative Shredders in support of the Extended Term Act?" she asked.

Hands went up in the air all around the room, but Millicent wasn't listening. Her arm, freed from its cast, still felt not quite like her own, and ached slightly. When she'd mentioned it to her father on the way to school that morning, not complaining, but informing her conscientious parent of her physical status, he reached over and tousled her already unruly locks, a habitual gesture his daughter found mildly endearing and not quite annoying. "That's because it's still healing, making itself stronger than it was before," he said, not taking his eyes from the road.

"Why does it need to be stronger?" Millicent asked.

"Maybe it's afraid you might decide to throw yourself off some high place again."

"I won't do that. I promised Mom I wouldn't. Not until I've learned how to fly."

"Well," Joshua said. Millicent could hear the smile he

was trying valiantly to swallow, "Practice on the ground until you're sure you can do it."

Millicent nodded. Her survival instincts were intact. She'd learned her lesson. She wouldn't leave the ground again until she was lifted up. She had every confidence that would happen any day now.

"Millicent?" Somebody was calling her name. "Millicent McTeer." Louder this time. It was Miss Hester. "You didn't raise your hand. Why should every loyal American citizen support the Extended Term Act?"

"It means that President Horne won't have to steal elections as often," Millicent said, repeating what Joshua had told her when she was studying at home the night before.

"Who told you that?" the teacher snapped, her voice sharp and quick as a snake bite.

"My father," but when she saw Miss Hester's dark and stormy face, she quickly added, "He was joking."

"Real Americans don't joke about our President," Miss Hester admonished, her voice hard and blunt now, like a hammer. "Joshua McTeer best bridle his humorous impulses before he receives a visit from Neighborhood Watch."

"Yes, Miss Hester," Millicent said meekly, waiting inside herself for the day when she would be raised up and fly away.

That evening, over supper, she reported the exchange to her father. He studied his glass of grenache intently for a moment, then looked at his daughter, soft and sad, and dredged up a smile as he said, "In our house, we share our minds freely. Out in the town, we shouldn't repeat any of it that doesn't need telling. The world is full of unfriendly ears these days. Some would throw our words back at us like stones to hurt."

His tone carried no blame, and Millicent didn't assume any, but she took Joshua's advice to heart. Something of her childhood's open innocence fell away. Hereafter, she never spoke of her parents' political leanings to anyone outside the family without first weighing her words.

———

Saturday morning in April, sun shining, birds singing, the whole world going green and flowery. A perfect day, thought Millicent, for sitting on the back porch at Hillhaven Inn and savoring the two cookies she swiped from the kitchen on her way out. Iris had seen her transgression, she knew, but the cook's covert smile assured the child that she would not be reported to parental authority.

Millicent had only taken two cookies after all, just enough for an adequate snack to tide over a winged child until supper. She savored the first one, studded with chocolate chips and spicy with cinnamon, taking small bites, not making any sudden movements so as not to frighten the pair of manic squirrels cavorting through the redbud tree whose limb draped down across the railing of the veranda where she sat. When Millicent had munched her way down to one cookie, one of the squirrels dashed out of sight up over the roof. She heard the tiny claws tapping and scampering over her head while the other squirrel remained on his branch, swaying slightly in the breeze, peering at her for a long minute with scarcely a twitch or a blink.

She wondered if the little critter were fixated on her person or her chocolate chip. Sitting still as a tree, Millicent willed the animal to come closer. Eventually, after several days, when her patience was almost depleted, the squirrel hopped down from the redbud branch to the porch rail. He sat there, the breeze ruffling his fur while his bright-berry eyes regarded the small human and her cookie. His quivering nose persuaded her it was the cookie that drew him, but the child who kept him distant.

I'm just a fat chair, she thought at the squirrel, holding her breath, trying to one with the chair she was sitting in. When Millicent thought she might implode from lack of air, the squirrel—she was confident he was a male and knew his name was Samuel—rewarded her concentration by jumping onto the arm of her chair, inches from her hand. Slowly, she let out her breath. Sam snatched the cookie from her fingers and bounded back into his tree, where he sat munching his largesse and gazing, thankfully, Millicent was certain, at his benefactor.

She was elated. Sam thought she was a chair. She could change her shape if she just concentrated on it. That might be a skill as useful as flying.

———

Millicent found her father up in his lair on the third floor of the old inn he'd inherited from his grandmother, which was the family's home and livelihood. Lost in the weave of the story he was writing, for a moment, he seemed unaware of her hand resting on his shoulder. When his inner voice paused, he reached up and put his large hand over his daughter's small one, looked up to bask in her smile.

"Have you been working on that story all night?" Millicent asked. It seemed to her that her parents, and especially her father, were always awake.

Joshua said, "No Angel, but I got up early when your mother left for Drovers Gap. She left without breakfast and I've been waiting to eat with you."

"Where do stories come from, Dad?" Millicent asked.

Joshua shook his head. "I don't know, Angel. I suppose I just make them up."

Looking serious as only a child can, "But stories are real, Dad. They were there before they ever thought of you."

"You mean before I ever thought of them, don't you?"

"No, Dad," genuine exasperation in her trilling voice, "The stories come looking for you when they want to be written. All you do is get in their way."

Josh couldn't hold back the laugh. "You might be right, Angel. How did such a dense man as I ever become father to such a wise soul?"

"I learned that stuff before I was ever your little girl," Millicent informed, "Back when I knew how to fly."

"Well, don't fly away from your old dad now. I'd be lonely without you, Angel."

The angel grabbed his hand with both hers and pulled. "Come on, Dad. Lucy says it's time for breakfast."

The rain slacked and thinning clouds threatened to cheer Drovers Gap with a sliver of sun by the time Amelia Montford, clutching two of Doug Bradley's infamous sausage biscuits in a plastic foam carton, extricated herself from Wardlow's Lunch. She had dallied too long, being helpful and friendly to a man who would never buy a house from her, and now she risked being late for her first appointment of the morning.

She glanced along Main Street, saw it clear of traffic,

and preparing to make her dash, nearly tripped over the gaunt man sitting on the curb. A hiker's backpack hung from his high-boned shoulders. His clothes gave the impression of perpetual homelessness, confirmed by his odor. This one definitely wasn't a hiker. More than a few of those stopped in Drovers Gap, taking a break from their trek and resupplying for the long trail just outside town. Some could be pretty ripe coming off the mountain, but this man's sweat was ancient, his dirt integral.

"Sorry," Amelia muttered, suppressing the impulse to scold. After all, she was the one who hadn't been watching her step. As she plunged into the street, a more pleasant aroma wafted from the biscuits she carried. She wouldn't have time to eat them now. Halfway across, she stopped, turned and looked back at the man sitting on the curb. Not a drunk, she judged. For all his unkempt appearance, he returned her gaze clear and steady. He still sat, just as before, perched like some bedraggled bird. For an instant, she saw him as such, a gangly, folded up crowman, his knees propping up a hand-lettered cardboard sign anchored by a quart canning jar, half full of coins with a touch of green among them. *Free Money, Help Yourself*, the sign read. The rain was already streaking and bleeding the message toward illegibility. Nobody read it, apparently, because, as she watched, a pedestrian wearing a red cap bent and dropped his pocket change into the jar as he passed.

The man on the curb, no longer crow, just shook his head, stood and smiled at Amelia as she walked back to him and held out Doug's aromatic carton.

"Breakfast," she said.

"Just in time, too," he replied, taking her carton before, unnerved by his unwavering grin, Amelia fled away to her client without waiting for thanks.

The clouds broke their promise, closed ranks, and as Amelia reached the door to her office, unleashed another deluge. She paused as she went in, shaking her umbrella, and glanced back across the street toward Wardlow's Lunch. The little man she nearly kicked off the curb was gone, no doubt to find a dry place to enjoy her biscuits. Just for a second, she wondered what had brought him to Drovers Gap, if he had a destination, had he come by her town on a journey, or just a wander. She closed the door against the weather and turned to face her day.

"Morning, Amy," she said to her office assistant, who looked to have partied late the night before. "Another wet one."

"Morning," said Amy, offering no further comment on the weather, "Mrs. Stephens called in, said she wouldn't be able to make her appointment this morning, that she hoped you wouldn't sell the house before she got a chance to see it."

"She wouldn't buy that house," Amelia said. "She likes to look at charming old houses, but she wants to live in a new one. We'll end up selling her a lot so she can build something impressive for her friends and inappropriate to her needs." To herself, Amelia thought, *I'm hungry*.

Amelia was still hungry as she drove out of Drovers Gap that evening on her way to Asheton. A trio of overweight and undergrateful adult siblings had taken most of her afternoon, having parked their aged and addled mother on the edge of town at White Oaks Eldercare. Armed with the appropriate paperwork from their lawyer, they converged on her office to render their matriarch's small house into cash. After an hour of hostile exchange, they hadn't even been able to agree on an asking price. In the end, they'd left to find another realtor whose office environment might be more conducive to consensus.

She had been on her way out the door to grab sustenance from the Wildhearth Bake Shop next door, when the black Hummer growled at her. A large-bodied man got out, dressed like a TV sitcom rendering of a Texas oil baron. His costume didn't fool Amelia. He had local property developer written all over him.

"Morning Missy," he purred from beneath his cowboy hat, maybe a half-size too tight for him. He was obviously in performance mode. Amelia half expected him to sweep off his hat and bow like a Rebel general in an old movie.

He kept his hat on. "Don't run off just yet, young lady. I'm here to do business."

Amelia stepped back inside, held the door open as wide as she was able, and cringed inwardly when Business contrived to brush against her despite the ample passage she'd allowed him. Without waiting for an invitation, he sat down, not in the customer chair, which was nearest, but walking around her desk and sitting back in her chair. Amelia, thinking he might put his feet up on her desk, was prepared to whack his ankle with one of the walking sticks she kept by her door. Perhaps he read her mind. In any case, he seemed to realize he had overstepped his welcome, and stood again, stepped aside, and gestured an invitation for Amelia to sit in her own chair.

She stayed on her feet, arms folded, the desk between them. "I'm Amelia Montford, the chief broker here. What sort of business are you about, Mister...?"

"Heath." He dropped the word out into space like a stone into a pond and paused a second, as if expecting a splash. When Amelia returned only blank silence, he went on. "Carter Heath. I'm sure you've heard of us, Heath and Porter Development. Luxury mountain communities. Most of the big residential projects within sixty miles are ours."

"Oh, yes, I know about you folks, Mister Heath," not in Amelia's esteemed customer tone. "You've spoiled some of the best scenery in Marshall County."

Heath had obviously heard it all already. "Well now, Amelia, honey, there isn't much profit in scenery, though it is good for bait. To make money, you must build houses, big houses and a lot of them, and to do that, you have to turn over a little dirt here and there. I didn't drop by to talk about the scenery, though. I'm here to help you make a lot of money today."

Amelia suppressed her urge to tell Carter Heath where he might best hide his money. "And just where do you plan to make this windfall, Mister Heath?"

"Carter, please. We are friends now, aren't we?" Carter came around the desk, and would have stepped up close, had not Amelia moved at the same time, so that a chair intervened. Sensing his charm was running thin, Heath changed tactics. "I don't need to take up much of your time, Miss Montford. Ransom Ridge is just the property I need for our next project. It's the largest parcel of prime mountaintop near Drovers Gap and you have it listed."

"The sellers just signed a letter of intent this morning to convey Ransom Ridge to the Drovers Gap Community Land Trust."

"I'll pay four times what the Land Trust can pay. The contract is still on your desk. I've talked to the sellers. They want to go for the money."

"If the sellers want out, tell them to come talk to me. If

the Land Trust will release them from the deal, they can sell to you."

Carter gave up on his smile. "That will take time, Amelia. I don't have much time and I have lots of money. I can sweeten the deal for you off anybody's books if you'll make it easy for me. I need to tell the bankers this week that I have the property nailed."

Amelia knew better than to laugh, but she did anyway. "I don't do business off the books. I have a contract agreed to by all parties. As far as any of them have informed me, all are happy about that and intend to sign. If I hear any different, I'll let you know."

The few words exchanged after that were not pleasant. The developer left in his boisterous Hummer without ever removing his hat. Amelia felt certain that if she ever saw his driver's license, it would show a man with a gleaming scalp. It was not the first time someone had threatened to put Amelia out of business. It was not Carter's attempt at intimidation that unsettled her. It was the palpable stench of greed lingering in her office after he drove away.

———

Millicent enjoyed hanging out in the Hillhaven parlor among all the guests and local diners. There were people she knew, and people from all sorts of strange places she thought she would never see or want to. There were people who spoke in languages that she had never learned in school, but sometimes, just sometimes, she was sure she knew what they were saying. Some people Millicent saw nobody else seemed to notice, as if they were visible to no eyes but hers. Some of them wore old-fashioned clothes, like the vintage photographs around the walls of the inn. Now and again, she thought she recognized a face she had seen in one of the old pictures.

Once, when she tried speaking to a young woman in a long flowery dress with a lace collar, her mother had asked, "Who are you talking to, Angel?"

"Just imagining," Millicent lied.

"Don't imagine out-loud in public," Amelia said. "People will think you're talking to ghosts. We wouldn't want them to imagine Hillhaven is haunted, would we? They might be afraid to come back."

"No, we certainly wouldn't want that," Millicent agreed, although she knew for a fact that Hillhaven was probably the most haunted hotel in a town that homed as many unbodied spirits as live ones. She knew this with the same certainty she was convinced that one time she had known how to fly. Sometimes, when she was by herself with no grownups around, shadows would become real and speak to her. Hillhaven was a happy house. Nobody who came there ever wanted to leave. And some who had left came back if there were eyes innocent enough to see them.

Tonight, though, as Millicent scanned the room, everybody she saw was breathing. Most of them were watching her favorite program on the television when her mother came in from work. Joshua got up and crossed the room to meet her. He put his hands on her shoulders and they leaned toward a kiss and Millicent thought there must have been hundreds of couples over the years before she was born who met like her parents just inside the entrance, to bless one another with smiles and kisses, but probably none but Amelia Montford and Joshua McTeer ever had a daughter who could fly.

Amelia was away up the stair before Millicent could catch her eye. The program ended after a while and as she set out to search for her mother. Cora intercepted her. "Bath time, Missy."

Nobody, not even Joshua, argued with Cora Paige.

———

Amelia had settled into her steaming tub, only her face above waterline, drifting on the border between dreams and waking, when she heard the knock on the door.

"Wine boy," Joshua's voice.

Startled back into the world, Amelia set up suddenly, sloshing water over the brim of the tub. "Come in," she said, swallowing her reflexive profanity, "and mind the floor. It's wet." As her husband sat on the edge of her tub, she added, "Where's our child?"

Joshua laughed. "I left her in the parlor with the guests, watching *The Winged Child* on PBS. As soon as it's over, Cora will nab her to get a bath."

He handed Amelia the glass of Malbec, and while she sipped, took the sponge from her hand and rubbed her back and shoulders. "You look better," he said. "Still want to sing?"

"Wouldn't miss it for the world," Amelia said. "I love you."

"I love you, too." Joshua whispered in her ear. His breath tickled. "That's what I was made for." He lifted her damp hair, kissed the back of her neck so lightly she wasn't quite sure of the touch, though she felt his breathing. He stood. "Full house tonight," he said, and without further word, left Amelia to herself.

She thought about the hectic day behind her now, for a brief instant her mind was snared by an image of the homeless man outside Wardlow's Lunch, then Carter

Heath and all the other complications of Drovers Gap lost their urgency and fell away from her like autumn leaves, the residue of a dream. Amelia realized she was looking forward to singing tonight, the same way she would look forward to sunrise after a night of cold wind and rain.

Cleansed and dressed and full of music, on her way down the stairs, guitar in hand, she met Cora Paige herding Millicent bathward. Bright as morning, the child hurtled toward her mother, who barely had time to hand her instrument to Cora before her daughter was in her arms. "I've missed you today, Angel," she murmured into sweaty hair, smelling something like a hayfield after a summer rain.

Millicent wriggled free, stood holding her mother's hand as if she feared she might float away into the air. "I missed you, too, Mom. Can I come down and listen to you sing tonight?"

"May I, you mean?"

"May I?"

"Have you done your homework?"

'Oh, yes. I did it this afternoon. Cora helped."

Cora nodded.

"As soon as you've had your bath. You can sit on the stairs. But in bed by nine o'clock."

"Nine o'clock." Millicent echoed. "Bed."

When Amelia came down to the dining room, dinner was well underway, the usual contingent of tourists augmented by a more than usual crowd of locals. Amelia recognized some of the faces, smiled and nodded to a few near and familiar ones, as she sat on her stool by the unpiloted piano and strummed a few chords on her guitar. Over the next forty minutes she sang a progression of Appalachian folk ballads that were all somebody's favorite. She sang a couple of songs comprising her husband's lyrics set to tunes of her own devising. Most people ignored her singing, engaged their groceries or impressed one another with witty conversation, although she noticed a few here and there would stop to listen from time to time, their attention snared by the soft soulful music.

Then she came to a place suddenly, where her mind went blank, and Amelia had no idea what she would sing next. Lucy brought her a glass of water. Amelia sipped and scanned the room, noted the thin man sitting alone at the table by the kitchen door. He looked familiar. Where had she seen him already today? When she saw the little girl perched high on the stairs in the hallway, barely visible through the door, Millicent met her gaze and became a smile.

"This one's for Millicent," Amelia announced. and opened her heart and her mind to the song and sang the words that coalesced around the tune of an old hymn she had once heard in a little church up on Slick Rock Creek:

There is a world behind the world,
woven deep beneath the curled
and folded realm we see unfurled
each morning as we're rudely hurled
into wakefulness undreamed.
There is a deep beneath the deep,
a far height beyond the steep
mountain's summit where we leap
to grasp the thing we cannot keep,
though it most treasured seemed.
There is a music past all song
that sings to righteousness all wrong,
that stills the war, however long,

and tolls healing to the throng
of broken souls redeemed.

By the time Amelia sang through three verses, the entire room had fallen silent and all eyes were looking to her and the music. Servers stood rooted in their places. When no more words came to her, she went back to the beginning and sang her song through again, and a scattering of voices trailed after. As she came to the last line, another song lodged in her brain and she poured it out. This time, everyone was singing with her as if they had known the words from childhood.

Welcome to the wanderer, the stranger at our door,
It matters not your origin, if you be rich or poor,
We only ask your right good will to share our humble feast,
We'll drink health to the mightiest and drink joy to the least,
for none is lesser than the rest and none the more than all
who gather at our table here to fill our love-lit hall.

When the singing ceased and the room went into motion again and all the social noises had resumed, Amelia, aware they'd all been caught up in a holy moment, looked again into the shadows on the stair beyond the door. She had a vague impression people stood on the stairs, but it was past nine o'clock and Millicent was not among them. Amelia blinked, realized they were just a confusion of shadows and lights from the traffic outside. Good. Her daughter had gone off to bed, just as she promised. Stifling a yawn, Amelia looked again at the table by the kitchen door. Cora Paige was clearing the table. The man who ate her breakfast biscuits in Drovers Gap had gone.

Millicent still sat on the stair long after her bedtime. Amelia didn't see her daughter there, although she might have. The girl hadn't rendered herself invisible. She had so attuned to the surrounding shadows as to appear one of them. Anyone who might have peered beyond normal expectation would have seen her. She hadn't disappeared, just ceased to be obvious. As Millicent would have said it, she had simply dimmed herself, blended with what had been there before she arrived.

For her part, Millicent saw with forbidden clarity all that grownups, bound by habit and skepticism, were blind to. She saw the skeins of power twining out from the spidery man sitting to himself beside the kitchen door. She saw a glowing thread touch her mother as she played and sang, the music exciting chords and tones heard not with ears but vibrating within the bone. She watched the spell that was the music spread out across the room, riding on Amelia's song to settle over the whole gathered throng, like a shining pulsating blanket. She watched faces soften as hearts melted. She saw, or perhaps only felt, the stillness of creation well up like a rising spring within each soul, as shoulders relaxed, chins lifted, fingers unclenched and hands opened ready to receive the blessing of the song.

Millicent listened with the shadows on the stair, who she knew now to be people as real and present and alive as she, whose breath in their own time was as warm as hers, whose hearts beat in their own moment as steady and full of purpose and desire as her own. Beside her stood her great-grandmother, Alice, who had appeared in her room the night after she broke her arm. She had come a long way toward understanding what she'd been told on that first meeting, that now and forever are the same place.

"We'll always be here, Grandmother, won't we?" Millicent whispered. "Together in the music?"

Alice, fading fast now. Millicent felt a smile she couldn't quite see, heard within her the airless voice. *Yes, little Dearest, the Music never dies and we are in it.*

She watched the grasshopperish man by the kitchen door take his bill from Cora, and quick and quiet as any of the shadows on the stairs, she flowed away to intercept. By the time he came out Hillhaven's front door, Millicent was ensconced in a big rocker on the porch waiting to ambush him. He looked down and smiled at her as he went past, as if he were genuinely and thoroughly happy to see her, like a long away relative come home at last.

"What did you do in there?" She called as the man started down the steps.

He stopped, turned, gazed at her like she was a grown-up. "I didn't do anything. It was your mother's music."

Millicent slipped from her chair and stood at the top of the steps, her eyes level with the man in the yard. In the uncertain light, his face resembled a big black bird's more than a man's.

"But you made the music real," she insisted.

The face became a man's again and smiled. "Music is always real," he said. "I just helped them to hear it."

Before Millicent could call up another question, he turned and walked away across the yard. She heard his feet crunching in the gravel and watched him move away into the fog, his form dissolving in the shadows of trees. She was about to call after him, ask his name, when a spark of fire ignited between his shoulder blades. He seemed unaware that he was burning as the spark flared into flame, unfurling like the wings of a giant butterfly until Millicent couldn't see the man at all for his fiery wings. She watched, silent and astounded as the wings closed like the pages of a book into a thin vertical line of light against the night. Then all was dark, and the man was gone.

"Did you see that?" a woman asked the man with her as they came out from the inn onto the veranda. Millicent blended with her chair, and they didn't notice her at all.

"Just a reflection on the fog, from the traffic in the street," said the man. "Looked weird, though. Thought I was seeing aliens for a second."

"Looked like a dragon to me," said the woman as they went laughing to their car.

There was nothing left then for Millicent to do but slip upstairs to her room and pretend to be asleep when her mother came in to kiss her goodnight. She lay in bed, not daring to move, lest she break her concentration, staring at the dark until she could see the light that always burned at its center. She thought long and long about the threads of brilliance that had ridden on her mother's music. She thought about the mysterious birdman who had rendered Amelia's song more than any song had a right to be. No one had seen that but Millicent. She knew without knowing how she knew that the man intended her to see it. He hadn't come to meddle with the music. He had come looking for her.

Finally, when there were none awake but owls in the town, and the moon blessed her room with a pearly glow, Millicent McTeer fell asleep, certain of two things. There were more wonders in the world than most people allowed themselves to see. And there was more than one way to fly.

Some slight stirring in the dark woke Joshua McTeer from his sound sleep. He listened to the night, to Amelia's soft breathing in the bed next to him. She murmured something in her sleep. Instinctively, he reached out and touched her shoulder, warm and comforting, the shape of love. She turned toward him, throwing an arm across his chest, and fell quiet again, just the faint brush of her breath in his ear.

Joshua stared up into the night, imagined he could see the slow turning of the blades on the ceiling fan above their bed. Barely, just barely, he could hear the whispering arc they cut in the shadows. *Do shadows bleed?* A crazy, rootless thought, shriveling to nothing as soon as it sprouted somewhere between awake and asleep. Through the open window came the rhythmic chatter of crickets, and the pulsating anthem of tiny frogs that thronged the trees in the yard. The city beyond lay asleep and silent, the only clue to urbanity the faint drone of a big truck on the distant interstate.

He wondered about the noise that woke him, thought maybe it wasn't a noise, maybe just a dream. He could almost summon his sleeping world into consciousness, even while it was slipping away. Joshua realized then he was happy. This ordinary life, so different from the life he and Amelia had anticipated and planned for out west, had fulfilled and joined them beyond all hope and expectation. He'd been writing television plays in California, reaping awards and good money, and about to get married to a beautiful woman from a rich family when his grandmother, whom he'd never actually met, died at the other end of the country.

Joshua arrived in Asheton to find himself the new owner of a vintage hotel plus a few wild acres on a mountaintop outside town. By the time he found a prospective buyer for the properties, he had fallen for the place. When Amelia came to bring him home, armed with an ultimatum to either forget about Asheton or their wedding, she lingered, looked around, then to her astonishment, stayed. When they weren't running the hotel, Joshua wrote his own novels now, and a continent removed from her overbearing father's expectations, Amelia had found a calling selling houses for ordinary folk to live in rather than fabricating commercials to feed Fred Montford's media empire. But their greatest gift to one another and to the world, Joshua thought, was their beautiful and precocious daughter, their winged child, Millicent. Joshua breathed a prayer to the night that tomorrow would be just like the day before, that their life and love could continue uninterrupted to its end, unaltered in any essential way but to grow ever deeper.

Joshua waited to fall asleep again, and surprised when he didn't, wondered what happening he was watching and waiting and listening for. A firefly drifted lazily past on the veranda outside their room. Not a firefly, exactly, the light too steady, too red. It flared slightly for an instant and Joshua glimpsed what he thought was a face. Somebody was smoking a cigarette on his no-smoking veranda. He hoped it was a guest who needed to be reminded of the house rules.

Joshua slipped from bed, careful not to wake his wife, shrugged into his robe, and on the way out, took a trekking pole from the closet, just in case. He opened the door and looked at the middle-aged man leaning against the railing. Some trick of the moonlight made the figure appear semi-transparent. Joshua imagined he could see faintly the railing behind. The man smiled at him as if Joshua were the guest. The cigarette disappeared. The man didn't toss it. It was simply gone. The erstwhile smoker just stood there, in his old-fashioned suit, looking like an extra in a Great Gatsby movie.

"May I help you?" Joshua said, because he felt he needed to speak to the situation and nothing else came to mind.

"I'm here to help you, Joshua McTeer," the man said, wavering like a reflection on troubled water.

"At the moment, I don't need anything, thanks." Joshua retorted, feeling slightly foolish, slightly annoyed, not quite amused.

"You need to pay attention. There is something you ought to know," said the ghost, dissolving into a smoky cloud that shimmered for a moment under the moon before it bled away into night.

When the weather was good, Millicent walked the three blocks to her violin teacher's house. Lisa Charon was a friend of her mother's, and occasionally performed at Hillhaven during dinner. Sometimes Lisa and Amelia worked together, but as much as Millicent liked to hear her mother's music, she preferred the evenings when Lisa played alone, either singing, her fiddle tucked under her arm, with only her voice to carry the song, or just letting her instrument sing for her with a voice so like Lisa's that the only difference was the words.

On these occasions, Millicent, hidden on the stair with her great-grandmother Alice and the other shades of Hillhaven past, drank in the intoxicating sound, watched the music's light gather around the fiddler as she played, and weave across the room a luminous labyrinth that only Millicent, and perhaps Lisa, could see, until it rested upon every head at every table and no one was hidden and no one was alone. Before the close of the last song, Millicent would fly up to her room so she could pretend to be asleep when her father came in to kiss her head and whisper to her what she already knew, that she was loved and treasured beyond all things in his life.

When Millicent told her parents she wanted to learn to play the violin like Lisa Charon, Amelia tried not to look hurt and Joshua asked, "How about the guitar? Your mother could teach you."

"That, too," Millicent said, putting on her grown-up voice, "but Lisa's fiddle all by itself makes people alive in the music."

Eventually, she persuaded her parents to allow violin lessons with Lisa provided she let her mother teach her to play the guitar. Millicent had music in her bones and both her teachers were gratified at her progress.

About half-way along the street to Lisa's home, Millicent passed what she named the Castle, a three-story Victorian-style ostentation with ornate trim and turreted towers, set back from the street and surrounded by an unkempt treeless yard bordered by a rusted fence of iron pickets that retained here and there a few semidetached flakes of black paint, and were topped by viciously pointed spikes intended to discourage anyone with a mind to climb over. Whether their purpose was to repel curious children who passed, or dangerous children hidden within the house, was a source of recurrent speculation among Millicent and her friends. Most of her peers agreed that the Castle was haunted, but Millicent doubted it. All the ghosts she had met at Hillhaven were friendly, and the Castle smelled to her like anything but.

Whether or not any menacing juveniles were

sequestered within the Castle, none of Millicent's cohort ever discovered, but the three huge canines that roamed the yard definitely qualified. Any unsuspecting human innocent passing within ten feet of the fence was subjected to a heart-stopping display of untempered ferocity as the dogs exploded en masse from beneath the Castle porch, resembling for a second one huge three-headed hellhound, before they dispersed to range along the fence, pressing their drooling snouts between the pickets, all teeth and snarl and slobber until old ladies fainted or fled the walk to totter on past in the gutter, or until babies bawled in their trotting mother's arms, or until children ran screaming in delight at being so close to annihilation but barely safe from actual dismemberment.

Millicent, who by nature was a friend to the world, made repeated attempts to be neighborly to the beasts. She knew in her own mind that they were not really dogs but dragons, who could fly, and might be helpful in recovering her own aviatory talents. Once she offered her sandwich to one of them, who ignored the food and came within a hair of chomping her fingers. Eventually, she gave up her overtures, and studiously ignored the three terrors when they came roiling out to assault the fence as she passed on her way to her lessons.

This tactic sufficed until one summer afternoon when the largest of the ravening trio hurled himself against the gate as Millicent passed. The latch sprang with a loud clang as the gate swung open. For an instant, the fiend just stood there, as surprised as the child at their sudden mutual access. Then he leapt through the opening before the gate could swing shut behind him. Millicent jettisoned her case with her three-quarter size violin inside and ran for her life. Without thinking, she dashed into the street, praying the dog wouldn't follow, glanced back to see him gaining, huge and black, maw red and gaping, right on her heels. She screamed in her head. *Bad dog. Die.*

The shriek of brakes and blaring horn declared the truck that loomed up over her. *Don't hit me*, she prayed, closing her eyes as she ran. She felt the wind of the truck rush at her back. Another step and she heard behind her a crushing thud and a horrible soul-rending confluence of yelp and scream. The truck barreled on down the street as she reached the opposite curb. She turned to see the big dog on his side, spinning in circles like an unbalanced top until he lay still.

Millicent looked both ways. There were no wheels in sight. She walked to the center of the pavement and stared down at her erstwhile pursuer. His flank heaved once with a long shuddering breath and there was no movement at all except for the blood trickling from the dog's exposed ear to gather in a dark pool, glistening on the pavement beneath his head.

Millicent knew then that her thoughts could kill. She vowed to be very careful in the future about all her thinking regarding anything that breathed.

CHAPTER TWO

Millicent McTeer saw the dragon for the first time on her twelfth birthday. Once she had seen, it was impossible to unsee, so Millicent encountered the entity repeatedly after that, in various hues and shapes, amid all sorts of wild and unforeseen circumstances. Millicent had read about dragons, of course, but assumed they only inhabited screens and paper. She was not looking for dragons on that spring morning at her family's cabin in the mountains above Asheton. It didn't occur to her until much later that the dragon may have been looking for her.

Her father, Joshua, inherited the cabin from his grandmother Alice, who had inherited it, along with Hillhaven Inn, from Millicent's namesake, Alice's life-long friend, Millicent Robbins, who had inherited the place in turn from her mother, Claire Robbins. Claire's husband left the country shortly before her daughter was born. He was not the father. Millicent Robbins didn't meet her father until he had become one of the resident ghosts at the inn. According to family lore, he was still liable to manifest suddenly in Hillhaven hallways during seasons of impending crisis.

Her first husband was a logger, who died young and by accident, as forest workers were prone to do in those unregulated times. In her middle age, Millicent Robbins married Benjamin Drum, whom she loved longer if not more. Drum was a mildly famous local photographer, perhaps better known for the quality of his friends than for his published images, which appeared in widely circulated nature magazines for a generation. A number of his photographs still adorned the walls of halls and guestrooms at Hillhaven.

It was rare for Millicent McTeer's parents to take time away from their inn, especially in the spring, when tourists and day-trippers generated traffic jams in Asheton's winding and tilted streets. But when they asked Millicent what she wanted for a birthday present, she said, "A weekend at the cabin—just us and no more."

They made it a long weekend, not coming home until Monday, though it meant their daughter would miss a day of school. Millicent was weary of school, where she'd been consistently at odds with her teachers of late, to the point that Amelia and Joshua were discussing in low voices when they thought their daughter beyond earshot, the possibility of hiring a tutor to home-school her. Millicent, of course managed to overhear, and relished the notion, provided she might be granted approval of her mentor. Millicent, one way or another, contrived to become aware of most plots and plans of well-intentioned adults regarding her situation present and future. She also usually, through subtle maneuver and counter-logic, evaded any directive not her own without appearing to offer outright resistance. Early on, Millicent evidenced an adult's negotiating skills. As

Amelia would say of her in a later life, "My daughter never was a child."

All through breakfast on the morning she saw the dragon, Millicent observed fleeting touch and glance between her parents, concluded that they might have some transaction begun between them during the night that required further resolution. As she anticipated, when she asked if she could walk on her own to the waterfall a quarter-mile down the ridge below the cabin, they assented with slightly less than their customary reservation, and she was free and away, duly permissioned and cautioned, with instruction not to wander farther than her declared destination.

"I'll be down in a little while," Joshua said to her back as she went through the door. "Maybe I'll bring our gear and we can try to rescue a pan-full of trout from the pool below the fall."

"Great, Dad," Millicent called, glanced behind her on her way out to see Amelia standing with both hands on Joshua's shoulders. She suspected they would be into each other's clothes by the time she was across the yard.

Ten minutes into the woods, the steady, throaty rumble of the waterfall swallowed the breathy conversation between breeze and leaves. The torrent roared with a hundred liquid voices, spoke against every stone and ledge in its path, calling, inviting, commanding her in chorus with the unmovable mountain, water and stone shaping her name in the bright air, the sound sliding and dropping like the plummeting stream, in a cascade of descending syllables, the final *t* terminating in a stuttering crackle like an electrical spark.

Millicent ran the last hundred yards to the falls and arrived breathless at its bouldered glen. She collapsed on a large flat-topped rock to gather herself. A thick carpet of moss gentled their meeting. The easy green felt slightly damp in the faint mist from the waterfall, and cool under her palms and her tanned calves. She lay on her back, feet dangling over the churning eddy below, and swallowed as much true-blue sky as she could hold. While she tried to identify the large bird circling high above, smalled by the distance between them, Millicent McTeer was asleep.

From her dream, she looked down at herself out of the eyes of the hawk as it rose on the thermal currents ascending the ridge from the valley northward. She watched herself, sprawled on her rock, slowly turning and receding. The wee human female, just a pale and not particularly important cypher in the pooled shadow of the glen. Too large to be prey and too small and earth-bound to be predator. Hawk was not afraid of her and for less than a second, barely curious.

A sound called her back to her own mind, if only half awake. A word, spoken with the liquid ease and slide of water and the arresting click of stone. She lay there in her blood-tinged dark, still as the stone under her, not daring to open her eyes, waiting, listening until she heard her name again. *Milliccenttt...*

It wasn't just the water, then. She sat up so quickly it dizzied her, stared at the tumbled rocks and turgid rapids, until in the dappled, flickering light admitted by the wind-tossed trees, several adjoining crags arranged themselves into a face, vaguely reptilian and grotesquely human, with burning slanting eyes above a long nose and dark fanged mouth that would have been at home on a wolf. The mouth morphed to form her attenuated name again, accented and modulated as the stream itself might have spoken, *Milliccenttt MccTteerrr*.

She opened her own mouth to answer when a shadow fell across her mossy throne, and Millicent looked up to see her father's face smiling down at her. Beyond him, grim clouds roiled and rolled, obliterating the blazing blue that had homed the hawk. Millicent blinked, looked back at the waterfall and saw only transient water tumbling down immutable stone.

"Storm coming," said the comfort of her lovelit days and the assurance of her darksome nights. A familiar and beloved hand reached down. Millicent took it and let it haul her to her feet. Then, as the first drops of rain rattled the leaves over their heads and glistened the rocks at their feet, Joshua McTeer and his daughter, hand in hand, made a dash for home and shelter.

Millicent didn't think about the dragon again until after the storm and supper and her bath, as she lay gazing out her window, the waxing moon bathing her face. No dragons lurked in the shadowed forest surrounding their cabin. She listened to the calls and stirrings of all the creatures inhabiting the familiar night but none of them spoke her name. Finally, Millicent released her world to sleep, certain of two things—a dragon had spoken her name, and she would see him again.

The next morning, as soon as they finished breakfast, Millicent helped her parents neat the little cabin and pack up to go home. Amelia drove. Millicent and her father gazed wistfully out the window at the trees sliding by as their old crew cab pickup crunched up their gravel track toward the paved county road. Though neither of them ever said it aloud to anyone, they felt more themselves, more akin to their world, when free on the mountain than encumbered with their city lives. Millicent knew her mother was attuned to a more orderly and controlled existence and felt no less loved for that. She also knew that Amelia Montfort had her own dark wildness that she kept hidden deep, even from herself.

They rode in silence down between the mountains, twisting and turning toward the interstate that lay in the valley like a lazy snake, shining under the sun, trucks and cars flickering along it's back toward destinations that might have seemed important to the humans riding in them, necessary, at least, if not desired. Up the access ramp and they were in the peopled world again, streaming live toward acknowledged routine. As she drove, Amelia began humming to herself a scrap of tune that had caught in her head. Millicent guessed she would be hearing some refined iteration of it one night soon in the dining room at Hillhaven Inn. Joshua, frowning in concentration, scribbled something in his notebook. Millicent listened to the roar and drone of traffic and the rush of wind past the window. Eyes closed. Concentrating on the song the tires were singing to the asphalt. Waiting to hear something whisper her name.

When they reached the high bridge over the Long Broad, the song shifted key and tempo, transitioned abruptly to a rhythmic click, click, click on the hot concrete. Millicent opened her eyes, saw the water flashing eighty feet below, saw the city of Asheton crowding the far shore.

"It looks different," she said, not aware she shared her thought aloud.

Her father looked up from his notebook, closed it, and dropped his pen into his shirt pocket. "It is," he said.

"But it is still Asheton," Millicent said.

Joshua nodded. "Still Asheton, but not quite the same as we left her. Some souls have died, some have been born while we were on the mountain. People have arrived, folk have departed for some other place. Strangers have met and become friends. Friends have become lovers and lovers have fallen out. Fortunes have likely been made and lost in Asheton over the past three days. Some have become rich for the last time, and some become poor for the first time. Asheton is the same only in that she still changes."

"Nothing is lost, though, even if everything is changed," Millicent said quietly, repeating something her great-grandmother's ghost had told her on the stair at Hillhaven.

"That's a good one," observed Joshua. "May I steal that for my next book?"

Amelia had quit her humming, listening to her beloveds. She shook her head as she pulled off the freeway onto McTeer Street. "Philosophers," she said, laughing. "I hope you'll suspend your inquiry into the nature of things long enough to help me unload our stuff."

When she looked back years afterward, Millicent would say the summer of her first dragon sighting was the last summer of her childhood. Until then, she had believed in magic the way children do. Not entirely fantasy but not quite real, either. A practice that might change the way one saw things, but not necessarily change the things one saw. Before she survived her teen years, the deep world behind the broken and beautiful world she lived in would become frighteningly real and powers and forces she had consigned to her imagination would intrude into her ordinary life with startling consequence. In the process, Millicent would discover powers within herself that weighed her with more adult responsibility than adolescent thrill.

The summer began innocently enough, promising to be a variation on a seasonal theme that played out every year Millicent could remember. Hillhaven once again overflowed with eager visitors lugging expensive electronic gadgets to record the mountains and waterfalls encircling Asheton and to facilitate real-time sharing with their circles of social media contacts.

Millicent, like all her peers at school, had a smart phone. Everybody did. But unlike her friends, Millicent had never taken a selfie. She agreed with Ted Mura, a long-dead photographer whose sharp-focus photograph of Myrtle Mountain hung in the Hillhaven dining room. One day Joshua was explaining to her the antique process whereby captured images were fixed on chemically treated film. She was entranced that the sepia-tinted monochrome would seem so immediate and present.

"But it looks so real, Dad," she said. "I can smell the trees." Then Joshua told her that Mura claimed the purpose of a photograph was not to inform the viewers that the photographer had been in a place, but to convince them that they were there.

"It's a good one then," she said.

Hillhaven was full of photographs, on every wall in every room or hallway. No paintings or contrived images among all these frozen glimpses stolen from their moment, become now windows into the close and far past, all looking out into the same familiar place. The architecture almost as constant as the landscape that homed it. Only the faces changed, the styles of their accoutrement reflecting succeeding seasons and years and generations. Among all the images sequestered in the inn, Millicent loved best the small sepia-tinted double portrait in a plain black frame that hung over the desk just inside the front door where arriving guests wrote their names in a big book, and departing ones left their room keys in a large celadon ceramic bowl. In the photo, two women stood on the hotel veranda, close as lovers, smiling their welcome. Millicent couldn't remember who had told her the taller one was her great-grandmother, Alice McTeer. The other, shorter, not so thin, maybe a bit older, remained a mystery to Millicent until one day she asked her mother, "Who's the other woman with Alice?"

Amelia informed her, "That's Millicent Robbins. She owned Hillhaven before your great-grandmother. You're named for her."

Millicent was curious. "Why wasn't I named after dad's grandmother?"

"That was our first thought," Amelia said, paused a moment, as if searching for some alternative fact, then proceeded to tell the truth. "But my parents divorced when I was a teenager. Dad re-married to a woman named Alice. We would never have convinced Mother that we weren't currying favor with Dad. Then, I had that dream."

Millicent picked up the scent of a genuine adventure. "A dream?"

"It had to be a dream. I thought I was awake at the time, and I don't believe in ghosts, so it had to be a dream."

"Tell me, oh, tell," piped Millicent, shrill athrill with curiosity and anticipation.

Amelia drew a deep breath, assembled her thoughts, and made her confession. "I was sitting on the veranda reading. I could feel you kicking inside me. I was tired and must have fallen asleep. I thought I saw a woman standing just by the door. I recognized her from the photo over the reception desk. It was your great-grandmother Alice

McTeer, dressed just as she was in the picture. *What's troubling you, child*, she said to me, or at least, I dreamed she said it. I told her, *we wanted to name this one...* I remember I patted my tummy as I said it, *we wanted to name our girl for you, but my mother will have a fit if we do.* Then in the dream Alice laughed the strangest laugh, not a sound, but little splatters of silence. *Then, name her after my dear Millicent Robbins. Nothing would please me more.* I must have been sleeping, because I didn't think it at all strange to be talking to a dead woman in broad daylight. *Why Millicent?* I asked her. Alice flickered like a leaf in the wind and said, *Because I loved her and because she was a wild and winged soul. The life growing inside you now carries all her gifts.* I would have asked her more then but she was gone and I was awake again."

Mother and daughter sat silent for a time, weighing the dream in their minds. Finally, Millicent asked, "Did I bring you any gifts?"

Amelia laughed, pulled her child close and kissed her head. "You are the gift, my angel. The light in our day. Joshua and I couldn't ask or hope for more than you."

Millicent McTeer had never met her maternal grandmother. She'd seen her skyped, of course, a smartly garbed woman who endured costly and sometimes painful maintenance in an ultimately failing campaign to keep herself looking younger than her daughter. Calista Montford communicated with the family on birthdays and holidays. On these occasions a forced benevolence thinly veiled a vague air of disapproval that filtered through the world-wide web all the way from California. Millicent's mother, Amelia, didn't appear cheered at all by these conversations.

Millicent, always trying to get at the thorny heart of appearances, asked her father once, "Why doesn't Grandmother ever come to visit?"

Joshua glanced at his wife across the room to be certain she wasn't listening, then leaned toward his daughter and whispered, "Happiness is a loving close-knit family who live at the other end of the country." Millicent figured that saying it aloud practically guaranteed that her father's definition might soon be tested. And very soon, it was.

On a Monday evening, when there were fewer guests and Hillhaven Inn didn't serve dinner, a short day for most of the staff, a welcome respite from the summer tourist invasions, Millicent's family sprawled in varying postures around their personal upstairs veranda. With her current book-of-the-day, she lay on the floor, propped on her elbows while her bare heels made circles in the air. Joshua was scribbling in his notebook as usual, ensconced in a yellow-painted rocker that revealed, season by season, more of its previous green. Joshua called it his bleached blond. Amelia was communing with her laptop on an aging sofa camouflaged with a bright, intricately patterned blanket sent back by an elder relative from a small country in South America while he was negotiating contracts with their state-owned oil company. None in present company could recall exactly which country.

Asheton traffic raised just a low murmur behind the calls of wrens and robins and the conversation between poplar leaves and the warm wind. The three humans were each lost in themselves, silent and intent, until Amelia softly demolished their peace. In a voice full of surprise and tinged with alarm, she said, barely above a whisper, "Hell's bells."

"What's up?" Joshua breathed, not looking up from his notes. Millicent, without giving any sign she heard, suddenly all vigilant.

"Mother's coming," said Amelia, emitting a sound that might have been either a laugh or a moan.

Millicent came to her feet in a flash, almost airborne in her glee, "When?" she shrieked.

Joshua, his notebook closed now, queried quietly, "How long?"

———

Calista Montford descended upon Hillhaven with all her accustomed style and flair, a calculated extravagance that, had she been only slightly less tasteful, would have been counted as ostentation. She had been born into a moneyed family who taught her growing up that everyone had a price and she should sell herself dearly. The only person who had successfully dented her illusion of privilege and entitlement was her ex-husband, Amelia's father. Calista's lawyers insured that he still paid regularly for his transgression.

Time, experience, and expensive cosmetic procedures had transmuted the beauty of her youth into a steely sheen, impermeable, not quite human. Women half her age felt at an undefined disadvantage in the same room with her. Calista's *doesn't everybody* reaction to any perceived criticism, veiled or otherwise, was intended to maintain that effect.

Millicent, though fascinated with the grandmother she had never seen except on some screen or other, had always been cautious in their interactions. When she saw Calista pull into Hillhaven's yard, purple scarf trailing in the rush of her rented sportscar, the girl determined to maintain her stance. Calista Montford, she thought, was indeed a force, though not entirely of nature.

Calista stepped out of her car, as it sat blocking the drive and crowding the steps before Hillhaven's front entrance. She stood staring at the building, lifting her glasses with three fingers. From her expression, she might have been looking at the aftermath of a plane crash or observing an execution.

As Amelia and Millicent came down the steps, she held her keys aloft and said, "Where's the valet?"

"I'll do it, Mother," Amelia said, taking the keys and pulling the car into a marked parking space.

"And who do we have here?" Calista purred, regarding her granddaughter as she might have appraised a stray puppy.

"I'm your granddaughter," Millicent said. "We've skyped."

"So we have," Calista said, bending over and kissing the air several inches from the child's face. "You look smaller than I thought you'd be."

She straightened, as Amelia returned, carrying two of her bags. "Dear, don't you have people for this?" Calista said, waving a hand at the day.

"They're busy with the paying guests," Amelia said. She set down one of the bags and intercepted her mother's lofted hand with the car keys.

The older woman responded with the same sort of virtual kiss she'd bestowed in Millicent's direction. "You look tired, dear. Have you been taking care of yourself?"

"Yes, I have. I look older, Mother," Amelia said. "We haven't seen you since before Millicent was born."

"That's twelve years," Millicent added. She picked up the bag her mother had put down. Together they followed the self-crowned Queen of Despond up the steps to the door.

"Where's what's-his-name?" queried the queen as she sailed through the door like a frigate rigged for battle.

Millicent sat on the veranda waiting for Joshua when he came in from his meeting. "Dad, she's awful," she warned her father. "She talks mean even when she smiles."

"Calista is your grandmother, Angel." Joshua said, since he couldn't argue with his daughter's assessment.

"That isn't my fault," Millicent barked. "Don't blame me."

"I guess it's my fault then," said Joshua, trying not to laugh, "I wanted to marry your mother, and that meant Calista had to be your grandmother."

"She and my grandfather are divorced, right?" asked Millicent.

Joshua nodded, sitting down in one of the big green rockers, momentarily unoccupied by guests. "That's right, Angel. Fred Montford is married to a woman named Alice now."

"Dad, can children divorce their parents?"

Joshua's laugh finally escaped, "Don't think so, Angel. The best we can do is move to another state."

"But, Dad, she's followed us."

"Don't worry, Angel. She's just curious. She won't stay long."

"What's she curious about?"

"She's wondering how we can be happy without all her money."

"But she isn't happy."

"You can tell, can you?"

"Yup, Dad, I can tell, but I don't know why. I mean, she has everything."

"Calista doesn't have what we have, Angel."

"What's that, Dad?"

"What do you think it is?"

Millicent didn't need to think about her answer. Immediately, "We have us."

Joshua nodded. "And you could say love."

"Same thing," Millicent said.

Calista Montford crossed her room, ashtray in hand, opened the door onto the veranda outside, discovered it was vacant, then fetched a glass from a bedside table and a bottle from one of her bags. She listened for a moment. The only human-sourced sounds she heard were faint and from the floor below. Nobody would hear her confessional. She closed the door behind her as she went out again, retreated to an aged wicker armchair shaded by a gangly redbud tree in flower and ahum with bees. When she was certain the bees were taking no notice of her, she brushed imagination off the seat of the chair, and sat down. She thought about going back inside for a towel to protect her pricey pants, but there was no one in Marshall County she needed to impress so she succumbed to inertia, poured herself a stiff and straight libation, lit an imported cigarette, and punched a number on her cell phone. She had time to fill her lungs with hazy carcinogens and exhale before her best friend

Irmy answered. Irmagaard Stieglitz was not only Calista's best friend, but probably the only real friend she had in the entire state of California.

"No, Irmy, I'm not having a good time at all," she responded to the inevitable first query, "I'm flying home tomorrow ... I suppose it is, but it is so, to put it kindly, rural here. Asheton is nowhere full of nobodies. Amelia has chosen to bury herself in this wilderness with her loser husband. That's her right, I suppose, but I'm sad for the child ... Millicent ... They're bringing her up like a primitive. She will never have any idea of what she's missed out on in the wider world. Likely, she'll grow up to be a village innkeeper just like her parents ... That's a laugh. Joshua McTeer is no Ronald Horne. I'd wager Hillhaven is his last resort. He can't even afford a decent chef ... Oh, yes, there are some local excitements. There's lots of insects and nature noises and sweaty tourists traveling on a budget. It isn't the sort of place for our kind of people, Irmy ... You are so refreshing, Dear. You look for the best in everything and everybody ... Ciao, sweet friend. Let's do lunch on the other side."

Calista stared at her phone as if it were a sick animal that had just died in her hand, stubbed her cigarette, took a sip from her glass, grimaced, crossed the veranda and poured her drink over the rail.

Millicent sipped her grapefruit juice and listened to the exchange between her mother and grandmother. Calista's breakfast lay barely disturbed on her plate while she surveyed the assorted tourists and locals starting their day in Hillhaven's dining room. As Cora poured a third cup of coffee for her, Calista continued her inquisition of her daughter. "I'm surprised the place is so full. The food you serve here is hardly outstanding."

Amelia had grown up with her mother's hostility toward life in general, so was unperturbed by it now. "You seem to like our coffee well enough, Mother."

"Well, yes. One must sustain one's edge. But what do all these people come here for?"

"Because they're hungry," Millicent said. Her grandmother gave her a look meant to kill, but it only amused. Millicent, being essentially a kind soul, gave no sign.

Amelia picked up the gauntlet. "If you mean, why do people come to Asheton, Mother, they come for the climate, for the woods, the waterfalls, to hike our mountain trails and fish our streams, to slow down and catch up with themselves."

Calista picked up her fork, as if contemplating a tentative skirmish with her omelet, raised a precisely drawn eyebrow and said sweetly, "And what do they do the next day?"

Amelia laughed, as if her mother had told a joke. "Why they come to Hillhaven for breakfast. I must turn to work now, Mother. Enjoy your breakfast. Cora will see to you if you need anything." She kissed her daughter and was away.

Millicent got up, declared, "School," and kissed Calista on her powdered cheek. Her grandmother pursed her lips without turning her head and realized she was alone. She forked her omelet, and delivered a hefty bite to her mouth. While she chewed, she took renewed interest in a biscuit, broke it open and slathered it with butter, hesitated, then drizzled it with a bit of honey from the little pitcher Cora had left her.

"Well ..." she said to nobody who was there and ate her breakfast like a good girl.

———

The next day, Calista Montford flew away to the west without promising never to return and the following week, Millicent walked home from school, sans books at last, with the whole summer before her to pursue her study of human and non-human nature at the University of Hillhaven. She reveled in the ordinary routines of the hotel, and though she was yet too young to be an official employee, she pitched in and aided the staff in their various chores and duties as much as they would allow. All the souls at Hillhaven she regarded as extended family, the live ones and the once alive ones. The rambling old inn was her home, her village, her country and her world.

Millicent was a friend to the world. A stranger to her was simply a friend whose name she did not yet know. She took an interest in all who came and went, contrived to strike up conversation with most of them at some point in their stay, and would be remembered fondly by some of them when they had forgotten all other details of their visit. She took a particular interest in the young man who came walking up the drive as she was sweeping the broad veranda on a cool Monday morning when the sun had just lit the tops of the tallest poplars across the yard.

With the sun in his face, he smiled unblinking at Millicent as he strode across the yard with his big pack. When he stepped up into the shadowed porch, the light of the new day still flared in his eyes.

"Where are you hiking?" Millicent asked. He was obviously a hiker. He looked like a hiker with his rough clothes and scruffy boots and oversized load. He smelled like a hiker, too, a musky aroma of sweat and earth and miles afoot and something else Millicent couldn't quite place, not smoky exactly, though it made her think of fire.

"The whole way," Hiker said, settling his pack gently to the floor and rolling his shoulders to loose them from the memory of their burden.

Most who came to Hillhaven were wheeled there by car or bus or sometimes in a chair, but occasionally some thru-hiker would stop and stay for a day or two, resting from the tall mountains south of Asheton to gather strength for the taller ones north. Hillhaven didn't advertise as a hiker hostel, but the few who found it were welcomed and sustained, and word got passed along the Trail.

"Do you have a vacancy, Miss?" Hiker asked.

Millicent pointed her broom toward the door. "Mom's just inside. Talk to her." She knew that even if the rooms were all full, he would still be offered a place on their upstairs porch to spend the night.

"Thanks," Hiker said, pointing to his pack. "Will you watch this for me while I check in?"

"Who am I watching it for, then?"

"Trail name's Dragon. Who's watching?"

"I'm Millicent. How'd you come to be Dragon?"

"Because I'm slow. I come dragging into camp after everybody else has already cooked their supper."

Dragon went through the door and Millicent went back to her sweeping. She could hear him talking to Amelia. His pack perched on the porch like a patient familiar, still radiating Dragon's presence. Millicent shook her head and pondered, *whatever you are, Mister Dragon, you're not slow.*

An indefinable something about the hiker captured Millicent's imagination. She wanted to taste for herself what it was like to live for days on the mountain, sleeping in the open under stars, or with only a sheet of canvas between the dreamer and the stormy dark. At supper that evening, she watched for his lean face, sharp features weathered to a sheen like ripe tobacco leaf, but Dragon had apparently found his supper somewhere else.

Lisa came that night and played her fiddle. During summer, Millicent was allowed to stay up later. Sometimes she would sit in the dining room and listen to the music with the guests, though the stair was still her favorite spot, high up among the shadow folk, seeing but unseen, listening and silent, present but apart. Already, this was becoming the pattern of her life. She was engaged with her world, but if any noticed her at all, she remained in their mind the elusive other, a vague impression who left a vivid memory.

She didn't see Dragon come in, but late in the evening, he was there, sitting in a far corner of the room while Cora brought him a cup of coffee. He downed it as if it were cold water on a hot day. He rested his elbows on the table and watched Lisa intently with his shining eyes. There was nothing to see, but Millicent could feel him reaching out with his mind to touch the music. Lisa must have felt it, too, because her sound began to shift and change by degrees, the fiddle flashing in her hands like a live thing about to consume her. The voice of her instrument grew throaty and wild, soaring and swooping like a rising wind. The audience sat still and rapt as if stunned to silence while the air in the room grew charged like a storm until suddenly the lights went out as a bolt of lightning blasted a tree in the yard and there was a storm, rain driving hard against the old building, wind rattling the windows, a steady rumble and roar that might have been the voice of a flood, or a dragon.

Lisa played on, more quietly now. The lights came back on again, flickering, then steadied, and people began to call for their checks and discuss among themselves how they might get to their cars without being drenched in the downpour.

Millicent got up, went down to the foyer to help hand out umbrellas to those who had come unprepared for the sudden weather. Joshua bought them for four dollars each at a local home projects store. Sometimes diners even returned them. She got no chance to offer an umbrella to Dragon, though. Then she remembered he wouldn't need one. He was staying at Hillhaven for the night.

When she thought no one was watching, she peeked into the register. There, next to S*imon Ryder,* Millicent saw his trail name in parentheses. She noted his room was directly below hers. As she climbed the stairs toward bed and sleep, a thought not like her at all flitted through her tired head, that she might fall into Dragon's dreams tonight. Whatever dreams she fell into before morning, Millicent forgot on the far side of sleep.

She intended to wake early, try to snare her Dragon at breakfast. When she didn't see him, Millicent asked Cora if Dragon had been up and about.

"The hiker?" Cora said, "He checked out early, paid in cash. He was a beautiful animal, wasn't he?" Millicent had never thought of boy or man in those terms, but when Cora said it, Millicent nodded and smiled, thinking to herself that he most certainly was just that.

Back in her room, after her pancakes and sausage, Millicent puzzled over an object on her dresser. She was certain she didn't put it there. It hadn't been there the day before. She picked it up, turning it over and over in her hand. It felt like stone, a small round pebble from a streambed, perhaps, but gleamed clear as crystal, and as she held it to the morning sun, she thought it flashed in her hand, like the light in Dragon's eyes. The stone, if it was a stone, felt warm, the heat of it pulsing slowly in her palm as if she held a live thing. After a moment, she realized the stone's throb precisely matched the beat of her own heart.

Carefully, as if it were a talisman or a sacred relic, Millicent homed it in the ornate little box, her birthday present from Calista, where she consigned her serious treasures. She knew without knowing from where it had come.

CHAPTER THREE

For their daughter's sixteenth birthday, Amelia and Joshua arranged a dinner at Yagi, Asheton's most authentic Japanese restaurant, where she could host her friends apart from parental scrutiny. Amos, the restaurant manager and close family friend, was not Japanese. His wife, Shizuko, owned the place, and maintained its standards with an iron rule. Together, they would serve as undercover chaperones for the evening as the young people celebrated.

Japanese cuisine was Millicent's latest consuming interest, and she presided over her table with flair and decorum, a striking presence with her flaming hair and white blouse, catching the notice of most of the male diners in the restaurant, regardless their age, while igniting varying degrees of envy and jealousy among her own gender.

Most of Millicent's party were classmates. One of them, a handsome athlete with a following, Francis Howard, was a year older than Millicent, but they shared an advanced foreign language class, and when she told Frank about her party, he practically invited himself. Frank had always been respectful and polite during their conversations, and Millicent felt flattered by his attention during the evening. She knew every girl there wished to be sitting in her chair. When the party was breaking up around ten o'clock, they could hear thunder and see rain glinting on the street outside. Frank helped her into her coat and said, "Do you have a car?"

"Not yet," Millicent said. "I just got my learner's permit."

"Let me take you home, then," he offered.

"Thanks, but my dad is picking me up. Hillhaven's not five minutes from here. I could walk if I needed to."

Frank laughed, "You know how dads are. He's probably watching a ballgame or something. Let me save him a trip."

Millicent knew her father wouldn't be watching anything on television, but several of her friends were monitoring the conversation while pretending not to notice, so she took out her cell and called her father.

"I'll trust him if you do," Joshua said.

Millicent did trust Frank, so was surprised on the way home when he slid a hand across the seat and began groping after the hem of her skirt. She pushed his arm away and snapped, "Keep your hands on the wheel and your eyes on the road, Frank. You're driving."

When they reached Hillhaven, instead of turning into the drive, Frank pulled into the park across the street and stopped in the shadow of an ancient, low-hanging maple. Millicent had her fingers on the door handle when he reached out with one hand and turned her face toward his mouth and slipped the other hand deftly inside her blouse to grasp a breast. The execution was quick and smooth. Millicent thought he'd definitely had a lot of practice at this. His lips brushed hers as Millicent tried to pull away.

"You're hot," He murmured. "Let me..." Millicent imagined herself in flames. Frank's eyes widened. He howled with pain and jerked his hand away so quickly that he tore a button from her blouse. He held up his hand and even in the dim light Millicent could see the blisters. It looked as if Frank had doused his paw in boiling water.

Frank cowered against his door, staring at Millicent from eyes wide with disbelief and terror. He opened his mouth but no words came, only a whimper that escalated into a thin whine as Frank fumbled at the door with his good hand until he found the handle and ejected himself into the night.

Millicent, astonished and dismayed, watched the boy crumpled on the pavement outside the car as she listened to his grizzly keening and the drum of the downpour on his new leather jacket.

"Frank?" she ventured, all her unaskable questions distilled into that solitary word.

Frank didn't answer or look up at her. He scrambled to his feet, manifest one last croaking sob, and clutching his seared hand to his chest like an orphaned babe, he lurched away into the storm, leaving his father's sports convertible unmanned, and Millicent McTeer to dash for home in the rain.

"Did you hear what happened to Frank Howard after your party last night?" Dianne Johnson stage-whispered over Millicent's shoulder as they shuffled along the lunch line.

"No telling," said Millicent, switching on her innocent face as she turned to her friend. "Something he deserved, I hope."

Dianne shot her a quizzical look and plunged ahead with her scoop. "He was driving home through that awful storm and heard something dragging under his car. He stopped and was trying to pull it loose and burned his hand on the muffler.

Millicent didn't bother to look sympathetic. "He put it in the wrong place, I guess."

Dianne shook her head. "You're just mean, Millicent McTeer. He's really hurt, all bandaged up. Says it hurts something awful. He'll miss the game Friday. You two didn't have a fight when he carried you home after the party?"

"I wasn't in his car long enough to fight, Dianne. Look, I'm sorry Frank got hurt, but he isn't exactly my favorite person right now." Millicent held out her tray to receive her day's ration of meatloaf.

"Not again," wailed Dianne. "Please, I pass," as she reached for a salad.

Apparently, Millicent was not Francis Howard's favorite person, either. For the rest of the semester, she never saw him if Frank spied her first. He dropped the class they shared, and quit pestering every pretty girl he knew for a date. Girls wondered what had come over Frank Howard. The few who did manage to rope him in for an evening out said he acted as if he was afraid of them.

A rumor began to circulate among the female student body that Frank Howard had fallen in love with a boy. When Dianne repeated it to Millicent, she said, "The only boy Frank loves is himself."

That summer was the wettest on record, according to the local weather bureau. The rain came almost daily, not as showers, but in torrents and deluges. Every week brought another storm warning and flood watch. Politicians argued on television about how much climate change was influencing the extreme weather, and whether human depredations were to blame. Experts gave wordy explanations about why this might be the new normal for Asheton. Several times during the summer, the Long Broad overwhelmed its banks and flooded much of the new Arts District along River Street. Two of the contractors heavily invested in converting the old factory buildings into studios, galleries, shops and condominiums went out of business.

Lisa Charon found a part-time summer job for her favorite violin student with a friend who ran a business in the District in one of the few buildings spared inundation. After their lesson one day, she asked, "How's the job search going, Millicent?

"Nothing yet. Everything I've been interested in has already been taken. I might have to settle for flipping burgers or waiting tables at Hillhaven for Mom and Dad. But I have my driver's license now. Dad says he'll help me get some wheels if I land a job."

Although she knew, Lisa asked, "What sort of job are you after?"

Millicent stood silent for a moment, searching for her words, "I'd like to work with live things, creatures or plants, you know, something non-human."

Lisa laughed. "Don't you like people?"

"Humans are the only animals," Millicent said, not smiling at all, "who want to be what they are not."

Lisa took a business card from her pocket and held it out to Millicent. "You should check this out then. Vesuvia is a friend. I've told her about you. There's a job there if she likes you."

Millicent took the card printed on heavy cream stock with a green ivy border around the edge. In the center, in a stately, old-fashioned serif font, one word, *Wildness*, followed by an address in smaller type.

"Wildness?" repeated Millicent, her puzzlement in her voice and on her face.

"That's her name and that's her game," laughed Lisa. "When you've met her, come tell me all about it."

"I'll check it out. Thanks a lot, Lisa," Millicent said sincerely, stuffing the card into the pocket of her jeans.

Lisa launched one of her inscrutable smiles. "When you get the job, make sure Vesuvia thanks me," she said.

"Don't you mean if I get the job?"

Lisa just shook her head. "I meant what I said. Some things are fated."

As soon as she got home Millicent called the number on the card, with the distinct impression that she was being set up for an adventure not of her choosing. She was curious, though, and when a heavily accented voice of indeterminate gender and nationality told her interviews would start at nine the next morning, Millicent said, "I'll be there."

That night she dreamed strange and violent dreams. In one, she was walking up a long hallway. Closed doors ranged on either side. The passage was dark, except for a light at the far end, where Lisa Charon and an indefinable creature resembling a large bird or a small dragon appeared engaged in earnest conversation. Millicent couldn't hear what they were discussing, but as she approached, they turned and looked at her and Lisa laughed when she said, "Here she comes now, and she's all yours." The bird/dragon opened its mouth and flames blossomed forth, filling the hallway and engulfing Millicent. She woke before she could scream and morning light rinsed her clean of all her nightmares.

After a quick breakfast, she caught a bus down to the Arts District. She had to walk the last block because of a wash-out repair in progress on River Street and when she arrived at the address, she stood in the shadow of a three-story brick building that looked to have had a former life as a warehouse. Now, if one could believe the signage, it housed on one side a painter, on the other a used bookstore, and between these two extremes, in tarnished gilt,

WILDNESS

rare and exotic botanicals.

Millicent pushed the door bearing on its glass a notice urging attendance at a Celtic band concert at the Tattered Turnip Bistro, and stepped up into Wildness. After the bright glare of the street, she had to stand for a moment until a counter and various other interior details gradually emerged from the shadows. Pods, seeds and cones heaped in bins just inside the door. Deeper into the gloom a crowd of vague leafy forms waiting for someone who couldn't bear to live without them waved gently at Millicent in the draft wafting from overhead fans. She wondered how they gleaned enough light to survive.

The narrow interior seemed to recede into an infinity of ever deeper shadows and rising darkness, illuminated here and there by bare light bulbs suspended on cords dropping from an invisible ceiling, lost in shadow or distance or time.

On the counter immediately in front of her, a huge antique cash register caught the light from the storefront glass and threw it back in fiery flares and flickers like coals on a hearth. The back of the machine bore a fantastic decoration that, once her eyes focused on the dimness, revealed itself to be some sort of winged serpent, perhaps a dragon.

Something stirred behind the cash register, and whoever had been sitting on a stool there, stood and faced her. Millicent gasped. For an instant, the woman seemed to tower over her, impossibly tall. She thought the dragon had come to life. Then, before the impression had fully registered, it was just a woman standing in front of her, tall, but in reality not much taller than Millicent, a luminous cloud of white hair around an angular face, thin, high-boned, homing sharp golden eyes that seemed to see through as much as to see. Millicent thought of a tiger's eyes, and for a second, she would have sworn a tiger peered at her over the counter, but it was only a woman gazing at her, fierce enough in appearance, though the voice issuing from the thin mouth sounded gentle and somehow, the only word Millicent could think of was *motherly*.

"I'm Vesuvia Wildness," the gentle voice said. In the dusky gloom, Millicent couldn't see the woman's lips moving at all, but she got the impression of a smile, and she heard the words, "This is my world, and you are Lisa Charon's favorite student, and you've come to learn how to fly."

"Actually, I've come about a job," stammered Millicent.

The job started at nine sharp the next morning, according to Vesuvia. Millicent left without any clear idea of what her duties might entail, other than to, as her new employer put it, "Companion my darlings."

"I got the job," Millicent told her parents when she got back to Hillhaven.

"What will you be doing?" Amelia asked her.

"I'm really not sure, but I suppose I'll find out," she confessed. "As far as I can make out, from what Vesuvia told me, I'm some kind of plant herder."

"Sounds like a rough job," Joshua said. "Plants can be a mite skittish."

The next morning, Millicent caught the eight-thirty bus down to the Art District. The sun blazed out of a true-blue sky when she left home, and the weather forecast called for a clear day ahead, but by the time her bus stopped on River Street, the clouds turned ominous, and as she stood from her seat to exit the bus, deluge commenced. The street reconstruction project was still ongoing. Beyond the traffic barriers, the whole block to Wildness Botanicals presented a morass of mud and broken pavement. She would arrive the first day of her new job looking like a drowned mouse.

As she stepped off the bus, shielding her head with her purse, Millicent thought, *I'm not really here.* To her own astonishment, as the door of the bus hissed closed behind her, it became immediately apparent that she wasn't quite. She could still see rain falling down around her, but as she lowered her purse, she didn't feel it. The disarray of the torn-up street still ranged ahead, but transparent and insubstantial, like the image on a phone display in bright sunlight. Somehow, behind the storm-drenched chaos, she saw a different scene, calm and sunlit, and the sidewalk whole and unmarked, as it had been until recently and would be soon again. Millicent focused on that desirable alternative and walked to work in her own personal and private beautiful day.

When she stepped inside Wildness and the door closed behind her, she heard the rain driving against the glass and turned to see the storm raging unabated in the street outside, but here she was, dry and unruffled. Behind her, she heard the voice that had spoken to her on the phone when she had first called to inquire about the job, "She was right about you."

Millicent turned to face the strangest little man she had ever seen. Not quite a man, perhaps. Not quite a woman, either. Maybe, not quite human. Nonetheless, an unthreatening and benevolent presence. Familiar, in some indefinable way. Millicent felt she ought to recognize him from some previous encounter. She saw first the dark and brilliant eyes, shining from a pleasant face, bearded or furred, Millicent couldn't decide which. The figure seemed taller the longer she stared at it, willowy and attenuated as the stem of a flower.

Disoriented, feeling outside herself, uncomprehending of anything that had happened to her since she got off the bus, Millicent stretched out her arms as if awaiting inspection. Laughing hysterically, she blurted out the only thing she could be certain of, "I'm dry."

"Indeed, you are," warbled the voice, shifting somewhere between a bird and a brook, "For a novice, your sense of place is extraordinary."

"I'm Millicent McTeer," Millicent stammered. "I'm supposed to start work here today. Vesuvia, that is, Miss Wildness, hired me.'

"Yes," said the voice, lower now, like the purr of a large

cat. "You are Dry and you are McTeer and I am Wendl VonTrier, Greeter and Guide, at your service."

Wendl, who had somehow adjusted height to bring his face level with Millicent's, brightened suddenly in defiance of the surrounding gloom, as he/she/it said, "Wildness is upstairs in the Preservation Department. Wendel will begin your orientation while we wait for her."

VonTrier turned abruptly, called over a shoulder, "Follow me, Dry McTeer.

Without another look in her direction, the elvish Greeter strode away through the dim toward a door hinting at more luminous regions beyond. Millicent McTeer, who early in her young life, had determined to follow no directive not strictly her own, chose to interpret Wendl's parting shot as an invitation rather than an order, and followed obediently into the light.

The door opened into a huge room, that looked to Millicent vast as an aircraft hangar, much bigger than the building she had entered a few moments ago. She raised her hand to shield her eyes against the glare, intense and warm as sunlight. She could feel the spaciousness. The ceiling hung so high above her it might well have been sky. She tried to locate it, but the light flooding down was too brilliant for her to see. Centered in the brick wall behind her, the door through which they had entered, now just a featureless black rectangle. On the other side there might have been deepest night, or nothing at all.

She gazed along the brick until it met stone, not cut and set, but piled and towered as if time and nature had done it. Wendl, ahead, seeming distinctly male now, appeared to have forgotten her. He leaned over a cluster of elegantly flamboyant flowering plants, muttering to himself, as if carrying on a conversation with them. When Millicent caught up with him, the Greeter straightened, his guise now as much fox as man, stared at her as if surprised to see her there, then barked a little laugh before settling into his more human face.

"Yes. Well. Dry McTeer, here you are. Behold the World behind the world."

Millicent stood speechless. She had no words and couldn't have summoned them if she had. Awe was too small a term for what she felt as she turned in a slow circle like a planet revolving before her star. They stood in a narrow aisle devolving steadily ahead into a narrower path. Flowering shrubs and berried bushes and rampant climbers crowded close in all directions. Vines and tendrils wrapped every available stem and branch and trunk. Mosses and lichen carpeted any surface that might have been soil or bark beneath. Except for flamboyant flowers and ripening fruits, green in infinite tint and shade was apparently the only allowable color.

Trees presided over the lesser foliates, some of them hung with fruit or cone, some graced with blossoms, some wearing needles and spines or broad succulent leaves. Some so tall their tops were lost in the light, their trunks as broad as Millicent was tall. It was a garden. It was a forest. It was a world. It was Eden, she thought, and the strangest aspect of it all, none of these verdant lives were familiar to her. For all the time she had spent walking the mountains with her father, she could not name a single plant she saw now.

She didn't feel a breeze but heard a constant rustling as if a light wind blew. As she watched, Millicent's eye caught subtle movement everywhere, shiverings and chatterings among the leaves, weavings and wavings among the vines and branches. She could feel within herself their reaching, their yearning toward the light, and toward ... her.

Something brushed her ankle. She looked down to discover a thin vine with brilliant emerald leaves and tiny magenta flowers had crept down into the path and was very purposefully twining itself about her leg. Millicent resisted the impulse to jerk away, reached down and began to gently disengage herself. The vine didn't resist, though it playfully flirted with her fingers as she removed it. She was sure it was making a sound, so soft as to be barely audible. It might have been speech and it might have been a song and it thrilled her to hear.

"They like you," spoke a familiar voice. "You'll do right well here."

Millicent looked up to see Wendl had gone. Vesuvia Wildness smiled down at her and a host of airy voices greenly gleed her welcome.

On her bus back to Hillhaven that evening, Millicent replayed her day in her mind, half-convinced it had all been a hallucination. The mobile vine, ringing in her fingers like minuscule sleighbells, a tone too high and slight almost to hear, then the whisper among the flowers and the sighing in the trees gathering to a rush, almost a roar in her head, as the whole forest sang her name to her, *Milliccenttt.* She had heard herself said before in just this way, sometime, somewhere, she was sure, when she was still a child.

But Vesuvia laughed, as if she hadn't heard anything, and said, "Quite impressive, when they're all together this way, aren't they? This is what we call the Welcome Center," waving her arm, "where we put the new specimens when they come in, let them acclimate to the unaccustomed weather and proximity. Plants get along together much better than people do. They have to, because what we strive for individually, they can only attain in community. That's the basic difference between our kinds, apart from the obvious physiology. Plants know as much as we do, maybe a lot more. They just have their own ways of knowing it. We could learn a lot from them if we could speak the same language."

Rapt in her remembering, Millicent involuntarily said aloud, "But I heard them."

"What did you hear, dear?" The lady seated across the aisle from her on the bus was looking at her strangely. "Are you all right?"

Millicent laughed, "I'm fine. I think I dozed off there. It's been a long day."

The lady went back to her worn and dog-eared paperback but kept glancing in Millicent's direction until she reached her stop. Then she gathered her bags and exited, but as she passed Millicent, she handed off her book, whispered, "This might be helpful."

Millicent took the book, too startled even to say thanks. She looked at the title, *The Forest Soul*, then opened it. The pages were blank. She flipped through the book. *Who would read a blank book? Who would write one?* then turned back to the cover.

THE FOREST SOUL
by Millicent McTeer

The bus lurched into motion again. Millicent looked out the window at the street sliding past the glass. The book lady smiled and blew a kiss before she disappeared behind.

As she walked up the drive at Hillhaven, Millicent saw her mother and father in earnest conversation just outside the front door. They appeared to be on the brink of an argument. As she came up the steps, Amelia saw her and lifted a bandaged hand.

"There she is. Home at last. How did it go on your first day as a working woman?"

Millicent gave her own query priority, "Mercy, Mother. What happened to your hand?"

"She couldn't wait for me to come help her, that's what," said Joshua, though it wasn't his question.

"My glasses fell down behind my desk, and I was trying to move it to retrieve them. You know how heavy that old thing is. My foot slipped and my hand caught against the wall and I sprained my wrist. Nothing's broken, thankfully," she said lightly.

Joshua threw up his arms, shot his *I give up* look toward his daughter and fled the scene.

Millicent put down her bag, took Amelia's wounded hand between both her own. "That must've smarted. Is it swollen?" She could feel the hurt in it, felt the pain in her own hands, let it slide up through her chest into her head and away.

The transaction left her dizzy as Amelia said, "A little, I think, but right now it doesn't hurt at all. Amazing what a little love can do."

"Oh more than a little," Millicent said, planting a kiss on the bandage.

Amelia flexed her fingers, "It feels pretty good right now, but I probably shouldn't play tonight. The medic at the Exigent clinic said I should give it a rest for a couple of days. Maybe Lisa could come fill in if she isn't busy."

"I'll do it," blurted Millicent. She had never played her violin for an audience, but she wanted to vent the emotions built up from her impossibly improbable day.

"Sure you don't mind?" Amelia said. "I can call Lisa."

"What's the matter, Mom? Don't you think your little girl is up to it?"

———

That night at dinner, about midway through the first seating of the evening, Millicent stood beside her mother next to the piano as Amelia took the microphone, and holding aloft her bandaged wrist, said, "Hello, everyone."

This incited a low communal groan of public empathy and sympathy. She began singing a cappella her improvised intro,

I cannot play, but never fear
Here's someone grand for you to hear
My daughter talented and dear,
The marvelous Millicent McTeer.

"Ah," the diners exhaled their collective appreciation, accompanying themselves with a smattering of applause.

Amelia retreated then, as Millicent cradled her violin and gave it her bow, easing into a strathspey, *Little John*, Lisa Charon had taught her. Once she had their attention, she followed up with several old ballads which she thought might have been better sung had she considered herself a singer. She took her break, downed a glass of mint tea, and resumed her set, was gratified to hear no conversation while she played a reel for them. The applause that followed was a shade more than polite. Seeing her mother talking to Cora by the kitchen door, Millicent laid her fiddle on the piano, reached down for Amelia's guitar, brought it to tune, and began to play a song she knew her mother would recognize. It was something of a family joke, the result of a game. Joshua had improvised the lyrics to Amelia's melody. Amelia looked up in surprise when she heard it. Millicent caught her eye, silently mouthed, *please*. Amelia shook her head, unfurled a rueful smile, then walked across the room and took the mic and began to sing,

The woods were lovely, dark and deep;
I brought along my map to keep
Me oriented to the trail,
Although it was to no avail;
I followed every turn and twist,
For miles, but then could not resist,
The shadowed path that beckoned me
To find whatever I might see
Among the fern and mossy stone,
Where many passed, but few had gone,
I pondered, then I turned aside,
To find what beauty might abide
Hid away across the stream

That laughed like children in a dream,
And so I went, quiet and slow,
To see what secret I could know,
And if you find me in that place,
Should Mother Nature leave a trace
among the laurel where I fell,
My story will be yours to tell.

The somewhat less then joyful song elicited a respectable round of hand-clapping, during which Amelia leaned over and asked, "Are we going to leave them in the dreadfuls?"

Millicent grinned, stuck up the evening's farewell, and Amelia lifted a brow, then gave it her voice.

Some roads hoist you high away,
Some roads lead you low.
Some roads invite to mystery,
And some roads' end you know,
Some roads simply wear you down,
And some roads make you grow.
Some seek the road that's paved and fast;
I'll take the one that's slow.

"You're in a strange mood tonight, daughter of mine," said Amelia when her mic was off.

In answer, Millicent sang to her mother softly so softly in a voice she hadn't known until now that she possessed,

Despair is black they say.
I walk somewhere between
There and hope today,
Closing in on green.

Later that night, alone in her room, drying her hair, Millicent remembered the book from the strange lady on the bus. She dropped her towel and rummaged through her bag. All she found was a battered old paperback by Stephen King. Rampant on the green cover, a multihued dragon.

CHAPTER FOUR

---

illicent, you have a drone delivery.
Millicent McTeer rolled over, mumbled "Thanks, Brigid. I'll get it now," and opened an eye. Her friends laughed at her for talking to her HomeZone device as if the Brigid were human. She agreed with them that it was a ludicrous habit, but she had never been able to break it. She spent more of her day talking to her computers than to people. She never admitted to anyone at the university that over the previous four summers at Wildness Rare and Exotic Botanicals she had talked mostly to plants. She never told any soul other than Vesuvia Wildness and Wendl VonTrier that the plants had talked to her. Millicent knew from experience that sentience was not confined to blood and bone. The newest quantum processors were composing symphonies now, although in her opinion, no AI author had yet written a good novel.

She climbed out of bed, padded across the room in her bare feet, opened her patio door, blinked in the sunlight, and the drone blinked back at her, *Millicent McTeer, here is your package. Please confirm receipt.*

Millicent reached down and pressed her palm into the sensor screen centered on the top of the shiny metallic cube at her feet. The lid sprang open and she lifted out the box inside.

Millicent McTeer, do you approve contents?

Millicent held the small square carton, heavy for its size, read the attached label bordered in green ivy, *Wildness Emporium.*

She read the rest aloud, smiling, "Rare and Exotic Botanicals."

The drone, adamant in its protocol, intoned, *I am sorry, Millicent, I did not understand. Do you approve or return the contents?*

"Oh, yes, I approve indeed," laughed Millicent.

Thank you, Millicent McTeer. Please allow access to the transport cube. The cube closed itself, the drone rolled forward and retrieved it, then backed away, whirred up and was gone.

Millicent hardly noticed the departure. She smiled at the little box in her hands, turning it gently, like a treasure. She had received her first present of the morning. Today was her twentieth birthday.

The Brigid's voice had been personalized by the user to sound like Vesuvia Wildness. *Your coffee is ready, Millicent. Would you like it here or to go?*

"To go, please," said Millicent, dropping her tablet into her bag. By the time she crossed her studio apartment to the kitchen counter, her full travel cup stood sealed and waiting in its bay. "Thank you, Brigid," She had done it again. Been polite to her AI device. Brigid was a tool, not her friend.

You're welcome, Millicent.

She shrugged into her coat, slung her bag over her shoulder and plunged into her day, closing the door behind her. She pressed her palm against the sensor panel on the wall outside, said, "Secure, please."

A flashing red light replaced a steady green one. *Premises secured, Millicent. Have a blessed day.*

Millicent trotted toward the elevator. She was running late. She hoped Inez would make the GO2 wait. As she came out of the elevator into the lobby, she saw Inez through the glass, standing on the curb beside the GO2, holding the door open. A yellow light flashed on the roof of the vehicle, indicating they were being charged for the wait. Inez mercifully withheld her scolding as they piled inside and palmed the sensors in front of them. The GO2 closed the door, in a crackling generic male-ish voice, repeated its pre-programed destination, *1509 University Court. Is this your destination, Inez Hagood and Millicent McTeer?*

"Yessir," said Millicent.

"Correct," said Inez

Millicent McTeer, is 1509 University Court your correct destination?

"Correct," said Millicent, "Sir."

The GO2 either tolerated or ignored the honorific, soundlessly and smoothly flowed out into the traffic. Near the opposite coast of North America, two thousand miles eastward, a government computer noted in the NTDB that Inez Hagood and Millicent McTeer were on their way to class.

When she returned to her apartment that evening after her forever day, Millicent wanted nothing but to sleep. Her scholarship at the university required her to work as lab assistant to one of her professors, a phytochemist named Irene Graves whose brilliant ideas were so obvious to herself that she had no patience for explaining them clearly to lesser minds. Most of Millicent's duties involved transcribing the professor's chaotic notes into comprehensible text. Millicent had been warned by several with experience that when her learned teacher got around to publishing her current research, the student assistant's name and contributions would not be credited. Millicent had ideas of her own that she'd shared with few of the souls she knew. The few who had heard them mostly failed to agree.

After she left the lab, Millicent joined Inez and several others for a late supper at the Student Union. The food tasted warmed over. The prolonged conversation degenerated into an academic row by the time it irritated the crew trying to clean and close the place. Millicent could not fathom how people who believed that the universe might be just one of an infinite number of them, or that the behavior of an electron could be altered by observing its action, would not entertain the proposition that living plants, whose capabilities to share information over long distances had been proven by controlled experiment, could conceivably be telepathic. As Vesuvia Wildness was fond of saying during mind-blowing summer afternoons down by the Long Broad on River Street, people would not accept any possibility, no matter how probable, if the illusion of certainty was more comfortable. When all her arguments got shouted down, Millicent took refuge in her conviction that green would have the last word.

"You leaving us?" Inez asked when the conversation took an especially absurdist turn and Millicent stood and reached for her coat.

"It's been a long day," Millicent said. "I need to get home and water my plants."

Good morning, Millicent. Did you enjoy your evening?" Millicent didn't respond. She was afraid if she said she had murdered one of her friends at the Student Union last night, Brigid would say in her Wildness voice, *That sounds exciting, Millicent. Would you like your coffee now?* Computers weren't kind or considerate, she knew. Computers didn't enjoy small talk. But just like humans, they had been programmed to fake it.

Your coffee is ready, Millicent, Would you like breakfast?

"No thanks, Brigid. I'd like to make it for myself this morning." Millicent looked at the time projected on the ceiling above her bed. Nine-thirty. She'd been a bad girl, indeed. Praise the Mercy, it was Saturday. She had no classes today. There was no one she need meet for lunch. No party to endure that evening. The day was hers to spend in the best company she knew. As soon as her brain established connection with her feet, she inserted them into her slippers, and made the trek to her coffee. She usually drank it black, but today, she wished she had some cream. When she took the cup from the bay and saw the caramel hued liquid it contained, she said, "Brigid, how did you know I'd want cream this morning?"

You arrived home at one-seventeen a.m., Millicent. When you are away past midnight, you always want cream in your coffee next morning.

Millicent opened the refrigerator. She was sure she had some real eggs in there. "You know me better than the people in my life, Brigid."

I am programmed to observe and serve, Millicent.

Millicent had three eggs left. "You're not at all like any humans I know, then."

"Is that a directive, Millicent?"

Millicent cracked the eggs into a bowl, began whipping them toward uniformity. "No, dear, just an observation."

My name is Brigid, Millicent. Am I Dear now?"

She set a pan on the range. "You are still Brigid. Low heat, please."

By the time Millicent salted her eggs and poured them into the pan, it was ready. She let Brigid make her toast.

She sipped her coffee. "Great caffeinated beverage, Brigid. Thank you."

You're welcome, dear.

Millicent looked over her toast, smeared with dewberry jam and real butter. The jam was part of the birthday box from her parents, delivered that morning by a breathing human as she sat to her breakfast. Amelia, she knew, had paid extra for that.

Across the room, on the table where she had left it the night before, the little package from Wildness Emporium waited to be opened.

"I can't believe I forgot," she whispered to herself.

Brigid beeped and came to life. *What would you like me to remind you, Millicent?*

"Shut up. I wasn't talking to you, Brigid."

Brigid beeped, went silent and dark. Millicent felt a momentary twinge of shame for being rude to her machine. She picked up the package, carried it back to her breakfast, and sat down. It took her a moment to find the tab, but when she pulled, the box sprang open. Inside, carefully cushioned in a crumpled page from the *Mountain Citizen*, was a small round ceramic container the size and shape of a yunomi three-quarters full of what appeared to be dirt, dried and hardened to the consistency of brick.

Underneath the cup was a note scribbled on the back of a Wildness business card. *She insisted on coming for your birthday. She will be thirsty when she arrives. Yrs- W.*

"Wendl," she murmured. "You would remember." Her eyes brimmed with tears. Her chin trembled. For a moment, Millicent was flooded with a child's homesickness for the mysterious woman who had mentored her last adolescent summers, for the enigmatic soul who may have been human or not, male or female or something totally other. Vesuvia Wildness had opened for her the door into another world. Wendl VonTrier had walked her through it.

"I'm sorry," she said to the yunomi. "I didn't know it was you." She tasted what was left of her coffee. It was barely lukewarm. She poured the last of it over the desiccated contents of the teacup, watched the soil darken as it absorbed the liquid. Then she gathered up her dishes and carried them to the dishwasher. She was loading them into the washer when she heard behind her the high, barely audible ringing that might have been either tiny bells or the onset of tinnitus. Millicent knew what she would see before she turned around.

That first summer she had worked for Vesuvia Wildness loomed in Millicent's memory like the beginning of the world, at least, the beginning of her life. That was the summer she had been born again her true self, acknowledging aloud at last all the certainties she had always held in her heart and been afraid to speak of to anyone other than the dead who met her in the shadowed corners of Hillhaven Inn.

Plants were alive, Vesuvia told her, in ways humans could not comprehend. Plants knew in ways people could not even imagine. They could speak to one another in a language we could not hear and perhaps they understood our speech better than the speakers. It was Wendl VonTrier who began to teach Millicent the language of green life. How to listen apart from words, deeper than emotion, calmer than logic. How to still beneath the storm of rational, linear analysis, to rest in the harmony embedded in all contradiction, to fall into deep awareness of the other until there is no longer any *I* and *Thou*, only *We*.

"They are calling you, Dry McTeer," he said suddenly one afternoon as they were planting a shipment of ferns that had arrived that morning.

"Who?" she asked, looking up, her trowel dropping fresh dirt on her tee. "Which one?"

Wendl laughed. At least he appeared to laugh. His laugh was as silent as his breath. "Not which, Dry McTeer. Only they speak. The green voice issues from all or none."

Millicent, closed her eyes, waited, held her breath. "I don't hear anything," she said when she finally had to gasp for air.

"We will listen together then," Wendl whispered, his voice sounding in the moment very like Vesuvia Wildness, "Take my hand."

Millicent reached out, felt his strong lean fingers wrap hers, felt the hair or fur or feathers that covered his hand according to his mood. She resisted the impulse to open her eyes to the mystery that was her friend. Was he really so different from the mystery that was herself? Could she describe Millicent McTeer in any greater depth or detail than she could describe Wendl VonTrier?

Without any words to say it, she knew that the girl and the Guide were united not by touch or sight or word of mouth, but in the unknowable Deep that had become in them both, in the same way the Unknowable became in the ferns they were tending or the earth under them or the trees beyond or that air they all breathed. And she heard a thin high tone that might have been bells and might have been song rising like a creek after a storm to a whisper and a laugh and a rush and a roar in her head. *Milliccenttt ...*

Suddenly present to herself and her moment again, she turned and said, "Yes?"

A lively plant she immediately recognized as Vinia, her old friend from her summers at Wildness Emporium, obscured her little teacup and covered half the table, her tendrils and branches weaving and waving hypnotically in Millicent's direction, a dance of brilliant green leaves and tiny magenta flowers.

Millicent poured her second cup of coffee and rescued her slice of wholegrain from the toaster. Once again, she'd set it too dark. She made her own breakfast every morning now, ever since she powered off the Brigid. The building superintendent had called immediately to ask if she knew she was off field. With great reluctance, he issued her a security code to access her apartment and enabled the keypad outside her door.

"Your Brigid is more secure," he warned. "She knows you. Keypads can be hacked, you understand?"

"But it won't try to talk to me," Millicent replied.

While she ate her own breakfast, without prompt or inquiry from the Brigid, she reveled in her new-found quiet.

"How do you stand living in a void?" Inez asked when Millicent confided her new house regimen. For her part, Millicent was happy to rediscover the silences from her childhood, not a void at all, but a sanctuary, rich and full of vital movements, her own unhurried and unfiltered thoughts, the voices that rose into her mind in measured cadence from the words displayed on the screen of her reader, or the sentences she scribed herself on actual paper, or lifted from the pages of an old book.

No newsfeed interrupted her morning and late-evening conversations with her soul, or intruded upon Vinia's wordless subliminal trilling in her mind. The plant, a nest of ceaseless subtle movement and transmission, seemed to be thriving in her little bowl on her diet of light, water and coffee grounds. As for Millicent, her own mind felt to her day by day more filled with that verdant presence and burgeoning with thoughts and notions that were not entirely her own.

Millicent would be going to the university on her own this morning. The term was over. Inez had left campus already, along with most of the students. Millicent had sat for all her exams, done pretty well on her required courses and very well on those she liked. All she needed to do today before she packed for the trip home was to meet with the new professor, a neurobotanist who would be her faculty advisor for next term. She didn't know much about him except he had come to her school from a research organization in Canada, right before the Horne Administration declared a cultural embargo against the Dominion. His name was Simon Ryder. Millicent was still trying to remember why it seemed so familiar, where she had heard it before.

Yesterday, she bought a hard copy of one of Ryder's books at the Student Exchange and was as surprised as delighted to see it contained a foreword by Vesuvia Wildness. Her summer-time employer had never hinted at her academic affiliations.

Millicent poured the remains of her morning coffee at Vinia's feet, stacked her dishes in the sink and hoisted her bag.

"Bye, Vinia," she tossed to her houseplant as she went through the door. She punched in her code on the keypad outside and, as soon as it flashed SECURE, trotted down the hall toward the elevator. She could still hear Vinia's warbling tone in her head as the elevator door closed behind her, and riding on the soundless vibration, like a leaf on a stream, she thought, but wasn't sure, she caught two words, which, she told herself on the way down, she probably imagined.

Later. Love.

Fifty-seven seconds after she exited the street door of her building, a GO2 whispered to a stop at the curb. The passenger door opened as she approached. Millicent eased inside, palmed the sensor panel and said, "153 University Court."

153 University Court. Millicent McTeer, please confirm, in a gravelly electronic monotone.

"Yes," confirmed the passenger, and the GO2 hovered for a moment, then whisked her away. The vehicle's exterior resembled a large egg with a door. There were no windows. Video screens on the interior approximated the scenes in the outer world they were traversing. Millicent heard the inevitable urban legends about hapless riders whose GO2 had shown them scenes of the way to their office while transporting them to fates worse than death, but no one she knew had any experiences resembling such a horror.

At the end of her ride, the green *egress* light flashed as the door opened for Millicent in front of the Thomas Berry Plant Sciences Building. She stepped out into bright May sunshine and when the GO2 droned, *thank you for riding with GO2*, she didn't hear it. There was a faint, high, tumble of sound in her head that might have been speech or might have been wind or might have been water trickling over stones and it was telling her something if she could only remember the words.

Once Millicent stepped inside the lobby, her inner music subsided but persisted on the rim of her awareness. Large-leafed, oversized foliage exploded from low planters of unadorned concrete, surrounded by clusters of uncomfortable chairs upholstered in muted woodsy tones. The resident plant life loomed over the few transient humans with an air of vague and undefined menace. A desk clad in faux-mahogany veneer huddled in the center of the room like a besieged outpost. It was unoccupied. The receptionist apparently had Saturday off, if the position had survived recent budget cuts.

Millicent gazed expectantly at the directory panel on the wall above the desk. Two full seconds passed before it came to life. *You are in the Thomas Berry Plant Sciences Building. Where would you like to go?*

"Neurobotany Department," said Millicent. She had quit saying *please* to machines when she turned off her Brigid.

The directory wasn't offended. *Third floor. Elevator 2.*

When the elevator released her on the third floor, brighter, warmer and not quite so arboreal as the first, a real live human awaited her at a smaller, less impressive desk made of real wood, that in more prosperous times, might have served a librarian.

The thin young man with glasses and intensely black hair looked up from his book, seemed surprised to see anyone in his vicinity as Millicent said, "I'm Millicent McTeer. I have an appointment with Doctor Ryder."

The thin boy, whose ID hanging on a lanyard around his neck bore his picture and declared him to be Eric Lee, leaned over his desk and pointed down the hall. "Second door on the right, Ma'am. If the door isn't open, just go on in and say hello. He doesn't like for people to knock on wood."

"Thanks," Millicent said, and started down the hall. *Ma'am?* She turned back and called, "Hey, Eric, are you from Carolina?"

"Yes, Ma'am," confessed Eric. "Asheton."

"We're a long way from home, Eric" she said, and continued town the hall. When she reached the second door on the right, it was open.

Professor Simon Ryder sat perched like a large waterfowl in a woven rope hammock, strung diagonally across his office, among file cabinets and a table burdened with computers and monitors and printers and other electronic gear for purposes unknown to Millicent. Plants of all sizes and descriptions, and some nearly beyond description, flaunted rampant in every space not otherwise purposed and occupied. The Professor busily scribbled with a stylus on the face of his OmniPad, seemingly oblivious to the world. Millicent raised her hand to knock, then recalled Eric's admonition. Before she could speak, Ryder, without looking up, gestured for her to come in. She took a few steps into the room, then, uncertain of what she should do next, stood silent, awaiting enlightenment.

Ryder dropped his pad into one of the many pockets in the canvas vest he wore, immersed her in his smile and said in a voice from her childhood, "Ah, Miss McTeer. We meet again, a long way from home."

His dark eyes flashed for a moment with the fire of stars over deserts, or sunsets over mountains or perhaps merely coals on a hearth. His face, lean and sharp but not unwelcoming, was tanned and weathered to the sheen of a ripe tobacco leaf. He had the look of a scholar who was as much at home exploring forests and savannahs as the dry pages of scientific treatises. Millicent recognized him immediately and remembered where she'd seen his name. It bothered her a little that he didn't look a day older than when he had stepped up on the porch at Hillhaven Inn.

"Dragon," she blurted.

"Millicent," he said. "Our trails cross again at last. I've been looking forward to it." Ryder unfolded long legs and exited his hammock with reptilian grace, gestured at two large pillows on the floor beside a tray overflowing with papers weighted under what Millicent thought was a satellite phone of some sort. "Sit down. Rest from the world. Let's talk about what trouble we might get into together next term."

Millicent sat, rather awkwardly, she feared. Ryder, already comfortably settled upon his cushion, his legs folded beneath him as compactly as the pinioned wings of a bat, opened her student profile before she could arrange herself. He'd obviously studied her data previously because he flipped only a page or two before he nailed her with his gaze. She saw now that his eyes were deep deep blue, like the sky over Hillhaven after a rain.

"What made you want to study forest management,

Millicent? There isn't a lot of money to be made in that, so you're not trying to get rich."

Looking into this young/old face, she felt twelve years old again, incapable of anything less than the simple truth as she knew it, "Because ... Because trees have been my best friends."

"Mine, too," said Ryder, and Millicent believed he meant it. He reached behind him among his aspiring jungle of domestic greenery and lifted into the air between them an old coffee mug chipped and dehandled, homing a prehensile-ish looking vine with brilliant emerald leaves and tiny magenta flowers. As she stared at it, trying to determine in her mind if she was really hearing it sing to her, the professor went on. "A forest, Miss McTeer, as you certainly have learned by now, is a lot more than trees. There are more kinds of living organisms resident in the soil in this mug than there are species of vertebrates on the whole planet. For that matter, there are more other-than-human cells within your own body than there are cells original to your DNA. What one thinks of as oneself is just the surface of the life that is there. Knowing, awareness, intention, run deep. Deeper than we can see. Deeper than we can imagine. Deeper than unto ourselves alone, we are."

He wasn't telling her anything she hadn't already heard in her classes, but Ryder, with his prophet's intensity, made it all immediate and real. She could almost feel her boundaries dissolving, nodding mutely like a new convert as he went on. "Trees are more connected with their universe than we are. They are not burdened with ego and intellectual constructs. They are not blinded by self-observation. They simply participate in the collective intelligence of all the life inhabiting their place. The ancient Celts believed that places in a landscape were possessed of awareness and intention, souls, if you will. Our research here is revealing that they were right. Trees are just the beginning. Do you follow me?"

"I think so," said Millicent, lost in the sky of Ryder's gaze. "The intelligent life of a tree, of a forest, of any definable life form, is in the sum of its connections with other life forms."

The professor looked pleased. Whether with himself or with his student, Millicent couldn't discern. "You're getting there. When you go home to Hillhaven this summer, Miss McTeer. I hope you'll think about making neurobotany your major area of study. If you do, I'll try to land you a scholarship as a research assistant in our department. If, on the other hand, you want to stick with forest management, and not see the forest for the trees, I'll advise you as best I can in your pursuits."

Suddenly, Ryder was on his feet, rising as smoothly and effortlessly as a tree might grow. Millicent scrambled after him. He shook her hand, held out a folded sheet of paper. "Here's a list of books to help you while away your summer. See you next term."

That night, Millicent began packing her bags for the morning's flight to Asheton. She thought back over her interview with her faculty advisor. The picture of the broken mug with the little vine was vivid in her mind. She had forgotten to ask the species of the plant. It was obviously the same as the one Wendl had sent her.

"Oh, poor Vinia. I'd forgotten about you. Who'll take care of you while I'm home?" she said, as if the vine could hear. She turned and looked. Vinia's bowl still sat on the windowsill where it could catch the morning sun. Vinia was nowhere in sight. Millicent picked up the bowl and poked the contents with her finger. The dirt inside seemed dry and hard as brick. Very carefully she wrapped it in a towel and stowed it among the other sundries in her bag.

The next morning, Millicent activated the Brigid, ordered her GO_2 for the airport. When she was ready to leave, she said on her way out, "Bridgid, I'm gone. Watch the place for me, will you?"

All scans are active, Millicent. Your GO_2 will arrive in five minutes twenty-three seconds. Your flight reservation is confirmed. Enjoy your trip. Goodbye.

The GO_2 sighed at the curb three seconds late, and swallowed Millicent and her bag. At the airline terminal, she found her flight was departing on schedule, a not entirely usual occurrence. She boarded without incident, and sat next to a willowy, dark-haired woman who spoke a mysterious language and made small talk via her obsolete hand-held Unitrans device. It turned out she was a Buddhist missionary from Nepal.

The big jet leveled above a brilliant floor of cloud, President Isadora Horne, who had been elected by the newly installed National Legislative Council to replace her father who had died mid-way through his fourth term, was speaking on the video screen at the front of the cabin ... *the elitist resisters certainly have the right to live their lives in whatever way they desire, so long as they don't impinge on the privileges of loyal citizens. At some point, for the sake of common harmony, it may become necessary to designate geographic areas for their residence, much as when reservations were established by our fore parents, to preserve their own society and, I might add, to ensure the safety and continuance of the aboriginal populations that refused to assimilate.*

Millicent tuned up her Earworld and drowned Isadora's declamation in Celtic ambiance that brought Professor Simon Ryder back to mind. Three of the books on his list would be waiting on her Redi Reader when she got to Asheton. She was eager to be back in a town where some people still drove their own cars, although the state legislature was currently considering a bill that would outlaw the practice. Joshua had insisted his daughter maintain her driver's license. Millicent was the only licensed driver she knew among her friends at university. New cars now weren't even equipped to accommodate a human driver.

As the aircraft banked into its eastward run, she could see the morning sun breaking above the overcast. Away toward the horizon, a long serpentine cloud writhed above the rest, spewing flamely light. It looked like a dragon, she thought.

CHAPTER FIVE

"I think I'll go down to River Street to see Vesuvia and Wendl," Millicent said to her mother over breakfast.

"But this is your last day home for a while," Amelia protested. "Your father says we never get to see you anymore."

"Don't make Dad your fall guy when he isn't here to defend himself," teased Millicent, "Don't you miss me a little bit, too, Mother?"

"Of course, I do," Amelia said with a wry grin. "I'm a typical selfish mother who wants her daughter all to herself." Suddenly serious, she went on, "But since the riots last month, I don't go to the Arts District. It isn't safe down there. Neighborhood Watch has declared it a resister area, which makes every firster in Asheton feel like they have agency to harass anybody on the street there."

"Would you feel better if I wore my *First Forever* hat?" said a smirking Millicent.

Amelia didn't smile back, "I pray no child of mine would even own such a thing. I know you want to see your friends but be careful. Anybody who looks like a resister gets targeted these days."

"Don't worry, Mother." Millicent lay a hand over her mother's. "I'll be dim. Nobody will ever notice I'm there. Besides, I don't do protests. I don't think a street cam has ever caught me in bad company."

Amelia didn't appear reassured. "Your professor Ryder qualifies. I saw his interview on RealTruth. I'm surprised they let him out on the street after that one."

"Simon tells the truth as he knows it, Mother, even if nobody in the room with him wants to hear it. That's one of the things I admire about him."

Amelia shot back, "Simon, is it now? Is there more to this relationship than you've been telling us?"

Millicent laughed, shook her head. "The relationship is strictly professional and academic, Mother. Researcher and assistant. Professor and student. Simon Ryder is married to his plants."

"You do spend a lot of time together," Amelia countered dryly.

"We do," Millicent confirmed. "I'm his research assistant. He does a lot of research."

"On plants?" needled Amelia with lifted brow.

"Precisely," said Millicent. "Besides, even if I were inclined toward a male attachment, he's way too old for me."

"He doesn't look it," observed her mother.

"No, he doesn't. A little bit spooky, isn't it?" Millicent stood, gathering up her plate and cup. "If I'm going down to River Street, I'd better be gone."

Millicent caught a bus to River Street, rather than drive one of the two old vehicles Joshua maintained, officially designated for business use. Private vehicles now were required by law to have location devices installed. Simon Ryder had advised her to avoid them.

"They'll probably track you anyway," he said, "but why make it easy for them?"

Millicent made considerable effort to avoid succumbing to the prevalent paranoia of the population at large, but she took the cap from her bag and put it on before exiting the bus to walk the last three blocks to Wildness Emporium. The street was eerily quiet. She only saw two other people along the way. Neither spoke nor raised their gaze to meet hers, but studiously focused on the pavement in front of them. She didn't spy any street cams perched above the sidewalk, but held little doubt her oversized dark glasses and *America First Forever* cap were being duly recorded in the Municipal Day Record.

When she reached the Emporium, Millicent found the front windows all broken out. Shards of glass still littered the pavement outside. Sheets of plywood had been nailed over the openings. The air stank of sewage. Spray-painted in a garish acidic yellow across the ornate door, the inverted *R* that was becoming a familiar symbol on media newsfeeds.

Wendl opened the door for her as she approached. Today, he projected a decidedly avian persona. Behind his hawkish gaze, Millicent sensed glistening feathers, piercing talons and rending beak. But it was his familiarly sharp though benevolent face that greeted her. "Hello, Dry McTeer," he murmured in that voice she heard as much in her mind as in her ear. "You have not been afraid of us, after all." Wendl's eyes ranged the street beyond as he held the door open for her and he locked it behind her when she entered.

Suddenly in near darkness, Millicent was momentarily disoriented. Emotion rippled her words as she spoke. "Are you and Vesuvia all right?"

"We remain unscathed." So softly that Millicent wasn't quite certain whether she heard the words or merely caught Wendl's thought.

"What happened?" she asked as walls and features began to emerge dimly from the shadow.

Wendl ruffled his feathers as he shrugged. Millicent heard rather than saw it. "Contrary to Wendl's counsel," in his near-human purr, "Vesuvia Wildness circulated a petition opposing the proposed government sale of Shaconage to private entities. The rabble were incited bigly."

Millicent shook her head, trying to damp the shrillness in her voice when she said, "But they can't do that, can they? Tell me the government can't really sell off a national park."

In the dusky interior it looked to her as if Wendl's head were morphing into a wolf's, all eye and teeth, glistening in the dark. His voice, when it came, a blend of equal parts sad resignation and implacable wrath, "Dry McTeer, once humans have sold their souls, they will delight to sell anything that doesn't belong to them."

Millicent swallowed tears. "I can't believe people would do this to you. Agree or not, they are still our neighbors."

Wendl raised his arms, or perhaps his wings, gesturing futility. "That may be so, Dry McTeer, and they are our friends no longer."

Bereft of answers, Millicent looked around her. She stood in a dark and empty shell of a building. The inner door to the plant nursery gaped black, open to nothing. Her eyes were insisting things her mind would not accept. "Did they destroy the nursery? What happened to all the living green?" She turned to Wendl for an answer, but he was gone.

Vesuvia Wildness stood beside her, reached out and lay a hand on her shoulder as if to comfort. "We sent them to a safe place. Otherwise, everything would have been trampled and burned."

Millicent wanted to weep. She wanted to mourn and wail. She wanted to kill somebody. "But why?" she whispered, "Why would anyone want to destroy so much sacred beauty?"

Vesuvia didn't reply. Instead she gathered Millicent into a wordless embrace. The two women stood wrapped in their shared wound, for minutes or days until Vesuvia pulled away and said, "Evil has a profoundly bitter flavor, but those who feed on it long enough develop a taste for it."

———

That night, Lisa Charon joined Millicent and her parents for dinner at Hillhaven, and stayed to play her violin. Amelia sang and Millicent longed to go sit up on the stair among the shadow souls, a wee ghost girl, high and hidden, but hearing and seeing all. In her mind, she was eight years old again, surrounded by the shades of the past. She thought she could hear her great grandmother speaking to her now across all the years, *Millicent?* Suddenly she was a twenty-four-year-old woman again, about to leave one more time the place and the people she loved most in the world.

"Millicent?" Lisa Charon was talking to her. "Where are you? Come play with us the last song of the evening."

"I can't, Lisa. I'm way out of practice."

"Don't give me that," Lisa said, holding out Millicent's violin. "Amelia said she heard you playing in your room this afternoon."

"Therapy for a broken heart," said Millicent.

Lisa's reply came half entreaty and half riddle. "One more happy song then before we all fly away."

In spite of herself, Millicent felt the music welling up inside her. She took the fiddle and stepped into the song. She played drone to Lisa's melody and Amelia sang.

I've dwelled in the city
and lived on a hill
with trees all around
where everything's still.

I've run with the crowd
and walked all alone
at peace with myself
when friends were all gone.

I've wandered this country
on roads up and down,
found no place to fit me
so well as this town.

Half the locals knew the song by heart, having heard it before they could walk, and as Amelia sang other verses about lovers lost and friends found and journeys started and wanderers come home, more voices joined in. In the music there were no Firsters, no Resisters, no religion or politics, not one a stranger and every soul a neighbor. When the song was done, the three women played on and diners forgot their meals to dance.

In the whirl of their playing, Millicent saw her beloved shadows flow down from the stair and mingle among the breathing, flickering and twinkling like stars, riding on the love-lit sound.

Finally, after a time none present could guess, the room fell silent and people stood gazing silently into one another's faces, unready to release the spell they'd woven. Millicent, who always had protested she had no voice, without premonition, tucked her fiddle beneath her arm, in a high clear voice, began to sing:

Just give me a sky that's wide and blue
and a winding road to walk
together with a friend who's true,
should there be a need to talk,
one fellow pilgrim to lift a song
when spirits are getting low
and the way is steep, the day too long
and the end too far to know.

And everyone knew the evening had come to its end. They paid their bills and cast last kind looks toward one another, spoke their final gentle words of parting and drifted away into the dark and divided town waiting in the night to swallow them again. Amelia Montford, Millicent McTeer and Lisa Charon stood mute, smiling sad sweet smiles at one another, slightly abashed at their own powers.

Although Millicent had reserved a GO2, Joshua insisted on driving her to the airport next morning in his ancient Cherokee. "Hillhaven service to all our guests," he joked as he hoisted her bag into the back. Even though it was early, the sun not quite risen yet, Millicent saw a man and a woman sitting on a bench in the park across the street. They were drinking coffee from Mountain Ground cups, appeared to take no notice of the traffic around them, but Millicent had a distinct impression they might have been watching Hillhaven until she and her father came out of the inn.

As Joshua pulled out onto the street, Millicent said, "Don't stare, but do you know those people in the park?"

Joshua said, "I saw them. I think they're the same couple who have dined at Hillhaven lately. At least, they order food, which they hardly touch. Your mother thinks they are Neighborhood Watch, but they're nobody we know."

"They were here last night," Millicent said. "Sat in a corner to themselves. Didn't sing. Didn't dance or talk to anybody. The man kept fiddling with his phone the whole evening. I think he might have been shooting video or recording."

"Strange," said Joshua. "Somebody up there wants to keep an eye on us, I guess."

As they turned the corner, Millicent glanced in the side mirror and caught a glimpse of a black SUV pulling out of the park onto the street. After two more turns, she looked over her shoulder to see the SUV still behind.

"Dad," she said, "I think they're following us."

Joshua didn't act surprised. "When we get to the

airport, I want you to get out of the car, take your bag and get inside the terminal. Go to the restroom or someplace where you won't be easily spotted. When I text you, come back out and we'll go."

Millicent couldn't keep the fright out of her voice when she whispered, "Okay."

When the jeep stopped in front of the terminal, Millicent got out.

"Wait," Joshua said, climbed out and retrieved her bag. He handed it to her and said, "Kiss me goodbye, hide and when you get my text, get moving out of there."

Inside the door, Millicent looked back through the glass, saw the Cherokee pull away from the curb as the black SUV parked in a handicap space and the mysterious watchers got out.

She sat in a waiting area screened by plastic greenery where she wouldn't be seen from the door. She saw the backs of the man and woman as they hurried down the concourse toward the departure gates. They weren't scanning the crowd. They already knew where she was supposed to be going.

She waited until they turned the corner, picked up her bag, and a moment later heard her text ping. She saw the Cherokee pulling to a stop outside, checked to make sure the watchers were not in sight, and bolted.

"Where are we going?" she asked Joshua once they were on the street again.

He looked grim. "To the Amtrak station. I'm going to buy you a ticket."

"It'll take three days to get back by train."

"You're not going back by train, although that is what your ticket will say. Ride at least until you are clear of

Carolina, then get off, text me where you are, and hitch a ride."

"I won't know anybody," Millicent said.

"Just stay put and somebody you can trust will come along going your way."

At the train station, Joshua bought a ticket with cash at a kiosk.

"You always carry that much money?" Millicent asked.

"It pays to be prepared. Knoxville might be a good place to jump the train. Remember to text your location." He handed her the ticket.

"Dad, what's going on? Will you and Mom be all right?"

"Don't talk to strangers unless they offer you a ride," Joshua said, then turned and walked away. Millicent remembered she had forgotten her plant.

"Don't forget to water Vinia," she called. Joshua waved but didn't turn around, kept walking to his Jeep, got in and drove away.

———

Millicent turned off her phone as the train began to wind through the Shaconage, descending with the Long Broad toward Shelton Crossing and Tennessee. She supposed she was some sort of fugitive now, though clueless as to what her transgression might be. Perhaps merely guilt by association. Vesuvia Wildness and Wendl VonTrier had obviously been targeted by someone, and her own father had reacted like a practiced subversive when she'd pointed out that they were being followed to the airport. Now, mystified and truly afraid, Millicent scanned the few passengers who shared her car. A woman with a small child, a couple who appeared to be in their late seventies, two teenagers with backpacks, dressed for earnest adventure. None of them triggered an alarm, or even caution.

Hypervigilant all the same, Millicent jumped, swallowed her gasp when the conductor came through. The male of the teen pair stopped him. "When do we get to Farport?"

"Farport isn't a scheduled stop."

"We didn't know," the girl stammered. "We're supposed to meet our hiking group there."

The conductor pulled an old-fashioned watch from his vest, consulted it and said, "In that case, we'll arrive in forty-six minutes. You'll have five minutes to disembark."

When he passed Millicent, he didn't say anything, let his too-green eyes rest on her face for a half-second, nodded and smiled as if he recognized a neighbor, then walked on into the next car. Millicent didn't know whether to be comforted or afraid.

After a brief and unscheduled stop at Farport, a straggling foothills settlement not much beyond a village, the Shaconage fell behind, subsiding into low rolling hills like the sea after a storm. The tracked straightened and the train gathered speed. Millicent watched Tennessee flow past the window, the distant ridges moving slow as an obsolete analog clock's minute hand, the brush and signage along the track a blur, time too fast to apprehend. Like her life, she thought. Only the past made sense. The present, a whirl of sensation, feelings, warnings and temptations. Computers could keep up with the unrelenting input. Humans merely did as they were told.

The landscape on the other side of the glass began to slow like a widening river. Buildings appeared and Millicent recognized a few. She didn't need the conductor's announcement to know Knoxville had arrived. As soon as the passenger station embraced the train and the world on the other side of the window was still, she texted Joshua. *Where you said.*

Before she could pick up her bag, she saw among the people moving past on the platform outside a familiar woman and man walking together toward the front of the train. She was certain they were the same pair who had followed her to the airport in Asheton. Millicent almost ran in the opposite direction, bumping and apologizing to startled passengers, a salmon swimming against the current. The green-eyed train conductor stood at the end of the last car. He smiled, saluted, and opened the rear door. Millicent hesitated, went through and heard it close behind her.

She glanced along the platform, saw people boarding the train several cars forward, but her pursuers weren't in sight. She hoped they were on the train. She went into the terminal, and, pretending to study the posted schedules, watched the train through the window. After several minutes that seemed to Millicent like several hours, the train began to move again, and the Evil Twins hadn't reappeared. Her RailPass said her destination was New Orleans. With any luck, they wouldn't start looking for her short of Louisiana.

What to do now? Joshua's instructions had been as vague as they were brief. Text him when she reached Knoxville. Don't talk to strangers unless one offers a ride. Not especially good advice coming from a concerned father, but Joshua was trying to tell her more than he was saying. Millicent knew that much.

She took a deep breath, looked around to get her bearings. Ahead were the doors to the street. Left of the entrance, an elevator, on the right, a Mountain Ground coffee shop. Millicent realized she was hungry.

She estimated the coffee had ceased to be hot about thirty minutes before she ordered it. The Purple Pig Panini eased her lightness of being but wasn't as succulent as she recalled it from her childhood. She asked the attendant for a cup of ice and poured her coffee into it. She sat sipping as slowly as she dared and pondered her future, toying, as she often did when at odds with herself or her world, with the little stone pendant hung on a chain around her neck. She'd had the stone half her life since she was twelve and found it on her dresser the morning after the hiker Dragon had stayed at Hillhaven. She regarded it as her charm, her talisman and growing up had done nothing to diminish the magic it held for her. She had always kept it close. When she was thirteen, she became so terrified of losing it, her father fashioned from gold wire the little cage that contained it now, and attached a chain to wear it.

She slipped it out from her collar and peered at it as if it were a crystal ball, full of portent for her future. It might have been just that, except for the size, smooth and round, small as a wren's egg and clear as glass. She could see her face in it, and as she turned it in the light, she thought she glimpsed Joshua's face, then Simon Ryder's lean and hungry visage. Once, in an incautious moment, she'd accused him of leaving it for her at Hillhaven, as she'd always suspected, but his look of baffled amusement was so convincing that she'd never dared bring up the subject again. Now she recalled he'd never really denied the gift.

Millicent was almost done with her coffee when she felt a hand on her shoulder. She looked down, summoning her depths for fight or flight, and recognized immediately the thin, furred fingers, looked up unbelieving into a face she knew as well as her parents'.

"Wendl," she gasped, jumping up and throwing her arms around him, burying her face against a shoulder that smelled like spruce and woodsmoke. Wendl's calm flowed through her then and her mind was clear and still.

"How can you be here?" she said.

"How can Wendl be there?" he smiled, answering, as was his habit, a question with another query. "Where can we be but here?"

Wendl reached down and hoisted her bag. "Come, Dry McTeer, we must hurry. Your friends from Asheton have discovered you are not traveling with them. They will be back and we will be gone."

Wendl led Millicent past the entrance to the two elevators beyond. "Strange," she said when he stopped. "I'm sure I saw only one elevator here when I got off the train."

"We see what we need to see, Dry McTeer," Wendl murmured as the nearest elevator door slid open. "Quickly," he said. "It won't be here long." And ushered her inside.

Millicent heard the door sigh to closure behind her and turned to see no door at all, just a blank wall with a keypad to the right.

"Wendl, we're trapped," she gasped.

"We're waiting for you to press the appropriate key," Wendl said as the keypad's only button came alight.

Millicent stared at the glowing lemniscate. "Infinity. That could be anywhere."

"Where do you need it to be?" said Wendl.

"Home. I want to go home," Millicent whispered.

Wendl took her hand and gestured toward the keypad. "It's your call."

Millicent pressed ∞. Her field of view narrowed to a thin vertical line, bright to pain, then everything went dark and she was falling. She shrieked in terror and felt Wendl squeeze her hand and heard his voice in her head, "Be dry, McTeer."

They fell for years. Gradually, a web of glowing strands emerged from the black. Millicent fixed on them as they were all she could see, a web surrounding them above and below, all around as far as her eye could trace, a tangled everbranching shining alive tapestry like the mycelium underneath a forest. They fell near one of the strands and it glowed brighter and reached to meet them and they were in it being carried along faster than thought.

Where are we going? thought Millicent and heard Wendl in her head,

Are you not there?

The lights came on and the elevator slowed and stopped. Her bag sat beside her and nobody held her hand. The door opened. Millicent stepped out onto the third floor of the John Muir Plant Sciences Building at the University. Eric was not at his desk but Professor Simon Ryder was in his office smiling at her when she appeared at his open door.

"What the hell is happening?" she blurted.

"There's more than one way to fly," he said, apparently not at all surprised to see her there. "Let me take you to dinner and I'll explain some things."

"We live in interesting times," Ryder said, smiling across the table over their mujaddara and coffee.

"That's an ancient Chinese curse," said Millicent.

In the background, a televised voice was elucidating the current crisis:

The state legislature this afternoon approved the Articles of Secession which Governor Longley is expected to sign. In Washington, President Isadora Horne has vowed to send in federal forces in that event and arrest all participant parties on charges of treason. The President is scheduled to address the nation on this constitutional crisis at seven o'clock this evening.

"Strange, isn't it?" Ryder said, "That most people don't get interested in public affairs until things start to fall apart."

"Well, I'm interested now," Millicent said sincerely.

Ryder took another sip of his coffee, set down his cup and folded his hands beneath his chin, gazed at Millicent with eyes that seemed to contain all the green in the world. "We don't have much choice, do we?" he said. "In a nutshell, the non-human world, which comprises most of the intelligent life of this planet, is not pleased with us humans at all. While we are doing our best to kill each other off, we are destroying the health of the world. We are like cancer, eating away at the body that homes us. That can't continue. Earth will not allow it to continue."

"You speak of Earth as if she had her own mind," said Millicent, not to disagree but to clarify her thinking to herself.

"And how would you speak of it?"

Millicent sat silent for a moment, gathering her reasons, then answered, "Dad used to tell me stories about how the ancient Celts believed that we don't have souls, but that our souls have us, contain us, people, animals, even places all ensouled and every soul embraced by a greater soul, holding all of them. I guess that's how I see the Earth. As Gaia, if a word will do.

"Precisely," said Ryder. "All this," he waved at the television screen suspended over the bar across the room, "is just transient static." Empires, especially this one, are short-lived. The music of the universe is slow and deep. Our species hasn't been around long enough to hear a measure of it."

"I don't think we've even been listening," Millicent said.

"No, we homo sapiens are deaf and blind. We look and look at the world and never see the first thing about it, much less see the world behind the world."

"The world behind the world?"

Ryder laughed. "You caught a glimpse of it on your way here today, Millicent."

———

"Thanks for lunch," Millicent said as they stepped out into natural weather. "What do we do now?"

"We can't go back to the university," said Ryder, gesturing at the armored vehicles rumbling past them on the street. On the corner ahead, two police officers stood, garbed in riot gear. "Probably shouldn't go to your apartment, either. They obviously consider you one of us now."

"Who's us?" Millicent asked.

"We'll take a little walk, and I'll introduce you to your new family," said Ryder, "Or maybe the oldest family in the world."

The two cops standing at the intersection began

walking down the street in their direction. Ryder stopped in front of a shop window bearing the logo, *FLR Outfitters.* "Just in time," he said. "Let's get you dressed for our expedition."

They stepped through the door into another world that seemed to belong more to a primeval forest than to the impermeable and sterile city outside. Cool and shadowed, green plants everywhere, nodding and weaving gently over the heads of the customers. It reminded Millicent of Ryder's office, only this space was much larger, as if they'd stepped out of a building rather than into one. Soft lighting from the vague ceiling highlighted islands of merchandise among the verdant canopy. Millicent couldn't think of another word for it. They were wandering a deep wood. She wondered if there were a wicked witch somewhere in the maze, stoking her oven and watching hungrily for stray children.

Ryder seemed to know where he was going, so Millicent followed, futilely attempting to note the twists and turns that might lead her back to the street. He stopped before a desk emblazoned with gilt letters promising *Customer Service.*

A woman crowned with a fiery cloud of hair emerged from a copse of monumental ferns that might have been transplanted straight from the Pleistocene.

She nodded to Ryder. "Greetings, Professor, you're back again. I see you've brought your flyer with you this time." Then she turned toward a clueless Millicent, and with an eagle's gaze that seemed to see the whole world, said, "Hello, McTeer. I'm Mathilda, Daughter of the Stone. Welcome to the Free Laurel Republic."

Joshua McTeer was walking to the post office to fetch the day's mail. He still retained his operator's license but his jeep and pickup sat idle in Hillhaven's garage since the Transportation Authority had revoked his permit to purchase fuel for them. Not that he minded walking at all. He had plenty of time for it. Business at Hillhaven had declined somewhat since Neighborhood Watch had posted them on the Unaligned Businesses list.

It was a beautiful day for a stroll, Joshua thought, as he became aware of the dark sedan creeping along the street about half a block behind him. He pulled his First Forever cap from his pocket and wedged it atop his unruly thatch, tinged now with the first hint of gray, and tried to ignore his stalkers, concentrating instead on the mockingbird holding forth from the top of a dying hemlock by the walk. Joshua stared straight ahead and kept walking, pretending to be oblivious to the whisper of the vehicle pulling alongside. He didn't look around until the driver's window slid open and a polite voice said, "Joshua. It's good to see you out and about. We'd like to talk to you if you have a minute."

Joshua stopped. The car stopped. He'd seen the driver and the woman seated beside him before. He didn't recognize the second man in the back seat, who opened the door and beckoned for him to get in.

"What do you want to talk to me about?" Joshua said. "I doubt anything I've done lately would be of much interest to you."

"We need to talk to you about your daughter," said Back-seat Man, as he slid out onto the street and held the open door.

"My daughter's away at her university, as I'm sure you know." Joshua strove to keep his voice neutral and uninflected, like his interrogators'. "I've not been in touch with Millicent since she went back there. If you want to know anything about her, you should ask her directly."

"That's the thing. Joshua," said Back-seat Man, putting a heavy hand on Joshua's shoulder, "She's disappeared from the university and we thought you might want to help us find her before some truly bad people do."

Joshua tried to hide his relief. He would trust his child to the truly bad people any day before he would deliver her to these goons. "I'm sorry I can't help you," he said, calmly, he hoped, "I don't know where she is."

"Would you rather we discussed your daughter with your wife?" said the woman beside the driver.

"Get in, please," Back-seat man said, tightening his grip. We have lots to talk about."

Joshua got into the car. Back-seat man climbed in beside him and closed the door. As the car pulled away from the curb, the woman in front turned around and smiled at Joshua, "Take off that silly cap. It doesn't suit you at all."

II

INTO THE TREES

Into these silent woods I go, still as frost, quiet as snow,
And what I might find there, the Lord only knows,
So I'll follow closely, wherever He goes.

CHAPTER 1

M illicent hadn't slept at all. All night the trees had been whispering, murmuring, chanting in her head, their music woven of wind and water and starlight, like a stream, a river, like the blood pulsing in her veins. Try as she might, she couldn't catch the conversation, though a single word lodged repeatedly in her mind as she opened herself to the flow of voices. *Coming.*

Who was coming? Why? So, she had lain awake all night braced for arrival of friend or stranger, nemesis or lover. Now dawn cast a thin line of rising light between the overcast and the rounded summits of mountains away southward. Quietly, so as not to wake the two sleepers, she dressed and stepped out onto the porch. A drowsy bird roused from somewhere among the branches overhead and offered a single note to the morning. *One.* Knowing it would be repeated, Millicent waited until she heard it again. *One.* Nearer now, she recognized him and set off down the path to the place where she had seen him first, sixteen years before to the day, in another life, another world entirely.

Dew sparkling on the mossy path gleamed too precious

to oppress, so Millicent passed over it, not quite touching. There was no one here to see her skimming, as she called it. Practice was always a good thing. She didn't relish or indulge her emergent powers, but knew that sooner or later, they might prove useful, even vital.

She heard the falls before she was there. The sound of falling water growing until it drowned the voice of the rising wind. A fire burned in the tops of the trees eastward as she sat on her favorite boulder, hovering involuntarily for a second before easing to rest on the chill damp.

Gathering her presence into the stillness, Millicent watched the paling sky and waited. She was certain of it now. He was almost here.

She felt the arrival before she saw him, a subtle vibration that might have been from the stone where she sat or might have been in the water that tumbled past her feet. Something felt in the bone, as if the whole mountain were focusing all her awareness and becoming on this place, this waterfall, these tumbled boulders, this rushing and falling stream, this womanly soul, open, expectant, unafraid.

And where there had been only rock and shadow an instant before, there was something like wings and fire more than anything else describable, that folded and condensed into the shape of a human male. He climbed down among the boulders, carefully and deliberately as any ordinary man would do, found a narrow point in the stream to jump across, and stood smiling down at Millicent, who smiled in return.

"Happy birthday, McTeer," said the familiar voice. "I hope I'm in time for the party."

"Hello, Ryder," she said, as he reached out a hand for her to pull herself to her feet. "You're just in time."

Together, they took the path away up the glen toward

Joshua's cabin. "I left my parents asleep up there. They look exhausted. They would be better off in containment with the rest of our kind."

"Except," Ryder reminded her, "they are not precisely our kind."

Millicent bristled, "Distinctions like that are what started this mess. You know better, Simon."

"Yes, I do. I'm sorry. It must be hard for them out here."

"Anybody who hasn't been sickened by now is targeted, branded as carriers in the minds of most. Wellness has become a sin since the Affliction," Millicent said.

"How many have died now?" asked Ryder.

"If we can believe NewsReal, four million in this state. Dad thinks it's probably more than that. Asheton is a ghost town. Those who aren't dead are leaving if they have anywhere to go. The Firster gangs are looting or burning whatever gets left behind. Mom and Dad are talking about closing Hillhaven when they can. They're planning on moving up here."

Ryder shook his head. "You're right. Joshua and Amelia would be much better off with you in the Laurel Creek Containment District. The Feds don't even count heads in containment anymore. Maybe I can talk them into it while I'm here."

"I've tried," Millicent said. "Mom insists she needs to be with Dad, and he says his friends need him here."

"They're fortunate more than most if they still have any friends," mused Ryder.

At that, they left words behind and climbed up through the trees in silence until they saw the cabin ahead in the morning bright. Amelia stood on the porch, watching the path for her winged child's return.

"And here must be the infamous Simon Ryder, who

lured this daughter of mine into the subversive netherworld of autotrophic eukaryotes," she said, laughing, as they stepped up onto the porch.

Ryder performed a courtly bow and kissed her outstretched hand. "I am found out, Lady Amelia. You must have encountered my wanted poster at the post office."

"Actually, I saw your photo on the back of your last book," Amelia said. "Do they let you publish anything in Yosemite Containment District?"

"We don't publish there," he said, reflecting her smile. "We just sit around the campfire and tell everything we know."

"Sounds dangerous," Amelia said. "Come on in and meet Josh. He's preparing our feast."

"Look who's come to dinner," Amelia called, as she ushered them through the door.

Joshua looked up from the bowl he was stirring, wiped his hand on his apron and reached for Ryder's. Ryder noticed the tips of two fingers were missing. "Accident or Firsters?" he asked, nodding at the hand grasping his.

Joshua held up his abbreviated paw, and shot Ryder a rueful smile. "DHS interrogators, actually. That's why I'm still outside. When I didn't exhibit any aberrant abilities under duress, they decided I was harmless. That was their mistake."

"We could use you in Laurel, Dad," Millicent said.

"Out in the big world, I can be a tiny force for change, Angel."

"But in the districts, we are becoming the change," countered Ryder.

Joshua liberated a mirthless little laugh. "At my age, I've become about as much change as I'm capable of, Simon. By the way, don't you people ever get old?"

"I just look young, Josh," Ryder said. "And there's some question among the experts about whether my kind even qualify as people."

The day being clear and pleasantly cool and the cabin being cramped for partying, Amelia spread a cloth over the long table Joshua had built in the yard for festive occasions. "Set seven places," she said, handing Millicent a basket full of plates and utensils.

"Is Lisa coming?" Millicent asked, taking the basket.

A lively fiddle tune from down the path toward the falls provided an answer. The music was interrupted when Millicent set down her basket and ran to wrap her arms around her old teacher. "How did you get here?" she asked when they untangled. "I didn't know you had wheels."

Lisa pointed with her bow back down the path. "I came with them."

Two figures climbed up through the forest toward them. In the dappled light and shadow beneath the trees they seemed to shift and flicker, one second seeming to merge into a singularity, the next step, distinctly two and apart. As they came closer Millicent saw Vesuvia Wildness garbed in some sort of long flowing robe, green in a thousand transmuting shades and tints, that touched the ground, seemed to flow into it, giving the wearer an air of a tree who had achieved the power of mobility. Beside her, furred or feathered or scaled, depending on the angle of the light, inordinately tall and impossibly thin, like a forest vine become blooded flesh, strode Wendl VonTrier.

"Greetings, Dry McTeer," his voice in Millicent's head as much as in the air, like wind among leaves or water among stones. "Once more our place finds us together."

"Happy birthday, dear soul," whispered Vesuvia, taking

Millicent's hands together in her own and kissing her firmly on the lips. "We've been far but not apart."

The sun rose higher into the unclouded day and under the trees kindred spirits shared news and gossip until Amelia and Joshua populated the table with food and drink and Joshua called, "Let's eat. I'm starved."

"So you're still on the outside, Lisa?" said Millicent between sips of Joshua's homemade dandelion wine. "How have you managed?"

Lisa pointed to her violin resting on the porch. "I keep my mouth shut and play my fiddle. The Firsters like music at their parties. After the lights go out, I help your father and his friends guide pilgrims to the Promised Land."

Ryder lifted his biscuit toward Vesuvia and Wendl, who sat next to one another across the table from him. "And where have you ones been? I've put out feelers, but nobody has heard from you since the Affliction three years ago. Where were you up to all that time?"

Vesuvia exuded a mysterious mirth. "We've been tending our plants in the Otherside, Ryder. You should come visit us sometimes. The green lives are talking back to us now."

"Where's the Otherside, exactly?" asked Amelia.

"Closer than you know," answered Wendl. "Just a brane away."

"Closer to the Shaconage than to the High Balsams, apparently," Vesuvia put in. "The Greenlife tell us there are several points in the Laurel Creek Containment where you can essentially just walk through from one to the other, assuming, of course, you can find the door."

"The Greenlife?" said Joshua, "You mean the plants?"

"The major forbiddance in our attempt to be of the same mind with Greenlife," Wendl replied, with the benevolently patient air of a wise teacher talking to a slow student, "is our animal bias. We were trying to communicate with individual plants. Botanic mind expresses in all the contact and transfer between every plant."

"In other words," Vesuvia added, "plant mind is extra-self, a collective, global consciousness. A mind like Hawking's, for example, or any human genius you could think of, would be like a bacteria's compared to the awareness of Greenlife."

"They've had a lot longer to evolve than flesh and bone," mused Joshua. "We homo sapiens are just a last-second afterthought in the Earth story."

"At the rate we're going," Amelia said, "I don't think we'll be here long enough to catch up."

"In the twinkling of an eye, we shall all be changed," murmured Wendl.

"What?" Millicent said, her thoughts adrift in implausibilities.

"It's in your Christian scriptures," Vesuvia said.

"First Corinthians fifteen, fifty-two," Joshua confirmed, before he exited the conversation and disappeared into the cabin. He emerged after a few minutes and returned to the table and proudly bearing his daughter's birthday cake, iced in spring colors mimicking leaves and flowers. Ryder passed his hand over it and the twenty-eight candles atop came alight beneath his palm.

"Saved my matches," Joshua said with a grin.

"It looks alive," breathed Millicent, too happy to deny her tears.

"It will be," Lisa said, "as soon as we eat it. Make your wish and douse your candles, McTeer."

Millicent gathered her intention and before she could draw in her breath to blow them out, the candles lost their fire in unison, their smokes rising up into the morning like wee prayers.

"Speech," demanded Vesuvia, clapping her hands in Millicent's direction.

"No," Millicent protested. "I don't know what to say."

"No cake until she's spake," intoned Ryder.

Everybody laughed, even Wendl, all stilled to silent anticipation as Millicent stood. She sacked her mind for a song, and while she waited for words to rise, she lifted her glass of dandelion wine to the light and saw in it the faces of all she loved.

When her mind was quiet, she said, "So, here's to the dreamers, who held on to their visions after rude awakenings. Here's to the believers, who, when the Firsters said their wings were too small, took flight all the same. Here's to the Resisters, who, when they found no place to be and to become, made their own. Here's to the wounded, who, when their lives were broken beyond repair, built new ones. Don't give up on me, please, don't go away, any of you. I need you. I always have, but now more than ever, I need you."

Applause, pledges of undying friendship and fidelity followed, and the fellowship of outcasts sat upon their cake with innocent and uncalculating joy that powerful and respectable people in society never come to experience. When more crumbs than cake remained on the table, Ryder lifted his cup and declared, "Let Millicent McTeer eat her cake and have it, too. Presents, now."

"You've all come. That's present enough," protested Millicent, slightly embarrassed.

"Hold out your hand," commanded Ryder. Millicent held out her right hand. He touched her palm with the tip of his index finger and, like one of the candles on her nearly disappeared cake, a tiny flame flared. She gasped and involuntarily closed her fist around it. The flame didn't burn but she felt the warmth flow through her hand, up through her wrist and arm and into her chest. Something like sunlight, that she couldn't see but felt blazing within her, unfolded like a flower inside her head. Millicent opened her hand. The tiny fire left behind no mark at all. But she felt different in a way she had no words to describe. Not more powerful, exactly, but more…capable. She felt she could do anything she needed to do, be anywhere she needed to be.

The stone she always carried hung round her neck, pulsing against her clavicle like the beat of a lover's heart. She was sure she glowed, but if anyone there saw it, they didn't remark upon it.

"Give me your hand," said Vesuvia Wildness. Millicent obeyed. "No, the other one," said Vesuvia.

Millicent held out her left hand. Vesuvia placed in it a small bag of crimson velvet, embroidered in a golden tracery describing leaves and blossoms. Millicent opened the bag and turned out three berries, the size of grapes. One was hued a raging scarlet, one greener than spring grass. The third looked to Millicent like a hole in the world, blacker than a midwinter night, reflecting no light at all. She touched it with the tip of a finger to be sure she held it.

"Well," said Vesuvia, gesturing toward her mouth, "eat your berries."

"Millicent popped them into her mouth and they melted immediately on her tongue, liquifying into a thick syrup sweet as honey and sour as sorrel and bitter and spicy as dandelion. Before she could swallow, her whole body felt suffused with their flavor, the light of them and all their night. Everything she saw around her stood sharp against the air. She saw things, too, that were not in the light, Ryder's fire, Wendl's dark, Lisa's song, Vesuvia's reined and ready wrath, Amelia's binding love and Joshua's pain. Millicent's heart broke under the weight of it. She had never guessed her father carried such constant hurt. How long, she wondered. How far? She could also see that sooner than she wanted, he would lay it down.

Wendl reached out, took her hand and opened his palm over hers to drop a single seed into her possession, faceted and translucent as a jewel, but Millicent could feel the life in it. "When Dry McTeer comes at last to her heart's home," he murmured, "she should plant this by her kitchen door. However far she may stray, it will call her back."

"Thank you," said Millicent. She suppressed an urge to plant a kiss on that changeable face. At the center of his darkness, she could see Wendl's abiding love for all of them there, and his sadness, almost pity, that they could not be like him.

Joshua held up a hand. "Wait a moment," he said, looking at Amelia. She ran into the house and returned holding a little bowl overwhelmed with a profusion of lively vine, swathed in brilliant green leaves and tiny magenta flowers. They hadn't forgotten to water.

"Vinia," exclaimed Millicent, clapping her hands like a delighted child. She reached out to caress her plant and it twined immediately about her fingers. She had never noticed thorns on Vinia, but there were thorns now and one of them needled into Millicent's hand.

"Ouch, what's this?" she said, then watched unbelieving

as the vine sank roots into the flesh of her palm, and promptly drew its emerald and magenta in after them. She rubbed the unmarked skin. It didn't hurt. She couldn't feel anything until she heard the grass whispering around them in the yard, and the answering murmur of the overarching trees, and the humming drumming thrumming mantra of the mountain under her feet and she fainted dead away, undone by the great knowing of the place that held her.

When Millicent was herself again, a minute or a thousand years had passed, and all the faces gazing back at her looked pleased to see her as she was. Lisa knelt by her chair, holding her hand. The thought made Millicent feel foolish and selfish when it came, but she spoke it anyway. "What present did you bring, Lisa?"

Lisa Charon jumped to her feet and laughed. "All I have to give you is my song." And she took up her fiddle and played and everybody began to dance. Millicent recognized the melody as she took Ryder's arm. It was the first real tune Lisa had taught her to play, a reel called *The Winged Child*. Out of the corner of her eye, she caught Wendl and Vesuvia whirling together into a turn. She wasn't certain if she saw two or one.

They all danced, changed partners, then danced some more. Lisa played on and on, as if there were nothing left of her except the music. Amelia and Joshua retired from the circle. Millicent could feel her father's weariness and her mother's concern, though their faces were still lively with laughter. The mountain herself seemed to suffuse them all with her everlastingness. The afternoon stretched on and on for centuries.

Millicent lost sight of herself in the theirness of the dance. None were separate, none alone. The circle spun and turned and they lived only in the movement of the music. Then the fiddle slowed, and Amelia found her guitar and sang a song everyone there remembered. Joshua was out of his chair and reaching for his daughter's hand, and everyone stood silent and still as Quakers at meeting while the two McTeers turned slowly, slowly toward the silence where the music died.

"When I was as young as you," Joshua whispered, "when my life was turning to a place I didn't know, I came up here and was found."

"Who found you, Dad?" Millicent asked, her cheek against his shoulder, breathing in the scent of his slow dying and his rising life.

"All of you. All of this," he murmured. "My life. My soul."

"Promise me, Daughter," he said, suddenly breaking off the dance and standing back to look into her eyes. "When you feel your Turning, on that day when you cannot see your future, come up here alone, as I did, and let this old mountain call you home."

"I promise," she said, her eyes brimmed and ashine with all the sadness and joy of her love.

Then they all looked at one another, felt the cool of coming night reaching out to them in the long shadows of the trees. Millicent's party had come to its close. It was time to go.

The last smudge of dimming day lingered in the clouds when Millicent and her friends gathered below the waterfall for goodbyes and departures. Bats wheeled overhead, seining the air for mosquitoes. Owls voiced the shadows among the trees.

Lisa had stayed at the cabin. She would ride back to Asheton with Amelia and Joshua. Hillhaven had been commandeered as temporary housing for evacuees from the Carolina coastal cities, now mostly underwater since Superstorm Ivanka, Joshua was committed to maintaining his standards as host insofar as was possible under the current Federal rationing programs.

Ryder had plans of his own, "The Feds want to abolish Yosemite Containment, turn it into a private resort. They don't call us Resisters anymore. We are Aberrants now in official parlance. Still, there are over three thousand souls there that I must have gone before the troops come in to relocate us to the cage camps."

"There is the Otherside," Vesuvia said. "Bring them over with us."

"Some would agree to that," Ryder said, "but more than a few want to join the Secessionists and fight rather than be displaced one more time."

"Ryder is adept at persuasion," observed Wendl.

"Reason and logic are not in vogue at the moment," retorted Ryder. "I'll have to make something up."

He began climbing up among the boulders flanking the waterfall. His gray angularity blending with the stone as he climbed until there was only rock and shadow and a shimmering thread of laughing water against the dark.

Millicent watched after Ryder until she saw no shifting trace of his going, then turned to Vesuvia, who stood alone beside her.

"Where's Wendl?" she asked. "I didn't even say goodbye."

Vesuvia waved her hand over the pool at their feet. "Within," she said. She reached out and took Millicent's face gently between her hands, bent and kissed atop her head, murmured into the damp hair, "Remember, we are always close, however far," then stood back and said, "Happy birthday, Millicent McTeer. You're one of us now, born again the mountain's child."

Vesuvia turned, stepped down into the water and waded deeper into the pool. Her dress floated about her, seeming to melt into the current as she went. She turned and waved, smiled a smile that lit the night, and there was only the reflection of the waxing moon upon the dark water.

Millicent stood for a long time watching, listening. It was time for her to leave, too. But for the moment she longed for nothing but to belong to this place, to relish her solitude and her solidarity with water and stone and leaf and wing and fleet running and slow becoming, with all the furred and feathered lives that she could see now in her mind, hear in her heart, as she spread her arms wide, over the pond and the falls and the rocks and the mountain, over Asheton and all the roads leading to other towns and away and away to the ever-rising sea. She wanted to gather to herself now every wounded soul and broken spirit she saw between, and in the instant realized they were her and she was them. They all suffered the same hurt and they all shared the same hope and hungered for the same healing.

From somewhere in the night, an owl called, and from somewhere farther away, another answered. She heard the bird again, the one she had never seen, but knew only by that single tone, a ringing, shining, briefly everlasting *One*.

As she gathered herself to be apart from this place, she heard something else, or felt it first, a vibration in the air around her, that gradually grew to audibility. Far out and high over the descending stream, Millicent caught a flicker in the moonlight, focused on the machine that hovered back and forth over the mountainside. She watched the pattern of its search as it swept east and west and back again, gradually ascending the flank of the ridge where she stood. She recognized the drone for what it was, reached out and touched it with her mind and knew its mission and took hold of it with her thought.

The little craft sputtered, wobbled in the air as if it might fall, then shot like an arrow back the way it had come. Millicent didn't release it until she saw the lighted window in a building in Asheton growing larger and brighter and startled, panicked faces of technicians fleeing their monitors and controls as their spy machine crashed full speed through the glass.

She wondered then, if that provocation had been her first mistake of this new life that had come upon her without her seeking or asking. She couldn't deny the solid sense of satisfaction her little defiance of Empire had aroused. Still, Millicent vowed to herself that she would be more prudent in the future. She was, after all, only human, gifted and endowed, a full-blown Aberrant now, yet a woman, easy prey for pride and retribution. She would be wary of herself after this.

She looked out over the valley toward Asheton. Her parents and her teacher would be on their way back to Hillhaven now in Joshua's antique jeep. She could see the red glow rising on the far edge of the town. Something or somebody had started a fire. Millicent walked slowly back up the winding path through the spruce wood toward the cabin. When she reached it, the windows were all dark. There was no sign anyone had been there at all.

She sat on the porch, listening to all the voices of the mountain, until the stars began to fade into the dawning day. No ghosts came to council, no fears arose to haunt. She felt no sense of duty other than to pay attention to her life and respond as honestly and truly as she was enabled. In her mind, Millicent played the memories of her becoming. Events arose clear and sharp from her childhood that she could not recall forgetting.

In that moment, she knew that, wherever she went from here, her heart belonged to this place. Here was where she would come back to in times of her deepest need. She knelt beside the cabin steps and scooped up a handful of rich humus and buried Wendl's seed in the mountain.

Finally, Millicent remembered the time when she had been able to fly. She stood in the golden morning, hands at her side, closed her eyes and released her body to the air and slowly, slowly rose above the trees, hovered there in the golden light as the sun broke over the mountain, fixed her mind on Laurel Creek Containment and Shelton Crossing, and began to flow. For a moment, Millicent McTeer manifest as a long ribbon of cloud resembling the contrail of a jetliner. Then she was clear air and gone.

———————

"Space, like time, is an illusion," Wendl told Millicent during one of her summers at Wildness Emporium. According to Wendl VonTrier, every place was the same place. To travel, he said, one had no need to traverse vast landscapes, but simply to change one's point of view. Millicent's present experience of flow seemed to confirm Wendl's premise. She had no sensation of passage. There was no between. She stood on the porch of her father's cabin in the High Balsams one moment and the next instant she stepped onto the flat stone outside her door at Shelton Crossing in the Laurel Creek Containment District. Nothing felt changed, except her point of awareness and presence had shifted, as if she had turned around to see in a different direction.

"Where and when are merely mental constructs," Wendl would insist when she professed to be confused. "Your thoughts are either your wings to fly with, else stones to weight you to your place." Then he added, "Most souls only dream stones except when they are asleep."

Whether Wendl was right or not in his belief, Millicent decided it was a good functional hypothesis, because she had become where she had willed herself to be, in a light drizzle on a warm spring morning. Weariness hung around her shoulders like a heavy blanket. Whatever Wendl had told her about time and space, getting from one place or moment to another obviously took energy, whether one traveled on a train or in a trance.

She reached out and opened her door, no one locked their doors in Shelton Crossing, and stepped inside. Millicent hung her coat on the rack in the hallway. Hungry now, as tired as if she'd walked the whole way, she went through to her kitchen to brew some chicory and forage something for a breakfast. Through the window she could see a man standing in her vegetable garden, facing away from the house, intently studying her okra.

She opened the window and called, "May I help you?"

The man turned a vaguely familiar face in her direction and a voice she almost recognized said, "Remember me?

CHAPTER 2

Millicent McTeer smiled to herself as she watched the man in her bed stir himself awake. It was hard to believe four years had passed since she had discovered him prowling in her garden, communing with her vegetables. The day after her twenty-eighth birthday, and her best present had come late and last.

She recalled now her own surprise and his evident embarrassment at her accusatory tone when she asked, "May I help you?"

"Remember me?" he answered. "They told me it was all right to wait for you here. I hope you don't mind."

She hadn't quite recognized either the face or the voice but together they ignited a memory.

"Eric?" asking herself as much as him. "Eric Lee, is that you?"

"All day long," he said, laughing, sensing welcome. "I asked Sharon at the café where you were, and she told me you were away but would be back today and I should wait for you."

"Ah, yes," Millicent said. "Sharon puts everybody in their place upon arrival. The Hungry Dragon is our unofficial immigration control office."

"I saw the sign. You don't actually have dragons around here, do you?"

Millicent laughed. "It's a long story. You'll have to ask your boss Simon Ryder about that one. So, why aren't you out in Yosemite with him? What brings you here?"

"Ryder sent me to you, Millicent. The Feds are about to clear our people out of Yosemite, and I've brought all our neurobotany research. Everything."

Millicent frowned and shook her head. "The Federals won't let us have computers here, Eric."

Eric tapped his forehead. "Don't need computers, Millicent. It's all right in here."

Eric sheltered in Millicent's house that night, and she invited him to stay the next. After a month of mornings it never occurred to either of them that he should leave. On this particular morning Eric's eyes opened, focused on Millicent, as if he'd dreamed asleep that she would be the first sight he'd have of his waking day. She knew that he probably had. That was the nature of the Sharing, which had grown past their union to embrace by now most of the seven hundred thirteen people remaining in Laurel Creek Containment. Two years past, the population of the Containment had been triple that. Then the Yosemite Removal, among other outrages and atrocities, precipitated the successful four-state secession that created an independent Pacificana along the west coast, whereupon the diminished Atlantic American Republic promptly accelerated its campaign to eliminate the remaining Containment Districts. Offers of financial incentives, free level-three housing, and "voluntary" Cultural

Rehabilitation lured many back into the Firster world. Those who had better memories resisted the government enticements and stayed put.

"We have real coffee this morning," Millicent informed her spouse. The mere mention of the beverage seemed to energize Eric considerably. He struggled free from his blanket and groped for his sandals. "How did that happen? Somebody raid a Firster supply convoy?"

"We're not quite that brave," laughed Millicent. "Not yet. No, Sharon found it when she unpacked a box of medical supplies yesterday, honestly labeled as *Granulated Caffeine Supplement*."

"Methinks I see Mathilda Stone's hand in that. The AFG should teach their inspectors to read," quipped Eric, buttoning his shirt and reaching for his kilt.

"Speaking of reading," Millicent said, "Trader Amos got hold of a newsreader somewhere. We're going to meet down at the Hungry Dragon and Sharon's going to serve free coffee to everybody who shows up to hear the latest."

"What is the latest from the world that never was, I wonder?"

"Amos was stingy with the details, Sharon said. He doesn't want to miss his chance at stardom, but apparently the Republican Guard has been sent in to clear the Acadia District."

"That's where Ryder went, last I heard from him," Eric said.

"He isn't there now," Millicent said. "According to Amos, when the troopers got in there, the whole area was deserted. Do you think that's a cover story? It wouldn't be the first time the Guard just killed a whole colony and shoveled them under."

"In that case, I think they would have come up with a

more complicated story," Eric said. "I'm going to make some inquiries."

"Who do you know to ask?" queried Millicent.

"The trees. Who else?" was all he said.

After they ate their breakfast, Eric went off to teach his Greenmind class. Millicent went out to weed her tomatoes. So far, the Sharing hadn't eliminated the need for weeding. Eric had tried to dissuade unauthorized plants from encroaching upon their crop rows, and there were fewer of them now, but plants were not entirely cooperative, even among themselves.

As she worked, Millicent let her mind reach out among the surrounding green. She still wasn't nearly as adept as her husband, but he was teaching her. He was teaching them all. Greenmind day by day became more and more human mind as well. The little band of homo sapiens in Laurel Creek Containment were evolving transapient.

The air felt weighted with humidity as Millicent brought her tomatoes to the house. She stopped by her door before she went in, listening for a moment. The trees knew the rain already falling on their kin on the western slopes was moving closer. The forest was responding in anticipation, increasing transpiration. Millicent sensed her own isoprene levels rising in sympathetic reaction. Deep down, green and blooded were all of the same mind. Greenmind had always known that. The remnants of humankind were just beginning to catch on.

As Millicent ranged the tomatoes on a windowsill, *Millicent?* Though she only heard the voice in her head, she recognized it immediately, *Sharon? I'm open.*

Can you come over to the café? Important.

On my way, thought Millicent. The Sharing that Greenmind opened to the Laurelites had in large measure replaced the communal connections lost when the exiled community's electronics were confiscated by the Republican government, but telepathy also had its disadvantages. Much was gained and some things, like privacy were lost in the process. Plants were not troubled with individual ego. Humans clung to it, and thus were being forced to learn a whole new etiquette.

By the time Millicent came in sight of the Hungry Dragon Café, more than a dozen people were milling around out front. As she approached, she caught a mix of emotions ranging from puzzlement to anger and outright fear. She didn't try to insert her persona into the mental cloud, but she gathered from a surface scan that strangers had come among them. Strangers these days usually proved unfriendly if not dangerous.

The gathering parted for her outside the door. She felt their questions crowding her mind as she entered. *I just got here*, she tossed to the general air. *You'll all know when I do.* The Laurel district was already accumulating a stock of quaint folk sayings to express their unique mindset and emerging social norm. The quip bantered about most often was, "The only sin in Laurel is a secret."

Inside the Hungry Dragon, Sharon stood with her hands spread proprietarily on her counter, where a half-dozen government-issue electronic gadgets lay scattered, their detached batteries piled separately beside. Most notable in the collection were three stunner pistols. Four women and two men pored intently over the artifacts on the counter. Millicent knew the foragers. The Laurel folk gardened but found it often easier and more tolerable to Greenmind to glean the forest for natural food rather than slay numbers of trees to clear land for farming. She correctly assumed the foraging committee had acquired some human presences among their mushrooms and herbs on their outing.

"Tell me," she said to any inclined to answer.

"These here," Sharon said, gesturing at the others, "came up on three of them, fast asleep, like babes in the woods. They had 'em tied up before they were awake."

"Who's them?" asked Millicent aloud, although she was already beginning to know. It wasn't considered friendly to appropriate another's knowing before they had a chance to say it by choice.

"AARP," said one of the women, a near neighbor of Millicent's named Allison Peacemaker. "Young boys they are. The Firsters are sending out children now."

Millicent looked at the assorted gear on the counter. "This all they were carrying? No lethal weapons or explosives?"

"Just the stunners," said one of the men. "They couldn't have killed anybody." He pointed to one of the larger devices on the counter. "They had two deep scanners in their stuff, though. They meant to spy on us."

"We'll need to check the woods hereabout," said Millicent. "Be sure they haven't already set some more active." She looked across the counter at the door leading to the storeroom. She could feel the anxiety seeping through the wall.

She pointed to the captured gear. "Put this stuff away and we'll have a conversation with these children you have shut up back there."

Sharon began gathering the items in question and

stowing them in a wooden box beneath the counter. There were no locks in Laurel.

"That's our salvage," said one of the foragers. "Finder's right."

"You'll get it back soon enough, and the Trader will tell you what it's good for. But I need Eric to take a proper look at it before it gets any more meddled than it already is."

"If you good folk will just clear the room now, we'll bring out our visitors and have a little chat," said Sharon.

"We prisonored them," said another forager, a woman. "We want to hear what they are up to."

"Then listen from out there with every curious body else. I don't want you spooking them any more than they are already. Spies get shot dead where they come from."

Offering no argument beyond protestual sighs, the foragers trooped out the door to stand with the rest of the spectators in the yard. Sharon opened the door to the storeroom and, sounding like a mother calling her children from an enforced nap, said, "You all can come out now."

The pitiful trio emerged hesitantly, as if fearing they were on their way to their own hanging. Automatically, they ranged themselves in a ragged row in front of Millicent and commenced an intense contemplation of their muddy boots.

"You boys thirsty?" Sharon queried from behind their backs.

"Yes ma'am," they chorused in unison without raising their gaze from their toes.

Sharon gave them each a mug of ginger beer, which they sipped, then gulped until they had it all down.

Emboldened by unanticipated mercy, the oldest policeman, who might have been twenty, asked, "What happens to us now?"

"That might depend on what mischief the Atlantic American Republic Police is up to in our District. The deal was that this is our place as long as we don't intrude on yours."

The prisoners exchanged furtive glances. A boy who could not have been eighteen, the youngest, apparently, ignored the warning stares of his companions and blurted out, "Somebody has been looting Republican supply shipments. We were just trying to find out how you knew schedules and locations that were supposed to be secret. It seemed like you had to have some electronics in here. We were sent in to set up scanners to detect your transmissions."

"The District violated the ban first," said the oldest, who was apparently in charge. "We're not military, we're civil police, conducting lawful investigation. You can't say that makes us spies."

Millicent gazed at the policeman for a long moment until he resumed eye contact with his shoes. *You're a brave one, son*, she thought at him, and he lifted his eyes for an instant, just long enough to catch her fleeting smile.

"Innkeeper," she said at last, "will you show our guests back to their room while we decide what we're going to do with them?"

The crowd outside the store had doubled by the time Millicent emerged. They waited, mostly silent, though the air was charged with their conversation. She knew they were aware of most that had transpired within.

"Any questions?" she said aloud.

"Will they be hostage?" a woman from the back of the crowd called. Millicent knew she had a brother in a Republican prison camp, accused of unauthorized disclosure.

"When do we get our salvage back?" from one of the forager party.

Millicent answered the second question first. "If we keep their stunners, we have violated the no-weapons provisions of our sufferance charter. That would give the Republic an ample excuse to descend on us in force. You can keep the power units, scanners and com devices to trade with Amos. As for the three police in there, they were sent because they were deemed expendable. They have no currency for prisoner exchange, and we have no facilities in the Laurel for keeping prisoners. My judgment is to let them go back to where they came from, but we need to be of one mind, whatever we do."

Proposals ranging from torture, execution, indentured servitude, to liberation and forgiveness stirred the silence, eventually coalescing into *send them back*.

"If we are consensed then, I will convey our humane intentions to the boys inside and you foragers, since you profit from this affair, are free to escort them to the Separation." Answered by assenting silences, Millicent said to Sharon, "Bring the children out then, and we'll get them started on their way."

"Should I feed them first?" Sharon asked. "They probably haven't eaten in two days."

We mustn't send visitors away hungry. The Republic would think us inhospitable. Millicent didn't quite say it aloud, but the thought caught, and sprinkled the crowd with laughter.

The captives devoured their cold lentil-and-root stew as if they hadn't fed in a week. "We don't get live food at home anymore," said the youngest, between mouthfuls.

"Can't get a gardener's license now," said the constable who had been mute until now. "They say the dirt's contaminated. There's just GovStor rations." A sharp glare from their Sergeant abbreviated the confessional.

"Here's the deal," Millicent said, as they mopped up the last of their stew with Sharon's biscuits. "We're going to send you home now. You will tell your people the truth, that you were treated humanely with due respect to your status. You will tell them that we will leave the Republic alone, if they will leave us in peace. We do not raid your supply shipments. If you have thieves and enemies, they are not us. And no more attempted surprises from your side. What one of us knows, we all know. If you even think about sending your people into the District, we will be aware of it. Is that understood?"

The three nodded, and since there was nothing left on the table to eat, they stood. The youngest remembered to thank Sharon for the meal. Millicent ushered them out the door, where only the foragers remained waiting.

"These nice people will show you back to the Separation," she said. "Remember our message."

Sharon handed them back their stunner pistols, unpowered now. They shuffled out into the yard, and the foragers began herding them away. Before they had gone fifty feet, the sergeant halted, looked back at the women standing on the porch. One of the foragers reached out to take his arm and usher him on.

"Wait," Millicent called. "He wants to say something."

The Sergeant glanced at his companions, then turned to Millicent. "May I stay here?" he said.

"Why would you want to stay, Sergeant?" she said, "You don't look like a convert to me."

"I'm the leader," he showed her a bleak face. "I blew the mission. If I go back, they'll shoot me."

"How do you know we wouldn't do the same?" Sharon asked.

"Well, you wouldn't let me starve," said the policeman.

"Do you have a name, Sergeant?" Millicent asked when their audience had dispersed.

"Roland, Ma'am," he said, apparently, in spite of his new uncertainties, relieved to be rid of rank and responsibility. "Roland Schlembach."

"Well, Roland," she said, pointing to Sharon, "you'll answer to her now. Do what she says and do nothing without her permission, or you'll answer to all of us, got it?"

Roland nodded.

"Why me?" said Sharon.

"You fed this stray," Millicent answered. "He's your responsibility now."

Sharon shrugged, grasped Roland's shoulder. "Then come with me Sergeant, and I'll show you how you'll earn your keep." With those words, she rechristened him. Ever after, the folk of Laurel District knew him only as Sergeant. Years later, Roland Schlembach would have to struggle to recall his birth name.

That night, Amos had big news to share that even the sharpest minds hadn't been able to pry out of him beforehand. Many already knew of the mysterious evacuation from the Acadia Containment, but ten Middle States had presented a declaration of independence to the Republican government in Washington. Dire warnings and threats were being issued, but half the Republican military assets had been based in the Middle States and apparently kept their loyalties local. The Atlantic American Republic would be outgunned if they attempted military intervention. Their former nuclear arsenal now resided mainly in the territory of the newly declared Continental Democratic Federation.

That night, over a late supper of sweet corn, roasted beets and sweet potatoes, and another version of their ubiquitous green salad, Eric observed, "In the main, that's good news for us. The Republic will have a plate too full to worry much about the little old Laurel District. We'll have some time to gather our mind."

Millicent caught the pun but ignored it. "What do you think of Sharon's new policeman?"

"I think she might enjoy his company."

Millicent ignored the smile, too. "Do you think we can trust him?"

Eric turned on his serious face. "I touched him lightly during the reading tonight. He doesn't know his own mind yet. But he feels safe here. He recognizes kindness and honors that in his thought. We should watch him for a while, but I think Sergeant is on his way to becoming of our one. Besides ..."

Millicent didn't quite catch the thought unspoken. "Besides what, Love?"

"At some point, the Laurel will need a policeman, and this boy has some training for it."

"Good coffee this morning," Eric said over his biscuits and gravy.

"Enjoy it," advised Millicent. "That's the last of it. We're back to chicory tomorrow."

"Aren't you having any?" he asked, noticing his wife's empty cup.

"No, my tummy's a bit off this morning," she said.

Millicent did not tell him that her tummy was off most mornings of late, and that coffee, of which she was inordinately fond, suddenly inspired nausea by its mere smell. Eric stared at her a second too long and she wondered if she had let her thought show.

"See Lucia," he said finally, got up from the table and carried his dishes to the sink.

He would have washed them, but Millicent took them from him and said, "I'll do that. You're late." A kiss, and Eric was away to his meeting with the Laurel Settlement Committee.

Dishes done, Millicent still had not found her appetite, so she took the path up through the garden and among the trees above the house to do her morning's listening. She did this every morning. Day by day she could hear deeper into Greenmind. The trees did not speak to her in words, although sometimes the impressions they sent shaped words in her head. She wondered if the translation was working both ways.

Today, there was an urgency in the air. The whispers in her mind insistent. She tried to still her rational thoughts, quiet her anticipation, just open and wait. Then, *Milliccennttt …* Her name came so weighty and embodied to her that she thought someone had spoken it aloud. Startled, she looked around, trying to catch some sight or sound from the speaker. There were only the trees, and the light wind in leaves, and the morning gossip of birds.

Eventually, she stilled, her brain quieted, she could hear the trees again, the flow of their collective knowing all around her like water in a stream. Then she heard it again, *Milliccennttt …* and realized the voice came not from without but within.

Lucia Kirk, the first and only trained physician in the

Laurel Creek Containment District, did not tell Millicent anything she didn't already know. She took her hands from her patient's still flat belly, smiled out the words, "You're pregnant. A girl, I'm pretty sure. Early yet, I'm surprised she's already talking to you. A precocious child, like her mother was, so I'm told."

Millicent wrinkled her brow. "Who's been talking out of school?"

"Nobody," Lucia said. "Just Eric. He said you would be coming to see me soon. Your child has been talking in his sleep, too."

"But he never said ..."

The doctor laughed. "Neither did you, but thanks to Greenmind, there are few secrets in the Laurel."

Millicent gazed at the trees beyond the window glass. "What will become of us, Lucia? Do you think that one day we won't be ourselves at all, just undefined drops in a sea of awareness?"

Lucia shrugged. "Speaking for none but me, I feel more like myself now than ever I did out in the Republic. We'll always have our boundaries. Even those trees you see out there retain individuality. You can commune with one as well as with all. If anything, I think we will each be more fully who we are for becoming more transparent to our neighbors as well as to ourselves. Humans evolved for community. Containment has freed us from all the cultural and economic forces that hindered that. The world we knew out there is self-destructing. Here in Laurel, we are just beginning to become all we were made for."

Millicent laughed, in spite of herself, felt some sort of inner release. "You should have been a shrink, Lucia."

Lucia smiled her doctor's smile, and lifted her hands in the air. "Like all of us here, I'm learning as I go."

"I need to go visit my parents," Millicent said to Eric over supper. She kept to herself the unsettling dreams that had robbed her sleep for the past three nights. The details always slipped away as soon as she woke, leaving her with only a vague and lingering impression of Joshua lying face-down on the floor and Amelia kneeling beside him, screaming.

"Now?" Eric said. "With the baby, I mean ..."

"We are the same body," she reassured, "she will flow with me, just like Wendl brought me here before I could properly fly on my own."

"I should go with you," Eric protested.

"No, Love," Millicent shook her head, "You can't fly. I'm not yet as adept as Wendl. I don't know if I could carry you in my flow. Alone, they can't touch me. I can be dim and I can be gone. Together, we are all at risk."

They were still debating travel when a knock on the door quieted them. Intent on their exchange, they had not sensed the arrival.

"I think it's the Trader," Eric said as Millicent went to the door and opened it.

Amos stood outside in the beginning of a rainstorm. "I have a letter for you." he said. "It's from your mother."

"You've seen my parents?" Millicent blurted, then, "I'm sorry, come into the dry. Have you had anything to eat yet?"

Amos stepped inside, his slicker dripping on the floor, raindrops glistening in his beard. "I've supped, thankee. I've not been to Asheton. The letter passed to me from Vesuvia Wildness. It came to her from Lisa Charon who took it from Amelia Montford's hand, so it hasn't been opened and spied."

Millicent took the brown square of paper, a single sheet, written on one side then folded into an envelope. She recognized Amelia's handwriting on the front, *Millicent McTeer, Shelton Crossing LCCD.* Swallowing her impatience, she spoke hospitality, "Amos, we have a little coffee left. Would you like a cup before you face the storm?"

Amos wrapped his weathered face around a dark and toothless smile. "Thankee, Millicent, but I'm abstaining toward stronger drink down at the Hungry Dragon. I'll be there for an hour, want ye to send an answer by me."

Before she had time to thank him, Amos had turned and found unity with the rain and the night.

Millicent closed the door, sat down at the table, lay the envelope before her and gazed at it with glistening eyes.

"Aren't you going to read it?" Eric asked.

"I'm doing that now, Millicent whispered.

Dearest, Darling Daughter-

I have nothing left to send you on your thirty-second birthday but a heart full of love and sorrow. Your father died three days ago.

The Republican Guard came to arrest him. They said he was suspected of aiding evacuees to evade assigned resettlement. He told the officer in charge, "You can't arrest a citizen without a duly issued warrant." The man said, "Here's my warrant," and put a stunner pistol to Josh's chest and shot him. It shouldn't have killed him, but you know his heart was weak. He had refused an implant, saying he couldn't trust RHA surgeons not to implant something else with the pump.

The RG has commandeered Hillhaven, pending

*relocation of all the evacuees here, which means those poor
souls (including me) will probably just disappear if Josh has
left his door open for us. I'll try to get this to Lisa to send on
to you. At least, I know my daughter is in a relatively safe
place.*

I so love you-
-Amelia Montford

Millicent handed over the letter when she finished,
although Eric had already read most of it through her. He
studied it for a moment, wordless, shook his head and gave it
back. Millicent saw tears in his eyes as he reached out arms
to her. She stood for a long moment wrapped in his love,
anguish and anger, an echo of her own, and comforting
because she was not alone in it.

"Will you walk down to the water with me?" Millicent
asked when they stepped apart. For some reason she did not
understand, it seemed easier to lift into flow near a stream.

"Need you go now?" Eric asked. "Your mother will be
gone. How will you find her?"

"She will have left the door open for me," Millicent
said.

Eric didn't protest further, just said, "Be careful then,"
and went with her through the silent village, reaching out to
take her hand when they came in sight of the Long Broad,
silvered under the moon emerging from the breaking
clouds. They stood together on the bank, listening to the
murmur of the water and the calling of owls somewhere on
the far shore.

"Finally," Millicent whispered. "Let me go, Love."

Eric kissed her forehead, dropped his hands, and stood
back while she gathered herself away from him, oneing with

the light on the water and the wind over it and the star-sparked dark above, becoming herself a ribbon of pale luminescent going, brilliant against the night.

Somewhere between the moon above and the shining river below, Millicent flowed eastward toward Asheton, a dim glow on the horizon swelling into a scattering of sparks against the dark mountain that flared and resolved into roofs and windows, a few with lights, and pavements glistening from a recent rain and she felt McTeer Street beneath her feet, deserted in the dark first hour of the new day. Hillhaven stood ahead, unlit, emptied of life.

She dimmed herself, being not quite there, so that any who might see the street would notice only a flicker of shadow as she passed. Yellow tape stretched across the drive. A large orange sign planted by the steps shouted to anyone not interested, *DANGER, QUARANTINE, DO NOT ENTER.* Smaller characters below affirmed the dominion of the Atlantic Republican Health Authority. She opened her mind to the night. Only the trees in the yard and the small nocturnal creatures who were awake and the flowers and grass asleep. No humans. Not even a guard posted. Millicent slipped past the quarantine notice and stepped up onto the porch. One of the windows had been broken out. The door, though intact, stood slightly ajar. Millicent pushed it and went inside.

Stillness. Silence in that inner dark. Not even the whisper of the fan overhead. In the dimness, Millicent could see the scattered pale of papers strewn across the floor. She listened for a moment, then crossed the hall into the dining room. Islands of moonlight, admitted by the windows, revealed tables stripped bare, a scatter of chairs, some overturned and broken. She heard a memory of music, Amelia's guitar. Lisa's fiddle. In the center of the floor, a man and woman, old and transparent, danced together, in a slow soundless turning. A younger man sat nearby watching them. Millicent could see through him to the chair he was sitting on.

He looked up, as Millicent came into the room, and when he spoke to her, Millicent only heard the voice in her head. *Hello, Angel. They're all safe and gone.*

The old dancers stopped, stood, holding hands, watching her. Millicent recognized her great grandmother, who sat with her on the stairs in another life, listening to her mother's sweet sad songs. The old man, who stood now next to Alice, holding her hand and smiling, Millicent knew without being told, was Edison McTeer, her great grandfather.

Remembering Amelia's letter, she looked at Joshua's ghost, "Dad, where's the door?"

The figure wavered and rippled like a flag as she spoke and Millicent realized it wasn't her father at all. About his age, perhaps, his size and build, but the clothes were wrong and it was not quite his face and not quite his voice as the ghostly simulacrum said, *we've left it open for you, Angel*, and Millicent stood alone in a room inhabited by moonlight and the wreckage of a broken dream.

When she could think of nothing else to do, Millicent went back across the hall and climbed the stairs to the floor above. As she reached the upper landing, memory incited a twinge in her arm. She stood for a moment at the top of the stair, rubbing the mended hurt, looking down at the child who thought she could fly. *Yes, you can,* Millicent told her.

Three doors down the hall she came to her room. The

unhinged door lay flat on the floor. She could see nothing she recognized among the jumble of smashed and broken furniture inside.

She hesitated when she came to her parent's bedroom, steeled herself, opened the door. The room had been ransacked. Dresser drawers pulled out and emptied into the floor amid tumbled bed linens. The door into Joshua's office stood open. She went through, expecting the same chaos, but the room was empty, stripped bare, no furniture, even the pictures on the wall taken. The window onto the balcony outside, just an empty square open to the night. Millicent felt the cool breeze that came down from the mountains just before daylight. The breeze, or perhaps a spirit, drew the door shut behind her with a sharp slam, shattering the quiet. Startled, she gasped aloud.

Millicent waited, not daring to move while her heart slowed and settled enough for her to hear her own breathing. When she was quite certain she was still alone, Millicent opened the door. Blinded by a midday sun, it was a minute before she could take her hand from her eyes. Before her, a foot path wandered down a grassy slope, to the Long Broad. Across the river, trees climbed up to crest the farther ridgeline. Beyond the ridge, blue mountains lifted themselves to kiss the clouds.

CHAPTER 3

All that was left of what had been Joshua McTeer came to awareness in light and pain. The light revealed nothing, a featureless intensity that impinged upon his consciousness from nowhere and everywhere. The pain rode into him on the light. Nothing he could identify hurt, but hurt was everywhere, within and beyond. Joshua searched for his tongue and could not find it. Neither could he find his hands or feet or face. He was a nothing strung out on a web of emptiness. He would have screamed if he had a mouth to shape it and lungs to give it air.

Not quite nothing. Something remained. Memory. Unbodied Joshua remembered the Homeland Security officer pressing the snout of the stunner against his chest. He remembered the feel of the cold metal through his shirt. He remembered Amelia screaming from some place he could not see as the man said, "Here's my warrant," and pulled the trigger, igniting fire and light through his whole body and stopping his heart.

Against all that he had been and lost, this memory still

held him in his present agony. He wondered if this was hell, to spend eternity strung out on the moment of one's death. Like a tortured spider, Joshua McTeer began to draw the threads of his being into his center, folding his past back into his now, until, at the heart of the endless light and suffering, he established a boundary where everything that remained himself endured. In the midst of the unbearable light, he found a shady place where he could rest. Like a tree. Like the redbud tree beside the veranda at Hillhaven. Joshua eased his wracked frame into his old bleached blonde and imagined himself a sigh, *I thought I was dead.* He raised his hands to look at them and watched his fingers stream away into beams of light that swallowed up his body and the chair and the veranda and the tree until there was nothing left but the bright sky, cloudless and unshadowed like an infinite sun.

YOU WERE, said the voice, familiar, though Joshua couldn't recall where or when he'd heard it before, YOU BELONG TO US NOW.

The voice spoke to him in his pain. Joshua let the pain carry his question, *Am I alive now?*

YOU ARE AN EXPERIMENT. YOUR EXISTENCE IS A MATTER OF DEBATE.

What are you going to do with me?

While Joshua waited for an answer, the voice spoke again, but not to him, to another, COMMENCE TRANSFER. Then Joshua McTeer felt all his knowing and remembering and hurting sliding away on the light until there was nothing at all.

Tell me the story again, Mill'cent. Like most of the children born in the Laurel Creek Containment District, Alice seemed to catch Greenmind from the air. She preferred the words in her head to words from her mouth and wouldn't speak aloud unless encouraged by an adult.

"What story is that?" Millicent asked the soon-to-be five-year old. Laurel children, especially girls, tended precocious in their grasp of language skills. Eric thought it was the effect of Greenmind.

About the door ... thought the child.

"I didn't catch that, Angel," said the mother.

"About the door to the Otherside," said Alice, using her voice, reluctantly. She laughed more than she talked and cried least of all.

Millicent told the story then one more time, about how she had opened the door to a room she'd just left, and walked into another world, just like the one they lived in now, except that world was still green and fresh and cool and bright, with no cities, no Republic, no trains or aircraft or bombs or armies or plagues, no pavements slicing through the forests, no mountains dug up and hauled away so greedy humans could get at the treasures underneath.

She told again, as if for the first time, how she walked down a grassy path to the river's edge, and a figure stepped from among the trees on the far bank and pushed a small boat out into the water, climbed in and commenced paddling toward her. Before he had come halfway across the water, Millicent recognized Wendl VonTrier. When he reached the bank, he stood in his little coracle and, without a word, held out his hand to help Millicent climb awkwardly aboard. Once she settled on her seat, Wendl pushed out into the current again. Millicent looked back up the path she had just descended. There was no door, just the canted meadow and trees beyond, and beyond the trees, blue mountains and bluer sky.

Neither boatman nor passenger offered words to the air as Wendl ferried them back to the opposite bank. Millicent brimmed with unspoken questions, but she knew better than to rush her strange friend to speech. She marveled at his adept handling of their odd little boat with neither bow nor stern, essentially a round basket of what looked like old tent or tarp fabric stretched over a frame of bent saplings with a couple of seats affixed. When they grounded on the far side, Wendl smiled just enough to reveal a glint of needle-ish canines between his thin lips, ushered her ashore, turned to the trees and unleashed a thought loud as a trumpet. *She's here.*

In another instant, Millicent saw as many people as trees around her, smiling, expectant, welcoming. Vesuvia Wildness emerged from the throng to embrace her. Before she could speak, Vesuvia stepped away and Millicent saw Amelia Montford reaching out to claim her winged child.

"Mother," she whispered. It was the only word in her mind.

They held to one another so tight and long that their arms ached, before Amelia drew back, kissed her forehead, and said, "You are your father's daughter. As long as you breathe, I still have you both."

"Tell about the party," Alice trilled.

"Oh, yes," said Millicent. "There was a party that night."

It seemed any new arrival was an excuse for a party. The Otherside was vast and humans were few enough that any increase in their presence on the land was cause for celebration. Some came to Otherside through a Door, either by intention or accident. Apparently, Joshua's was just one of many. A few souls were brought through by Fliers, like Wendl.

"There are others of Wendl's kind here," he said at table during the evening's feast, gazing intently at Millicent over his cup of juniper ale. Flyers, according to Wendl, not only traversed time and space, but possessed ability to alter their shape and substance. To the consternation of the adults present and the delight of their children, he proceeded forthwith to demonstrate, cycling through presences as bear, owl, wolf, eagle and finally what he claimed was his true and original conformation.

"Dragon!" yelled Alice, clapping her hands, levitating about six inches above her chair.

"He looked like a dragon to me," confessed her mother, laughing at the remembrance, "Afterward, he was just Wendl again. And after dinner we danced to the music while he told me what a fine daughter lived inside me."

I remember him, thought Alice.

"I think you just might," said Millicent.

"And then you went to sleep and came home."

Millicent nodded. "I was tired after all the talk and dancing, and I'd had too much to eat. Vesuvia Wildness had a little guest cottage in the garden behind her house. I was so sleepy I scarcely remember. I think she helped me get undressed and tucked me in bed as if I were a little girl. I was asleep before she closed the door."

"And then you woke up and came home." Alice thought that the best part of the story.

"And then I came home, and here we are," laughed Millicent, hugging Alice to her, kissing her fragrant hair. She remembered as if she were back there now, waking with the sun in her face, looking through the curtained window at a garden that looked like her garden at Shelton Crossing.

Getting dressed and opening the door and stepping into her own kitchen as she heard the front door of her house opening. She ran to meet Eric coming in raindamped from the dark outside.

"I thought you'd gone," he said, surprised.

This part of the story, Millicent hadn't told her daughter yet, how she had laughed at the puzzlement on her husband's face. "It's been two days, Eric. Didn't you miss me?"

Eric wasn't laughing. "What do you mean? It didn't take ten minutes to walk back from the river where you left me and here you are."

Here was where Millicent had been for nearly five years since that day, with the two loves of her life, with her garden and her neighbors in Shelton Crossing and the forests and the mountains. She hadn't flown away again, even to visit her mother. She hadn't opened doors to any other life but this one. Outside Laurel, the world continued to fall apart. The rising ocean had pushed the coast twenty miles closer to the Shaconage. The Atlantic American Republic reduced now to a loose and unstable aggregation of squabbling and rivalrous city states. Asheton was a ghost town, looted and burned and abandoned to vengeful ghosts and scavenging four-leggeds.

Where there had been fields and farms, the sterile and polluted soil now only yielded famine and pestilence. Re-processed garbage passed for food, packaged and distributed by a few mega-corporations in the industrial enclaves of the Middle States. People stood in long lines and paid a month's labor to get enough of it to stay alive. None from outside ventured into the Shaconage to claim her verdant plenitude, though. Rumors circulated in the shadowlands that devils lived among the trees there, or worse. Better to be hungry than to have one's soul eaten by Fairies.

Meanwhile, the Laurel Creek Containment District was known by those who occupied it as simply. The Laurel. It was a green and pleasant place where life was sweet and death came more often by age or accident than by disease or assault. The inhabitants rarely if ever felt need to venture into the Shadow the rest of the world had become. Some said the Earth was dying. Some said it was only humans who were passing away. A few said everything was waiting to be reborn.

———————

"We'll be back before sundown," Millicent said to Molly Deere, who governed the settlement's day school. Alice sailed away to join several other children who were cavorting among the topmost branches of an old hemlock. "Here's her lunch," the mother said as she handed a loaded basket to the teacher. "There's plenty in there to share."

"We'll be fine," Molly said, taking the food. "Don't get lost out on the mountain."

Millicent laughed. "Don't worry. We can't get lost anymore. The trees know us too well."

"You hunting today, are you?" Molly asked, as she glanced over her shoulder to ascertain that her squealing charges were still aloft.

"Yes. One of the foragers told Eric they had come across a colony of Queen's Crown. We're going to see if there are any suitable for transplanting in the Talking Garden."

"Children, come down from there before somebody takes you for fairies," Molly called aloud. *Get you all now to Learning Circle*, she thought at them when she had their attention. She turned back to Millicent. "Is it true what they say at the Hungry Dragon? Do Queen's Crown really speak?"

"Not aloud," said Millicent. "They're just lilies, after all. But Eric's starting to connect with them. They come through so wordy, it feels almost like they are voices. Eric thinks they might be a bridge into Greenmind, that we might be on the brink of deep conversation with Shaconage."

Be found, thought Molly, Laurel's equivalent of have-a-nice-day.

"You, too," said Millicent aloud. All who knew her said she was talkative. She still harbored a fondness for the soundful flow of words spoken. In her opinion, a stream lived in its music. Behind her, the air was a clamor with childmind as she turned and hurried away to meet her husband, who would have their gear packed and ready by now.

She found him waiting with Sergeant at the Talking Garden. Eric started the garden soon after his arrival in the district. There among the green lives he collected, he called them his "influencers," he pursued his neurobotany experiments, heavily biased by an obsessive conviction that, eventually, plants could become as communicative with humans as they were among themselves.

Sergeant, who grew up on a farm, and so far, having minimal policing duties in the Laurel, had volunteered as a practically full-time assistant gardener. He proved to have a knack for gleaning impressions, and occasionally, messages from Greenmind. "He grew up close to the ground," Eric told Millicent in a praiseful moment. "It shows."

When he saw his wife, Eric gestured at his companion.

"Sergeant wants to go with us," he said. "We might need some help carrying back our finds."

"My husband is so optimistic," Millicent said to Sergeant. "But there's a good walk in it for you, at least."

Sergeant just grinned and hoisted his pack, a large basket woven from white oak splits, fitted with shoulder straps. It was mostly empty. Eric's plan was that it would be filled with green life by the time they started home. He slipped Millicent's basket onto her shoulders and she adjusted it to comfort. She carried their rations for the day. She helped Eric settle his load, a small notebook he'd acquired from Amos, his collection tools, and their drinking water. When everybody was satisfied, they were fit for the trail, the trio set off toward the river. A couple of people spoke to them as they went down the street. Sharon waved from the door of the Hungry Dragon when they passed. Ten minutes later, they stood on the bank of the Long Broad, reduced by the current drought to a maze of meandering sykes amid rounded boulders that in a normal flow would have been inundated. Today, an adult human would be able to walk from one bank to the other without getting their feet wet.

Three flat-bottomed rowboats rested unattended at the landing, useless without enough water to float them. Though it was early in the day and the journey hardly begun, the hunters were wiping sweat and waiting for one another to be the first to mention drink. Eric's pack would be a lot lighter before they came back this way.

A mile's walk along the parched riverbank brought them to the foragers' trail. Once they began climbing up the forested ridge in the shade of trees, the heat was less oppressive.

"Where are the birds?" asked Sergeant.

They stopped, listening. Except for a quarrel among crows somewhere on the slope below, no avian conversation at all in the unmusiced air.

"Weird," said Eric.

"Maybe higher up, where it's cooler," Millicent speculated.

They resumed climbing and after another tilted mile, the air became a little cooler with a breeze lively enough they could feel it lapping up their perspiration. A wren spoke to them tentatively, promptly seemed to think better of it. Sergeant noted the lack of noseeums or bees.

"It's the dry," murmured Eric. "Even bugs need water."

By now the expedition were drinking liberally from their bottles. When they reached the point where they thought the foragers had seen the Queen's Crown, they found nothing but brown grass and briars. Another uphill hour and Eric called a halt for lunch. They still hadn't found anything to burden Sergeant's basket.

"We receive unworthily," Sergeant whispered as they broke out their cheese and nuts. He produced a pone of bread he had baked. "I've been taking lessons from Sharon," he confided. The bread was hard and dense, but they dipped it in their water and wolfed it down.

"A little farther," Eric said, when they had eaten and drunk as much as they dared. "A shame to go home now with nothing to show."

Millicent and Sergeant exchanged glances, tried to veil any thoughts they entertained that getting back home might be show enough. A half-mile further up the faltering trail they came to a rock outcrop that afforded a long view eastward. Past the dusty green and earthy blues of the Shaconage, they saw only an unbounded expanse of umbers and browns stretching away until lost in steely haze that might have been sky or might have been nothing natural.

"Dear God, can anybody still be alive down there?" Sergeant whispered.

"If they are," said Eric, "they're not like us anymore."

Sergeant made a brief reconnoiter of the narrow ledge ahead. "It looks like the end of the trail," he reported.

A sheer rock face rose above them for perhaps eighty feet. They could glimpse the green of fir branches over the top but discerned no crevice or niche that might give them purchase to climb. Eric passed around the water bottle. The drink tasted of disappointment. Faintly, they could hear birds singing somewhere up among the fir, and something else, Millicent thought.

"I hear water," she said.

The men listened, agreed, and they began to prowl the brush at the base of the cliff. Millicent found it in a fold in the rock, obscured by vines, a cleft so narrow they had to drop their packs to squeeze through. A glimmer of light ahead and a draft of cool moist air on their faces met them halfway, and another five minutes of confined squirming brought them through to a narrow glen. Dappled sunlight filtered down through towering spruce and fir. Beyond the trees, tumbles and steeps of fractured schist and gneiss rose on all sides. Variegated mosses and lichen clung to the stones and the trunks of the trees, pendanted from their lower branches, blanketed the ground. Everywhere, from this living carpet, emerged hundreds, no, thousands of Queen's Crown lilies arrayed in colors known and inconceivable. Hues that were seen with the eye and felt on the skin and heard in the ear, mind washing, soul cleansing color, pure and deep and intense beyond any measure and definition.

There was nothing for the three humans to do with this permeating glory but to kneel in its midst and surrender whatever prayers of praise and gratitude their minds could conceive.

Millicent felt herself dissolving in the shimmering glimmering silence and closed her eyes to retrieve her mind. She could see the colors flaring in her head. She could hear them, too, a whisper at first, but growing, swelling like a seed unfurling into a consuming chord of knowing sound, a melody, complex and profoundly simple, ever expanding and folding in upon itself, blending with her own being until she was part of the song.

She heard herself whisper, "Dear Lord, they're singing."

Then, from somewhere in the trees above, the bird she had never seen but heard all her life, called her solitary, silvery, sacred note. *One.* Millicent opened her eyes, looked at the men's faces and saw they had heard it, too. None of them breathed until they heard again. *One.* And the flowers were flowers again and the humans inhabited their own bodies and the world resumed its accustomed holiness.

Their sudden separateness left them disoriented and ungrounded. Instinctively, Millicent and Eric and Sergeant reached out to join hands. They stood untimed in a mute circle waiting, watching, listening for an answer to the question they had become. The answer, when it came, formed as another question.

The three hunter-gatherers stilled, measured their own breathing, counted their heartbeats until the flower music resumed, subtly different now, less in the ear, more in the mind. This time, the song became words. *How are you found?*

The humans responded with a thought in common. *We don't understand.*

The flowers sang to one another for a moment, a soft wash of sound blending with the laughter of the little brook that emerged from a crevice in the surrounding stone and cavorted across the glen to gather in a small pool before the mountain swallowed it again. Finally, more words. *Are you found three or one?*

The humans conferred in their minds in the manner of flowers until Millicent spoke for them. *We are found three in the one.*

The response this time was immediate and conversational. *You are found enough. Three in our one will go with you.*

The lilies began to fade, swallowing their colors until they were pale as trillium, like a flight of ghosts in the gathering shade. All except three by the little pool, who remained radiant as stars. When Eric knelt before them, they twisted and leaned out toward his hand as if accepting an invitation. Gently, he lifted them from their place one by one, careful to leave roots intact, and cradled the three emissaries in a bed of their own moist humus, then swaddled each one in a piece of his shirt that he wet in the brook. He handed one to Millicent and another to Sergeant to carry through the narrow way out. Holding his own close to heart, he said to the surrounding throng, "We are found thankful."

We are found one, came the answering radiance, splendoring their sight.

The way out took longer. They went slowly, carefully, embracing their charges gently as newborn babes. The lilies chirped and murmured in their heads until they were under the sun again. Eric was ecstatic, his joy contagious. Even back in the heat, they all three felt lighter, younger. Cumulous loomed ominously northward.

"A good rain would be worth the wetting," said Sergeant, hoisting his basket, a little heavier now.

"A good wetting would be a good end to our day," said Millicent.

"A good wetting is a good beginning," Eric said, patting Sergeant's basket as the policeman led the way back down the mountain.

They hadn't gone a mile before the rain overtook them in a sudden deluge that after a few minutes turned the trail into a creek. The going was slow and treacherous until they took shelter under an overarching bluff at a place the Foragers called Standing Stone. Previous trekkers had left a stash of dry wood and Sergeant built a fire.

The afternoon waned while the rain increased. As shadows grew, Eric said, "Maybe we should just stay the night here, and go down in the morning."

Sergeant agreed with him, but Millicent said, "I can't leave Alice with Molly overnight." While the two males courted their fire, she stepped out between the raindrops and let herself rise with the mists until she saw, away and below, beyond the storm, the Long Broad curling around the settlement at Shelton Crossing. She gathered her becoming into one dimensionless point of brilliant light and she was there.

"Looks like rain," Molly Deere said as Millicent walked into the schoolyard. When Alice saw her, she became a smile and ran to touch.

Millicent gathered up her daughter and said to the teacher, "It's on the way. Caught us good at Standing Stone. I left the boys holed up there."

"How was your walk?" Molly asked.

Millicent smiled and answered, "We were found."

As they walked home from school, Alice began her customary interrogation. "Where's Dad and Sergeant?"

"They'll be home in the morning. We got stormed on, and they're waiting it out up at Standing Stone."

"Did you fly home by yourself?"

"Well, sort of. Not like you do, though."

"Did you jump?"

"Yes, you're right, daughter of mine. More like I jumped."

"Why don't you jump everywhere? It's faster."

"Because when you jump, you're here and you're there. There's no between. Life is all the things that happen between there and here."

Alice reached up, took her mother's hand, swung their arms. "Like while we're walking?"

"Like while we're walking home together," Millicent said.

"Two in the one," whispered Alice, as if repeating something the wind had told her.

The storm besieged and assaulted them in a drowning fury for a week. By the time the sun finally reappeared over Shelton Crossing, the Long Broad brimmed her banks, too swift and debris-laden to safely cross in the stoutest boat. Creeks had become torrents. Trees that withstood centuries found no purchase for their roots in the slurried slopes and toppled into the mud. The town was awash. The gin was getting low at Sharon's Hungry Dragon Cafe. Unbedded streams and absented bridges had prevented Amos, the trader, his latest re-supply trip.

As soon as he sighted blue sky, Eric was intent on

getting his precious Queen's Crown into the soggy ground, although Sergeant protested. "This mire is too thick to drink and too thin to dig."

The lilies apparently were as much at home in the valley as they had been in their highland glen, for when Millicent and Alice walked down to the Talking Garden a few days later, the three had become a dozen.

"Mom, they're singing to me," said Alice.

Millicent listened inside herself, caught a lilting murmur of life lifting into light. "What are they singing to you, Angel?"

Alice tilted her head, as if in receipt of a secret. "They're singing about people, Mom. People in the water."

Millicent smiled. "Well, if the rain had kept up, we'd all be in the water by now, I imagine."

Alice didn't return the smile. "Not us, Mom. There are people coming on the water."

"Who's coming, Angel? What kind of people?"

"I don't know, Mom, but they're coming with the dragon."

"The flowers told you this?"

"Yup," Alice assured her mother. "It's all in their song."

The next morning over breakfast, Alice was telling her father about the lilies' song when her narrative was interrupted by an insistent rapping at their door. Millicent opened it to one of the foragers, a man named Slide Underhill.

"Miz Millicent, Sharon said I should tell you." He gasped, out of breath. He'd obviously run all the way from the Hungry Dragon.

"Tell me what, Slide?"

"Why, they's coming. I seen 'em putting out from their camp upriver atter first light and run all the way to tell youns. They's outerlanders."

"Outerlanders?" said Eric, coming to the door.

"Yup," Slide nodded vigorously, "And they don't look like they've fared right well in the Republic."

"It's them," piped Alice, tugging Eric's hand. "The Queen sang them all this way."

Before Slide had completed his rounds as self-appointed town crier, every soul in town had caught the news and converged on the landing at the Long Broad. The early morning sun ignited a brassy glow in the heavy fog that blanketed the river, receded somewhat by now from flood stage, but still flowing strong and deep. One by one a half dozen small boats and a couple of make-shift rafts emerged from the mists to reveal their cargo of forlorn and bedraggled humans crammed among their meager store of possessions.

Millicent wanted to weep. She wondered at the catastrophes these refugees had survived, if any of them were people she had known. All of the rivers in the Shaconage flowed away from the mountains, either to the Republic to the east or the Middle States in the west, except for the Long Broad, which sprang in the High Balsams above Asheton and cut through the heart of Shaconage to meander west, eventually mingling with deeper waters flowing southward into the Dead Gulf at Sunkentown.

As they drew closer, the forlorn flotilla began turning toward the landing. Everything above the waterline looked to be coated in ash. Craft, goods, clothes, even faces and arms, all bleached of color, eyes staring vacantly, as if drained of every hope and dream and promise of becoming, animated finally only by fear and a flagging determination not to yield quite yet to darkness.

One figure in the lead boat stood tall, radiated a vitality that Millicent could feel before the overburdened craft reached the shore. He seemed familiar to her, even though he was shrouded in a dark poncho that hung down to his knees. His broad-brimmed hat pulled down low shadowed his face, but Millicent caught the flash of his eyes as he gazed steadily in her direction. *Milliccennttt*, in her head, like wind through an open door, and the boats began to meet the land and her neighbors waded into the water to aid the beaching and she stood fast as if pinned to the ground until he stood before her and took off his hat so she could see his face, golden in the young light as a leaf of ripe tobacco, and looking not a day younger nor older than the last time she had seen him.

"Simon Ryder," she said, as if meeting a neighbor at the market. "Where have you been?"

"Let's get these people up to the Hungry Dragon," Sharon called after they had all the new arrivals on solid ground. "Get everybody fed and watered and then we'll try to figure out where all will sleep tonight."

Loads were hoisted, along with a couple of elderly humans hard put to walk on their own, and the refugees and rescuers made a slow uneven procession through town to a promise of food and rest at the Hungry Dragon.

Millicent and her former mentor walked at the rear of the flock, pausing occasionally to assist some weary soul who had fallen behind. "Are all these people from Asheton?" she asked.

"Most of them," Ryder said. "The rest, we picked up along the way. There's nothing much left out there. The Republic has no effective authority this far south. Those who aren't being preyed upon by their neighbors are preying upon them. Laurel is the only Containment District left, and that's because the Washington government has all its forces tied up skirmishing with the Canadians, who likely won't be satiated until they've occupied the whole East Coast to the tip of Florida. The Middle States are refusing any assistance. Some say that by winter Pacificana and the Continental Confederation will be all that's left of the America that stretched from sea to shining sea in our youth."

"They all look hungry," Millicent said, watching the tattered and bleak figures shuffling and stumbling along around them.

"Starvation is the new normal down east. Before it ceased to function altogether, the Republican government nationalized all agriculture. It was a prosecutable offence even to have a private vegetable garden. Food was the carrot and the stick used to control the populace. Unfortunately, the government wasn't very good at farming. They shipped in processed proteins from the megacorps in the Confederation until there was nothing left to exchange."

Millicent shook her head in disbelief. "Who's in charge of all this misery now?"

"Some guy named Thorn. When he isn't fighting his neighbors to the north, he's dealing with the purges and counter-purges among his underlings, and sending out raiding parties to glean the ruins for anything that might shore his power."

"Stripping the corpse," said Millicent bleakly.

"That's what it amounts to." Ryder might have said

more, but they stopped to help an old woman who had stumbled and dropped her battered violin case into the mud.

Millicent felt a thrill of connection when she handed the instrument back to the owner, who pushed her white hair away from her face and stretched out a gnarled hand to brush Millicent's cheek.

"Millicent?" she whispered, her voice all hope and question.

Millicent stared, then reached out and wrapped her arms around the tottering figure, "Lisa," she breathed into the snowy head against her chest. "Lisa Charon, you've brought us the music."

CHAPTER 4

The doors and windows of the Hungry Dragon were open to the warm spring evening and light spilled out into the street like a welcoming carpet as Millicent McTeer and Eric Lee walked with their daughter to her birthday party. Alice, humming to herself a minor-keyed and somewhat dissonant melody she'd learned from the Queen's Crown, darted like an oversized moth just above their heads.

"Come down and walk with us, Angel," Millicent said aloud.

Why? came the child's unspoken response.

Because it isn't polite to fly in public, Eric thought. "Not everyone can do what you do," he added in voicespeak.

Though capable of willfulness as any eight-year-old, Alice didn't argue. Perhaps the knowledge that her father wasn't a flyer compelled her obedience. She was an empathetic child. Molly Deere, teacher at the day school, had told Millicent that her daughter possessed a special gift for it, that she would be mightily surprised if the girl didn't grow up to be a healer. Alice came to ground between her parents immediately, light as a leaf, stirring not a mote of dust from the dry street. No rain had fallen on Shelton Crossing in weeks.

Two other children would also be celebrating birthdays tonight, Dorie, who was ten, and a boy, Patrick, twelve. Patrick would be receiving special attention. Two years previous, the human inhabitants of Shaconage decided in Consensus Gathering that clan names would not be perpetuated among them. Family designations as practiced in the Republic carried too many dark associations of prejudice and privilege. Parents would henceforth give their offspring a forename, but the child, on turning twelve would choose their own surname.

The sounds of laughter and dancing and the wild flight of a fiddle poured out into the dusk as the three walkers approached.

"Sounds like the old days," Millicent murmured. "Lisa's hands have healed, I think."

"We're fortunate to have Lucia," Eric said. "I doubt there was ever a better healer even in the old Republic."

Shaconage found Doctor Lucia with Greenpowers, thought Alice as they walked into the light and the music.

The birthday children were ushered to the table of honor and their parents blended with the other adults who hovered in the nooks and corners like the shadows Millicent remembered from her own childhood at Hillhaven. The parents at Shelton Crossing didn't worship their children, but were awed by them, gifted as most of the young were with powers and abilities their elders would never grasp. In most human societies, such progeny would likely have been spoiled and pampered to dangerous, but in Shaconage, the young, steeped in Greenmind from conception, were generally wiser and more generous than the old. Homo sapiens brinked extinction in the Outerlands, but here, humans had discovered their survival depended on becoming something more and other. At the end of their civilization, the seekers had been found. With every passing season they were less the many and more the One.

Everybody danced a couple of reels more before the grownups yielded the floor to their young who danced to a different music, a swirling curling murmuration, never touching one another and scarcely touching the floor, moving to the swift flow of the river and the slow pulse of the mountain and the sibilant shift and sweep of trees. Their young voices choired a song from their movement, a wordless, wondrous wilding upwelling, the sound of their oneing, too deep for laughter, too light for tears, leaving only amazement and joy in their wake.

After a time nobody thought to measure, there was a sudden silence and stillness and Sharon emerged from the kitchen with Sergeant and Slide behind her, pushing carts piled with the birthday feast.

"Let's eat," she called. And they did. An Outerlander might have wondered at the lack of conversation during the meal, but only because of not having ears to hear within. Laughter came frequent and audible, however. A mirthful spirit overflows the mind.

Following the desserts—there was a choice of three and some ate one of each—presents were presented, though not as many as might have been as Amos hadn't shown up for his scheduled delivery two days previous. None of Shaconage seemed to know what had become of him. Finally, Molly Deere called Patrick front and center to announce his grown-up name and his parents came to stand with him. He had kept his choice close, not even telling his parents what it would be. Alice confided to Millicent. "He's afraid he might change his mind." All of his friends had tried to guess, but he'd tucked it deep in his head past all their gentle and good-natured probing. They knew their friend spent most of his loose time in the river or along the creeks. The summer before, when he ventured onto the Long Broad in a "borrowed" boat while the river was in flood, he managed to tumble overboard. He might have drowned had not Slide Underhill seen him spill and fished him out. Slide had teased then that he weighed no more than a minnow, and the nickname caught on among his classmates. Now the air was filled with all manner of watery names said and thought and Patrick, grinning, shook his head to all of them.

When Molly decided there had been enough gaming, she lifted her hands and the whole assembly shouted, "Who is our Patrick found?"

Proudly and officially twelve, he released his secret. "I am found Patrick Trout," though to his intimates, he would always be a Minnow.

Cheers and toasts followed aplenty, until Alice slipped away from the birthday table and crossed the room to whisper to her father. Millicent caught the thought that slipped from mind to mind as the merriment subsided to a murmur. Everyone in the room stood silent as dread, staring at the door by the time Amos the trader appeared, bedraggled and footsore, minus hat, jacket, shirt and shoes.

"I've lost my load," he croaked, groping the air for support. "They took it all." As he tottered away from upright, two women who stood closest to the door rushed to help him to a chair.

"I should go with you," Eric protested.

Millicent remained adamant. "You stay here, Love. We'll have to flow if we catch them before they get back into Republican territory. Besides, Alice needs one of us home."

"What about me, then?" Sergeant ventured. "You'll be dealing with Guard. I might be useful there. I still have my uniform ..."

Ryder broke in before he could finish. "You're grounded, too. I'm afraid. We could carry you in our flux, but it would slow us and time is of the essence here. But if you will loan me your uniform, I can shift to fit it, if we need a bit of subterfuge."

Sergeant didn't look convinced, but Millicent further weighted the argument. "We don't know who else might be wandering loose, looking to pick our bones. Someone with experience needs to see to securing the town against intruders. That looks to me like a mission for you, Sergeant."

"Give me a minute," he said to Ryder. "I'll fetch my uniform."

"How many of them were there?" Ryder asked Amos, who, after several mugs of Sharon's pumpkin ale, honeyed and pokered, was marginally revived and restored from his depletion.

"Four of 'em, 'at I could see," wheezed the old trader between tentative sips of the hot drink in his hand. "All males, not much more than young'uns. They had lethal weapons, not stunners. I figure em' low on ammunition or they would'a kilt me."

Simon allowed himself a chuckle, "Old Son, they just felt sorry for you. If they'd wanted you dead, they wouldn't have wasted a bullet to do it. They wanted you left alive to tell their tale and frighten all us pitiful resisters."

"They was a scruffy lot, they was," said Amos, warming to his role as talebearer. "They acted 'bout as scairt as I was."

"I'm guessing they were," said Ryder. "Deserters or marauders, likely. The Republic is way undergunned these days. They don't generally issue lethals to interior patrols. Thanks, Trader, for the heads-up. Unless you've more to tell us, we'd best be getting to the chase."

"One more thing," Amos said. "They won't get out of Shaconage with that truck. Can't be a gallon of 'nol left in the tank. I had enough to get here and a little. Figured to trade for some fuel before I went on."

Distilling ethanol from the corn grown along the bottomlands flanking the Long Broad was a major cottage industry in the settlement, accounting for the greater part of Shelton Crossing's GDP. The few functioning vehicles left in the Shaconage had engines modified to run on it after a fashion.

The council was interrupted by Sergeant's return with his uniform rolled neatly into a tight bundle, which he handed to Ryder, who stood gazing at it intently while he turned it slowly in his hands. When he was satisfied with his inspection, Ryder handed the uniform back to Sergeant.

"Don't you want it?" he asked, perplexed and slightly annoyed.

"I took all the measures," Ryder said, as if explaining an obviosity. "I'll manifest a copy if needs must. Thank you, Sergeant."

The whole company left Amos nursing his ale and followed the two Fliers out into the starry night. Ryder looked at Millicent and spoke as if they were about to leave for a party, "Shall we go, then?"

Before she could answer, several of the stars above

wavered and flickered and slowly turned in a descending spiral, gathering and merging into a shining orb that upon settling to earth, morphed into the contour of a figure promptly proceeding into two and Vesuvia Wildness and Wendl VonTrier stood beside them garbed for battle.

Wendl voiced a thrumming sound somewhere between a purr and a growl and Vesuvia said, "We heard you might want some help."

"How did you know?" asked a mystified Millicent.

"I told 'em," said Slide Underhill, grinning from his perch in an open window.

"You a flyer?" Sergeant's question shot out more like an accusation than a query.

"Wellsir," said the forager, allowing a smile big enough to allow his toothless gums some light to shine in, "youns don't call me Slide for nothing," and without waiting for command or permission, he dropped down the wall and flattened himself into something resembling a shadow that slipped away in an instant across the yard to be swallowed by the night.

"We are found four in one," chirped Wendl, who in the flickering light from the lamps inside the Hungry Dragon seemed to be greening and sprouting leaves all over his body. Ryder's eyes were two coals burning in his face becoming scaly and elongated like a serpent or a lizard. The two women dissolved into clouds, or something that looked like clouds, one of them dark as the sky and one of them bright as the moon, shifting and dissipating and gathering again into themself as the four slowly turned and lifted above the earth as high as the tops of the trees bordering the yard. There came a sound like a spoon struck on a glass to call attention at a dinner. A single ringing note, not loud but heard by all, and the Flyers instantly imploded into one impossibly bright infinitesimal point of light that shot away into the night and was found gone, like a spark from a campfire.

Depending on one's point of view, it might have been a second or an hour later when the four-found-one hovered unseen above the hapless and hungry reivers huddled around their campfire. Amos's truck, still loaded with their plunder, sat cold and derelict at the side of the road. The hijackers appeared in the midst of an argument about which of them were to blame for their current predicament. Tempers were wearing thin and two of them kept fingering the rifles on the ground beside them. One angrily threw a stick into the fire exciting a shower of sparks toward the gathering clouds overhead. They all looked up, reached for their weapons when a shabby old man, obviously a resister, came walking out of the night.

"Maybe I can help if youn's don't shoot me first," laughing as if he'd told a joke.

"Maybe we'll shoot you if you don't," said a red-bearded man of indeterminate rank.

"I got some 'nol that I could swap for a leetle awhat's on that truck yonder. I got food, too. "I can bring it here, got us a deal," wheedled Slide. Four rifles pointed at him now, but his smile never wavered.

The men looked at one another, looked at the truck, looked back at Slide. Redbeard said, "Maybe we ought to go with you in case you can't find your way back here, old man."

One of them, a smooth-chinned youngster who perhaps wasn't old enough to grow a beard of his own, said to

Redbeard, "Earl, oughten one of us stay and watch the truck?"

Redbeard shook his head, waved the tip of his rifle at Slide. "That truck ain't going any place without some fuel in it. This codger might have some friends he ain't told us about yet. We'll all go. Lead on, old man. You got a name?"

"Slide," said Underhill, still smiling.

"Slide. What kind of name is that?" asked Redbeard as the four reivers trooped away up the dark road after Slide like a band of disciples following their teacher. Hardly had the fog closed behind them than the Four in One settled soundless as shadows around the truck. Wendl reached into his voluminous robes and produced a gallon jug of ethanol. Likely he could have found among the folds of his garment any item the occasion might have required. He poured it into the tank while Millicent got behind the wheel and Vesuvia climbed up beside her. Ryder opened the hood, signaled to Millicent, and breathed a whiff of dragonfire into the air intake as she pressed the starter button. The engine roared, flames shot from the exhaust. Ryder slammed the hood as Wendl clambered aboard with unaccustomed glee.

The raiders looked back just in time to see the truck turn in the road and barrel away toward Shelton Crossing. A dark blob of shadow shot past them and darted after the truck like the umbra of a tiny moon chasing its sun.

"They stole our truck," howled Redbeard. "Shoot 'em."

Before they could raise their weapons, they were blinded by a brilliant flash of light above the truck. For an instant, they thought the vehicle had exploded. By the time they knew better the dragon was hovering overhead spewing fire and despair all around them.

The beardless boy soaked his trousers, out of his mind

with terror, and pulled the trigger of his rifle before he thought to aim it. He blew a hole through his right boot, and fell to the ground, writhing and screaming. His companions stared at him as he flailed at their feet, splattering their legs with his blood.

"Wallace been shot," shouted the one closest to him, scampering backwards.

"We're surrounded!" Redbeard yelled, and all three left standing commenced firing wildly at their imaginations. By the time their magazines were empty, the dragon had swooped down and deftly plucked their wounded comrade from their midst and disappeared.

Somewhere in the dark over Shaconage, two found one flowed toward Shelton Crossing. Below him in the night, the wounded boy saw the lights from the trader's truck as it fell behind. *I'm dead. It's going to eat me now*, he thought.

Not until I'm hungry, said the voice that answered in his head.

The lights were still on at the Hungry Dragon Café when Millicent, Vesuvia and Slide Underhill drove into Shelton Crossing. Somewhere along the way they had realized Wendl was no longer aboard. It was his way to be out of sight when his presence served no purpose. A few people stood in the yard, obviously expecting them. They went inside to behold a young man in a much abused Republican Guard uniform lying on a table. Lucia Kirk leaned over his bandaged foot, securing the wrapping. Simon Ryder stood opposite, holding the patient in place.

"Is this one of the reivers who took Amos's truck?" Millicent asked.

"Yup," said Lucia, standing up from her completed task. "Gunshot wound."

"We didn't shoot at anyone," Vesuvia said.

"Friendly fire," Ryder informed.

The wounded boy didn't offer any explanation, just lay silent, looking afraid.

"What's your name, Soldier?" Millicent asked in what she hoped was a reassuring tone.

He looked up at her, didn't speak for long enough that she was about to ask again, when, his voice shaking with some combination of pain and fear, he whispered, "Wallace, Ma'am, but I ain't a soldier."

"Where came by you that uniform?" said Sergeant, who had been standing out of the way, watching.

"It's mine. We deserted."

Millicent said, "Why did you do that?"

"We lost a prisoner we'd been sent to arrest. They'd have shot us for that."

"More likely, you'd have been hung," said Ryder. "Bullets are scarce in the Republic right now."

"I reckon that's so," Wallace said. "Will you send me back?"

Lucia stuck an old-fashioned thermometer in his mouth. "First, we're going to get you mended and healed. What happens to you after that will be mainly up to you."

"Where's Amos?" Millicent asked.

Sharon said, "We put him on a cot in the storeroom. He's sleeping like a newborn. Lucia has the touch."

"When he wakes up, tell him we got his stuff back."

Lucia turned to Wallace, retrieved her thermometer and appeared satisfied by the information it provided. She smiled down at her patient, spoke no word, lay her palm against his chest and he was away from them all, wandering some private dream of deliverance.

Amos recovered from his ordeal in a few days, and his gratitude rendered him generous in his trading. Even so, his load gained more than it lost by the time he pulled out onto the long road that followed the river down to Beaverdam, the only other settlement in the Laurel District that might claim to be a town. Before the Republic established the Containment Districts, the Long Road, as everyone in Shelton Crossing called it, ran through the Shaconage from Asheton on the east in Carolina to New Town, just west of the mountains in Tennessee. Now the road only stretched as far as Beaverdam, and nobody seemed certain of what state that might be in. It was as if all the political and social upheavals in the Outerlands had somehow shifted the geography of the world. Connections were missing. Long had become short and short had become forever and a compass that guided true one day might lie to a traveler the next. GPS had become as extinct as GO2's and satphones.

The satellites were still up there making their rounds, so everyone supposed, but they weren't talking to anybody anymore. In the Shaconage, few mourned the loss. In a country where humans shared their minds with trees, rumors could travel faster than sound.

Young Wallace's wounded foot mended slowly. The tinctures and extracts Lucia learned from the forest staved off infection, but the heavy caliber rifle had shattered the bones beyond surgical repair. Wendl had supplied the doctor with a spirit made from holly nectar distilled in dragonfire, which she injected into the wound to good effect but hollies grow as slow as sure. Among the many lessons the reformed reiver was learning in the Laurel, patience was high on the list.

Sergeant questioned him thoroughly, but Wallace didn't know much more about what was happening in the Republic than the Resisters knew already. Beyond a disintegrating command and supply structure that left individual units to invent their own rules for survival, he had little military intelligence to offer.

When he wasn't trying to help Sharon with some small task at the Hungry Dragon, Wallace would hobble on his crutch to the Talking Garden and listen to the Queen's Crown. Whatever music he gleaned from them healed his heart and restored his peace, though it did nothing for his ruined foot.

Milliccennttt ... Again.

What? Everything trembling, swaying. Earthquake or storm at sea?

"Millicent!" Eric shook her shoulder one more time. "You're talking in your sleep again."

"I was dreaming," Millicent mumbled, opening one eye and groping for a smile, "What did I say?"

Eric laughed softly, pushed her hair back from her face. "It wasn't English or Spanish, That's all I know."

"I can speak one language you know," Millicent said, grappling his beard with her fingers and pulling his face down until their lips were found one. She felt his surprise and the answering hunger in him, as she sat up, kicked back their blanket and lifted her nightgown over her head. Then there was nothing between them but their love until they had said as much as their bodies knew to speak.

Later, after Alice had left for school, they resumed their original conversation over the last of their chicory coffee. "It was that same dream I've been having every night lately. At least I think it was. I can never remember any of the details once I'm awake," Millicent told Eric.

He looked concerned. Eric set much store by dreams, since that was often the way his plants communicated with him. "So you don't have any idea what it was about?"

"Not really." Millicent shook her head, stood to empty the pot into their cups. "I just come awake with a vague impression of storm and fire, peril, conflict. I wake up with my heart pounding and I'm hungry."

Eric smirked. "You certainly had an appetite this morning."

She bent down over him and kissed him loudly on his ear, making him flinch. "I'll always have a taste for you, Love," she murmured.

As soon as they finished clearing the table and washing dishes, Eric trotted off to obsess over his beloved Talking Garden and Millicent walked down to the Hungry Dragon Café. She had felt all morning there might be strangers in town, and Sharon had just thought to her that a refugee family had camped in front of the café overnight. There had never been an election, but by default, as she had never refused any of the duties requested of her in that regard. Millicent was generally accepted and expected as the Mayor of Shelton Crossing. Whatever disordinary event might ruffle the complacency of the townfolk, all assumed that Millicent McTeer would know how to address it.

When she arrived at the Café, Sharon and Sergeant were out front talking to a road-worn couple, who probably looked more ancient than they were, considering they'd ridden from wherever on a rusted two-seater bicycle with a cart rigged behind.

"Can I help?" asked Millicent, smiling at the strangers.

"They're looking for their son," said Sergeant.

"We want to take him home to bury," the old man informed. "Youn's kilt him."

"Nobody's been killed in Shelton Crossing," Millicent said. "Where did this happen?"

"Some mile back," said the old man. "According to Wayne. We didn't see no sign there, so figured maybe youns brought him here."

"Who's Wayne?" asked Sharon.

The old woman pulled a rumbled fold of paper from her bag and handed it to Millicent. "Wayne was in the Guard with our Wallace. He got this to us to show us what happened to him."

Millicent unfolded the paper and read between stains of tears or coffee or mud or blood or perhaps a blend of all.

Dear Mr. and Mrs. Williams,

I do not know if you will read this as I cannot send it by proper mail for fear of being arrested. If I did dare the Post, still it would likely get intervened by reivers or Guard along the way. Your son Wallace, who was also my best friend got shot and killed by Shaconage Resisters on the road between Asheton and Shelton Crossing about three mile inside the Laurel Creek Containment. We had to leave him there because of being set upon by a dragon. Dragons don't eat dead meat, so unless carried off by bears or critters, the body might still be found there for you to bury if you have means to fetch it home.

I am muchly distressed to need give you this woesome news. I will send it with someone I might trust.

Sincerely sorry,
Wayne Smathers

. . .

Millicent handed the letter back to Wallace's mother, felt the shadow of her last night's bad dream lift and vanish. "I believe I have some good news for you," she said.

The reunion went well. Slide Underhill and three of his forager colleagues were putting the finishing touches on the boarding house they had built for Lisa Charon just across the river from town. The carpenters would be paid with free meals for a span yet to be determined. Wallace was her first boarder, paying his keep with painting and cleaning. Lisa said the elder Williams were welcome to stay there until permanent housing could be arranged.

"All's well that ends so," said Sharon, but it bothered Millicent that two distraught and elderly souls had been compelled to undertake such a precarious journey for so uncertain a result.

When she told Eric about it over supper, he said, "It's almost like everybody who turns up here has been sent and guided to us."

"That may be," retorted Millicent. "But we need some reliable way to get messages beyond Shaconage where Greenmind doesn't reach. Even here, there are a few souls who still can't hear thoughtspeak at any distance. Besides, some things need to be scribed and set, so there's no mistaking meanings."

Eric took a sip of his hibiscus tea. "Maybe we could just post our mail at the Hungry Dragon, get Sharon to ask travelers to take a letter with them that's intended along their way."

"That much is already," Millicent said. "Travelers are too few and irregular. We need something like the Postal Service the old Republic had."

"With uniforms and everything," piped Alice, who had been listening raptly. "Molly Deere shows us pictures in old books."

"Well, Angel," Eric said, struggling to look serious, "what kind of uniforms would you give our courier corps?"

"Green," answered Alice without a second's hesitation. "They would have to wear green like Laurel."

When Millicent woke next morning, Eric was already up and gone. His Talking Garden had become a consuming passion, especially the Queen's Crown, which had proliferated to populate the entire grove. They resisted any attempt to contain them, and when Eric realized they spaced themselves so as not to displace any of the other flowering plants in the garden, he quit trying. Millicent teased her husband that his lilies had cast a spell on him. To herself, she wondered if there might be some truth to the accusation. At the very least, the plants had become his prevailing preoccupation, to the extent that Eric Lee had become, to all who knew him in Laurel, Eric Treetalker. When he was not tending his garden, he was thinking about it. When he was asleep, he dreamed it.

"There's a deeper language in them," he tried to explain to Millicent. "Something more subtle than the few words we catch. They want to teach us, but we don't have the tools to learn."

Millicent was sympathetic. She almost told him on occasion about Vinia, that abiding inner presence who sourced her powers, an isness intertwined with her own. But she dared not interfere with his process. Eric would have to be found by his own gifts, the way she and Ryder and Vesuvia and Wendl and Slide Underhill had found theirs, in the unique mediation granted to each and every by the Mind within all. Eric was seeking, she knew, because he was already found.

When Wallace found Eric asleep one day at the foot of an old hemlock with the Queen's Crown nodding and singing all around, Millicent wasn't surprised or concerned when Wallace said he couldn't get Eric awake. She had them carry her husband home, and she put him to bed and waited for him to return. Three days later, he did.

"They're not like us," he said when he opened his eyes. "They're not like us at all."

Millicent didn't answer, just bent and kissed his forehead, took his hand in both her own.

"But they are us," he murmured, wonderingly.

CHAPTER 5

Side by side, Millicent and Alice worked along a row in the vegetable garden. Today, they were gathering okra pods for pickling. "Your birthday is next week. Are you looking forward to your party?" Millicent asked her daughter.

"I guess so," Alice said. "But I'm still not found with my twelfth-year name. Why can't I just be Alice?"

Millicent laughed. "You'll always be Alice to me, Angel, but if you want to declare a name for yourself, we can go to the Alone tomorrow and maybe find one for you. I think I know just the place."

"Why do they call it the Alone?" Alice asked.

"Because it is the tallest summit in Shaconage, I suppose," Millicent said. "And because it stands apart from the others, with deep valleys all around it. And maybe because when you're up there, away from other people, it is easy to feel lonely."

"I could never feel lonely on a mountain," said Alice. "There's too much music in the air. Even the light sings."

Millicent dropped her handful of pods into their basket.

"I know what you mean. I'm only lonely when I'm in a roomful of people where everybody is talking and nobody is listening. Shall we go first thing in the morning, then?"

"Sounds like a plan," affirmed Alice, clearly more excited about a walk in the woods than the prospect of a party at the Hungry Dragon. "Will we take Dad with us?"

"No, Angel. I think it will be just the two of us. This is woman's work."

"Could I ask Lucia to come with us? She might find some medicinals along the way."

"If you like. You're fond of the doctor, aren't you?"

"She's offered to teach me about healing, but she said to think about it before I answer."

"Are you thinking about it?" Millicent asked.

"I haven't thought on much else since," confessed Alice.

"Then go ask her to join us in the morning. Tell her we'll leave at sunup. And hurry home to help me pickle this okra. We'll need to get them done tonight if we're going to wander the mountain all day tomorrow."

Lucia had patients to tend, so declined the invitation, though she did ask Alice to be on the lookout for bloodroot and bonewort and bring her some root if she found it in plenty but to spare any sparse or solitary plants she found.

"Mark where you see them, though," she said. "They might be adequate for harvest next year."

Eric got up early and packed their rations for the day, saw them out the door just as the sun tipped the crest of the nearest ridge above the town.

"I won't intrude but keep your minds open to me. If you need me, you'll have my attention," he said, planted kisses and wrapped them in hugs, then stood and watched until they were out of sight among the trees crowding their garden. By the time mother and daughter stopped to break their fast, the Long Broad was just a ribbon of sky threading the shadowed valley, and the only hint of Shelton Crossing, a thin veil of chimney smoke hovering low above the water in the cool air of morning.

Three mile's walking, mostly uphill, found the two pilgrims eating their bread and cheese and dandelion tea while sitting on a huge flat slab of schist, still barely warm from yesterday's sun, and watching the shine trickling down the ridge toward them like a slow stream of bright water. Before it was quite there, they had finished their breakfast and were moving again, ever upward, never hurried, present to each step of their way. A hawk in the high blue above called a greeting. A red fox crossed the trail just ahead of them, stopped for a moment to gaze at the two human females, then moved on into the day. She had mouths of her own to feed. Mother and daughter found no need to weigh the air between them with words. They were thinking the same thing, seeing what the hawk and the fox saw, feeling in their feet the same rhythm of root and rock, the slow deep music of the becoming world.

Unconsciously, Alice began humming to herself a warbling tune that went falling down and around through the air behind her like a brook finding her way among stones. Millicent, walking behind, recognized the song as a melody she had heard a long time past, before she had been found with wings. She remembered now how she knew, even then, that she was born for flight. Joshua had taught her the words that went with the tune, and she could still recall them all just as they had sung them together during their walks on the High Balsams. Not wanting to intrude upon her daughter's music, Millicent held the melody inside herself, but let the song run freely in her head.

Early on a morning,
between the day and night,
When trees surround me darkly
and the sky is going bright,
I mourn the things I didn't do
and dream of things I might,
Of all the times that went so wrong
and when I got it right,
of when I chose to run away
and when I dared to fight,
the days I stumbled blindly,
the nights I saw the light,
I recall then all who've loved me,
now vanished from my sight,
and thank the God who made me
and ever holds me tight.

When Alice turned and smiled back at her, and began to sing the words herself, Millicent knew that Greenmind had read them both.

By the time they reached the rocky ledge where way opened to the Queen's Glen, they had no extra breath left in them for song. They rested, broke out their lunch, and ate under the brilliant blue, while gazing out over the receding range of Shaconage to the low hills east, veiled now in a blanket of dense brown haze.

That's where the Republic was, isn't it? thought Alice. *Why do they stay there?*

Because that's all they know. Millicent answered in her head.

"What would happen to us if they all decided to come

here?" Alice asked aloud. Millicent could feel the troubled spirit beneath the words.

"We would need be found some other place," Millicent replied truthfully. "If we stayed, they would make us the same as them."

What if they changed? Alice thought.

Millicent raised her arm and pointed toward the murky distance below. "That is how they've changed, Angel," she said. "That is what our kind have made of themselves."

"But we aren't like that," Alice protested.

Millicent shook her head sadly. "But we are. We are exactly like that."

"No, we are different," her daughter insisted.

"The only difference is that we have been found. Shaconage has saved us from ourselves."

"If we're no longer ourselves, then what are we?"

We are the dreams that stuff is made of, Millicent thought.

Alice looked at her, smiled like an indulgent parent. *You're a mess, Mom*, she thought.

From somewhere in the trees crowning the tumble of boulders at their backs, the unseen bird voiced again her solitary note. *One.*

Millicent pulled a curtain of vines and brush away from the rockface towering above them. She pointed to the vertical crevice folded into a cleft of the stone. "That's where you'll find your name, daughter of mine."

In there? You've got to be kidding, Mom. Alice peered into the inky depth. "It's dark in there," she added aloud.

"Brave the dark and you may find the light," Millicent said, speaking more assurance than she felt within.

"What makes you think that?" Alice asked, with a hint

of petulance in her voice. She had no doubt caught a whiff of her mother's uncertainty.

"It's where your father found his," she said.

"Treetalker is not exactly what I had in mind for me." Alice said, "I was hoping for something a little lighter."

"We don't get to choose our name, Angel," Millicent said. "Our name chooses us."

"But you're still just Millicent," her daughter argued.

"That's because I haven't done anything for our folk worth being named for."

Not because she was convinced, but because she could think of nothing else to say on the subject, Alice shrugged. "Okay, then, here goes," and eased her body sideways into the opening. "Don't leave me alone in here," her voice echoed into the light.

I'm with you every step, and Millicent became of one mind with her child. It seemed to her that she was there in the narrow dark with Alice. She could feel the rough stone sliding across her back, the cool wet of water dripping onto her hands and face. She wasn't afraid, which meant that Alice wasn't afraid. *Good. Keep going,* she thought. They heard the scurrying of small creatures making way as Alice shuffled and slithered through her narrow passage. A thin ragged line of light appeared ahead and a sigh of relief emerged from two throats. As she neared the opening, Alice could see the stark outlines of parting stone and the glint of green beyond. The hum and drone and trill and peal of a thousand plantly voices filled her head. On her sunny ledge, Millicent smiled to herself at the remembered thrill.

When Alice stepped out into the sequestered glen, she stared unbelieving, two hearts stopped as two women whispered in chorus, "Holy Mother."

The dragon stood before her tall as the trees, filling her field of vision, a huge impossible creature beyond gender or species, its great iridescent wings testing the air as if any second it might be gone. Coals flared in its eyes and the innocent brook babbled around its feet. Pebbles buckled and broke beneath its weight and the air trembled around it, receiving its gaseous substance. The more Alice looked at this incarnation of contradiction the more insubstantial it appeared, as if moment by moment verging on becoming something entirely other.

Alice closed her eyes and took a deep breath and Simon Ryder sat on a stone on the other side of the little brook, smiling at her.

"Ryder," she said, because she recognized him and because Millicent on the other side had said it, too.

"The very same," he confirmed. "You're just in time."

Time? A question from two minds.

"Just in time for me to be found gone." he said.

"Where are you going?" Alice asked.

"Back to Earth," Ryder said, still smiling his sad, knowing smile. "To put it bluntly, I'm dying."

"How can it be?" Alice spoke it, but it was her mother's question, "You're no older than when I—Mom—first met you." *I thought dragons lived forever*, Alice added on her own.

Ryder shrugged. "Our kind don't age like humans do. We are what we are, and when we become worn too thin to contain our fire, we are found ashes in the wind."

Not yet. Please, Millicent thought. "We need you," Alice pleaded aloud.

"There is no light unless the candle burns," Ryder said

softly. He cupped his hands in front of him. "Come here, daughter," he said. "Take my light. It has grown too heavy for me to carry, but it will lighten your load."

Alice hesitated, but Millicent, knowing, thought, *Go to him.*

Alice walked through the singing lilies to the little brook and stepped across. Ryder held out his hands to her and flame burst from his cupped palms. Startled, she caught her breath as the fire swirled and drew itself in to a tiny point of blinding brilliance, forcing her to shield her eyes. She felt the heat of it on the backs of her hands, as if she'd lifted them before a summer's sun.

"Quickly, take it now," Ryder whispered. "I'm almost gone."

Alice closed her eyes and opened her mind, saw the light and let it shine through her, reached out then and closed her fingers around it. When she opened her eyes again, her hands were empty and the ground before her gray with ash.

Alice stood, muted by her awe, waiting for her world to change. Everything stubbornly remained as it had been. Until she realized the trees stretched not above but below, their crowns bleeding away into the well of blue between the vertical stone cliffs hemming the glen. For a split second a wave of vertigo seized her as Alice groped for something solid and rooted that might stay her from falling into the sky. Then the world settled, gravity resumed, the ground supported her feet and she didn't sink out of light into the mountain or fall away among clouds. The little brook chattered brightly in its bed of pebbles. The trees continued their conversation with the air and the Queen's Crown resumed their wordless and interminable song. Everything was the same as before. Stone was stone, earth was earth, sky was sky, trees were trees, water was water and Alice was still Alice searching for her name. Only the birds were silent, as if they had forgotten their music and waited with Alice to hear a note that would restart their life.

"Is this all?" she asked the day. While she waited for an answer she knelt among the flowers and dipped her fingers into the little brook, the water so cold it felt like burning. She plunged her hands into the chill and raised the cold to her lips and swallowed, felt it trickle down her throat into her belly like ice or fire. She stared at the ground as the gray ash that was left of Simon Ryder shrank and faded and disappeared into the humus like water on hot pavement.

He's gone, she thought, and heard her mother's response mind-to-mind. *None of us is ever gone, though all of us be changed.*

The little brook ignored their exchange, kept up its incessant babble. *Other, other, other*, it said to the pebbles in its flow. If the pebbles heard, they remained silent as stone usually does when confronted with the inevitable. *Another, another, another*, the water chattered to Alice, who listened, and almost understood as she gazed around her at the real world.

Alice rested. She didn't fall asleep but stilled her mind to a place deeper than sleep and let the Alone flow over and through her with the delicious intensity of a dream. She saw sights too far for eyes and heard sounds too soft for ears. Away at the foot of the mountain she watched a wide river flash and glint under the sun. In a village along its near bank people whose names she knew talked and laughed. Eastward toward the Republic, she saw and heard nothing but a wall of cloud and smoke, laced with lightning. It looked to her like the edge of the world, or the death of one. Overhead, clouds raced by swift as eagles in the blue sky.

The blue darkened as Alice watched, a star appeared, then another, as shadows thickened and settled around her, appearing dense as stone.

With a start, she called herself back to her moment. She had let the day run away from her. They would have to fly back to Shelton Crossing to be home before dark. She wouldn't be able to gather medicinals for Lisa as she'd promised.

I'm coming, Mom, she thought. *Have you left me?*

I'm still here. Take your time, Millicent answered in her mind.

It was pitch black inside the cleft, but once she began her transit, a soft glow lit the way just ahead. At first, she thought the light came from the stones, then realized they were merely reflecting light from some indefinable source.

She could feel Millicent's mind in hers, knew her mother was seeing what she saw. *Where's this light coming from?* she thought.

You.

What? not understanding what was apparently obvious to her mother.

You are the light, thought Millicent, *It's dragonfire.*

As Alice maneuvered the constricting passage, a ragged line of day ahead gradually opened into blue sky and green mountain. When she stepped out of the close stone into the early afternoon sunlight, she fell into Millicent's embrace like a runaway child home at last.

"That didn't take long. Did you find what you were looking for?" Millicent asked, when they stepped apart.

Alice looked around her, dazzled by the light. "How long was I in there?" she asked.

"About half an hour, I suppose. Did you lose track of time?"

"I think I was on the other side of time," Alice said.

If Millicent still wondered whether her daughter had found her chosen name, she didn't ask again as they walked slowly down the mountain, stopping frequently to harvest herbs and roots for Lucia's pharmacy. If Alice had chosen a name, she didn't confide it to her mother. Alice had another question burning in her heart.

They were almost back to town when Alice stopped and looked at Millicent, "Mom, is Ryder really dead?"

Millicent reached out, put a hand on her daughter's cheek. "Has his fire gone out?"

"No," Alice said, putting her fingers to her sternum. "I can feel it, here, drumming slow, like I have a second heart."

"There are many candles," said Millicent, "and one flame lights them all. We live as long as there is fire."

"What does that mean?" asked Alice.

"It means you should guard your light," said her mother. Though not satisfied with the answer, Alice could not persuade Millicent to say more on the subject that day.

When they reached Lucia's house, their packs stuffed with healing harvest, the doctor was duly grateful. She thanked them both, looked at Alice and knew without hearing words that she would be training a new healer for Shelton Crossing.

"Tomorrow night's your party," she said to Alice as they parted. "Will you tell us your name then?"

Alice launched a wicked smile. "I might just show you."

"Could you give your old doctor a hint?" Lucia teased.

Alice hesitated a moment, glanced at her mother, who smiled and nodded. She held up her right hand with her fingers close over her palm and her thumb in the air. She blew a breath lightly across her thumb and a little flame blossomed above the tip. The three women stood in that dim small light for a moment before Alice breathed softly on her fire, only a brief puff that left a spiral of unhomed smoke hanging in the air between them. A gust of breeze from off the river made the smoke a memory.

———

The Hungry Dragon Café could not hold all the people who came to the final Birthday night of the season. Seven turning adolescents were to be honored and relatives had come from miles away. A few even slipped in furtively from the Republic territories. Lisa Charon's hotel across the river had no vacancies. Several families had pitched camp beside the Long Broad. Anyone in Shelton Crossing who had an extra bed had welcomed a traveler for the night.

The weather was kind, so Sharon had her helpers bring tables and benches out into the yard and set up the feast under the sky. Fires were lit for light, and to ward mosquitoes, which in any case, had been fewer this spring. Vesuvia and Wendl brought Amelia Montford with them from Otherside to see her granddaughter claim her chosen name. "I'm not a traveler, anymore," she had protested, but the pull of family bond was too strong to resist and Wendl, in his peculiar way, rendered her journey swift and painless.

"Why don't you stay on with us here, Mother?" Millicent asked over supper, between sips of elderberry wine. "We have plenty of room. Alice is going to be leaving soon to live with the doctor and study the healing arts. Eric and I will be lonely in the house all by ourselves."

"No you won't," quipped Amelia. "You'll be all over one another the minute your daughter clears the door."

"We don't do that stuff indoors. Seriously, Mother, I miss you."

"We talk every day, Angel," Amelia reminded her.

"But it isn't the same," Millicent said, thinking she was sounding like her mother's little girl. "It's all in our heads. I want to have you close enough to touch."

Amelia lifted a brow. "Do you remember when my mother came to visit us at Hillhaven?"

Millicent couldn't contain her laugh. "Calista was a force of nature, wasn't she?"

"There was nothing natural about my mother," snapped Amelia. "The best part of her visits was her departure."

"You're not your mother, Mother," Millicent said.

"And happily, you're not yours. You're more like Joshua, I think. By the way, how is your book coming?"

"Slowly," Millicent said. "I have a lot of other things to do."

"One more reason not to be burdened with a failing parent," declared Amelia with a triumphant smirk.

"Just think about it, Mother," pleaded Millicent. "Talk to Eric. He wants you here, too."

"I'll think about it," murmured Amelia. She turned up her wine glass and drained it. "Could I have some more of this elderberry stuff. It's quite good."

Everyone, it seemed, had brought more food to the feast than they ate, and everyone ate more than they needed. Not so much, though, that they could not dance. As the musicians began to gather, Lisa came by with a fiddle under her arm. "Come sing a song for us, Amelia, like in the old time."

"I've lost my voice," Amelia said. "I don't sing anymore."

"Mother, I've heard you. It isn't like you to be shy," Millicent said.

With an exaggerated sigh, Amelia got up from the table and walked with her old friend to the little stage that had been set up in front of the café. When Lisa's fiddle launched the melody, it wasn't an old woman's music at all, and when Amelia looked over the crowd directly at her daughter and began to sing the words, it was with a voice rendered only deeper and richer by age.

Millicent recognized the song immediately. Her mother has always professed to dislike it. Not a children's song, it was a dark and morbid tale riding a rollicking tune. But as a young child, Millicent took a fancy to it, and had begged Amelia for it whenever she sang. Now she couldn't resist clapping her hands with delight as her mother gave it to her one more time, the bleak and bloody ballad recounting the hanged man's tale of a desperate ride beneath the hunter's moon to wanton murder and lethal justice.

We saw the Hunter's Moon take flight
across the deep October night
and aided by that baleful light
we ran our rambling road aright
until a tavern came in sight,
all its windows warm and bright
to welcome any soul who might
need respite there from toil or fight.

As we came near, the door flung wide,
the landlord bid us come inside,
find food and drink and there abide
in comfort through the eventide,

'til in the morning, we might ride
with sunlight for a better guide,
thus timely to arrive with pride
and toast the wedding and the bride.

We ate in haste, but would not stay
to rest at ease and wait for day.
We'd miles to pass before the gray
dawn broke upon us in our way.
A traitor had a debt to pay
to brothers fallen in the fray.
Before he with his love could lay,
the gladsome groom, we'd vowed to slay.

So we rode on beneath the pale
portentous moon, o'er ridge and swale,
through boggy slough, on ringing shale,
by wooded steep and grassy dale
upon our horses, stout and hale,
headlong into the darkling gale
and all by now have heard our tale
of faithless greed and friends for sale,

of how we found him by the stair
at Michael's Kirk with his bride fair
beside him on her golden chair.
My rapier parted his neat hair,

Lee's pistol barked in the bright air,
The comely bride shrieked in despair,
though none made effort to impair
our murder of young Richard Blair.

Johnny, lurking in the rear,
now swiftly brought our horses near,
the company, it did appear,
were one and all transfixed by fear
and holding their own lives more dear
than justice, left our passage clear.
The only sound that we could hear,
the rattle of our horses' gear.

But in good time we hunters three,
Johnny Muir, myself and Lee,
by our own vengeance came to be
here, chained together as you see,
waiting by this hangman's tree
to have our sorry souls set free.
Please say a prayer for them and me,
we'll say a shorter prayer for thee.

The instant Amelia dropped the last word of her song into the air, without missing a beat, Lisa's fiddle slid into a waltz as the other musicians fell in. Amelia started back to her table as Eric stepped up and took her arm and they turned with the other dancers.

"I wish Joshua could see this," she whispered to her son-in-law.

"Maybe he sees it through our eyes," Eric whispered back.

The dancing might have gone on until dawn, but Sharon stood on the steps of the café and assaulted one of her cooking pots with a steel ladle.

"It's time for the naming, folks," she shouted. "Sit ye all down and pay some attention." Sharon was used to being obeyed, and once again she was not disappointed. Within two minutes the yard was as quiet and collected as a church. One by one she introduced the birthday children and invited their families to stand with them as they were saluted by the gathering. One little refugee, ten years old, had walked into town one day all alone bereft of any relations. Molly Deere and his classmates stood by him as his surrogate clan while the crowd sang his birthday.

Alice was the last called among those being celebrated for their twelfth year. Her parents and grandmother came to stand with her as Sharon called, "Our Alice, who are you found at your childhood's end? How named the woman we greet this night?"

Alice raised her right hand over her head. Millicent tensed. She was sure her child was about to show off, but if that were so, her daughter thought better of it. She dropped her arm and stood silent for a moment, as if still trying to make up her mind, then, "I am found Alice Firehand," she said in a voice that convinced all who heard it.

The next morning, ways were parting. As soon as breakfast was done, Eric left with Alice Firehand to help carry her belongings across town to begin her apprenticeship with Lucia Kirk. Vesuvia Wildness and

Wendl VonTrier were saying final goodbyes before returning to Otherside. Amelia Montford announced over breakfast that she would be staying in Shelton Crossing.

"Don't worry, I won't clutter your homelife, Angel," she said to her daughter. "I'm moving in across the river with Lisa Charon. I'm going to help her run her hotel."

"What brought this on?" Millicent asked.

Amelia snapped, "Do you think I'm too old?"

"Of course not, Mother," Millicent said, "Old just means you're still alive. It seems a rather sudden decision, that's all."

"Not as sudden as you think," her mother said, "Lisa and I have been in discussion for a while now. I don't show you every thought in my head. But I wanted to see it for myself to be sure. I have now and I am."

"It isn't Hillhaven," murmured Millicent, wondering as she spoke why she said it.

"Nothing is what it was, Angel," said her mother. "Still, I've missed a big house full of friendly strangers. I've missed being surrounded by people on their way to their future. Joshua won't seem quite so gone if I can have some sense of continuity. I'll be here for you but I won't be underfoot. Lisa needs some help and we'll both be better for the company. Surely you can allow an old woman her final folly."

Millicent blinked back the tears provoked by a flood of memories, wrapped Amelia in a hug and said, "You don't need your child's permission to be happy, Mother. Having you close will make me happy, too." She looked around then to speak to Vesuvia and Wendl but they were gone.

"Back to Otherside, I suppose," said Amelia.

"I've been there and back," Millicent mused, "And I still don't know where it is."

"It's here, Angel," Amelia murmured. "It's just another here at not quite the same time."

Eric Treetalker threw off the quilt and sat on the edge of the bed until his feet recognized the floor. He waited until the dark ceased revolving around him before he stood. It wasn't entirely dark. Dawn leaked in through the curtains. It was quiet at least. Carefully, so as not to wake Millicent, he gathered his clothes and padded off barefoot to the kitchen to dress.

He had slept poorly and now had a headache. The storm had raged all night, thrown rain across the house with such force it sounded like hail. Several times during the blow, he heard trees crashing as they toppled somewhere off in the forest. Millicent had slept through the whole thing like she dreamed in another world. Eric wondered at times where his wife found her peace.

He slipped on a sandal, one foot on the floor and one hand on the windowsill. The clouds had blown east with the storm. It was still close enough to night that he could see one bright and morning star low over the mountain but light enough that he could vaguely make out the branches and debris strewn across the yard. He feared what his Garden might look like after this.

A bird called brightly as he crossed the yard. Just a single note. He reached the street and started toward the Talking Garden and heard it again. *One.* Inside himself, Eric was listening for other voices, airless and deep. When he turned into the garden the murmuring of the Queen's Crown chorused strong and clear, a crystalline cascade in his mind. Limbs and branches and untreed leaves lay all around, but as far as Eric could discern in the dawnserly light, his precious plantings had survived largely unscathed.

He set to work immediately, clearing and tending, mending the broken, straightening the bent, shoring the leaning, as the new day rose up around him, restoring his familiar world to sight and presence. The sun lifted above the ridgeline and instinctively, Eric gazed upward to greet it, saw high in an ancient and twisted holly, survivor of storms many and worse, a flash of brilliance, like a star.

Something alien was caught in the upper branches, blown there, Eric supposed by last night's wind. It seemed to flutter slightly in the light breeze and as the air calmed momentarily, it stilled again. The light shifted and the brightness vanished. Something hawkish in its shape, what he could see of it, and approximately the size of a red-tail, too, but whatever it might be, this wasn't a bird. Smooth and angular, the thing had been made rather than born.

Eric was not a climber at heart, but he was insatiably curious, and the old holly was many-limbed and accessible. He grabbed a lower limb and hauled himself up, tested his footing and reached for the next one. Five minutes later, the ground was fifty feet below and the mysterious object perched close enough to reach.

Eric stretched out his arm as far as he could and barely managed to touch the machine. The hard surface might have been metal or plastic. A whorl of blade-like projections appeared to be rotors. Wherever the wind had blown this thing from, it had once flown on its own. Something like an eye, dark and round, protruded from the nearest end. He could see his face reflected in the glass. A lens. A camera. Eric had captured a Republican spy drone. He could imagine the look on Sergeant's face when he showed him this thing.

Eric wedged himself in the fork of two stout limbs so that he could grasp the drone with both hands, very carefully leaned into his work, and after several minutes when his heart pounded in his ears and fifty feet seemed like five hundred, he managed to loose the contraption from its entanglements.

The lightness of the machine surprised him. It could not have maintained its flight against the storm gusts. Eric congratulated himself on his trophy. As he wondered how best to hold it on his way down, the drone, without any warning at all, came to life. The rotor spun, slicing his hand. Eric cursed, let go of the device, and glimpsed it whir away as his foot slipped on the wet bark and he was airborne himself. Something snapped in his back as a limb slammed into his spine, then he saw the ground rushing up and the world exploded in his face.

III

THOUGH ALL BE CHANGED

We merely think we know the path,
imagine that some mercy or some wrath
we might attain to muster on our own
will stay us when this flimsy world has flown;
In truth, we blunder blind and stumble
aimless as our burning cities crumble,
vast empires fail, their histories unread,
all virtues go extinct, all hopes lie dead,
and only then, when nothing is our all,
do we grow ears to hear our Shepherd call

CHAPTER 1

Millicent sat in her kitchen garden, gazing into her half-cup of cold tea. For the better part of an hour, she had been watching the images on the surface of the liquid as three craft hovered over the river, slowly meandering upstream from New Town in the Tennessee Holding. While she watched, they stopped frequently to reconnoiter the shoreline. The vessels reminded her of the helicopters in the old republic, squat and ungainly as dung beetles, but with no rotors. She guessed they were propelled by some sort of magnetic field. In her mind she heard the swish and hum of their tentative progression. *Like an obese GO2*, she thought. The memory surprised her. The Republic was another life. Another world. Had any of it ever been real?

She tried to sort the crew manning the lead hummercraft, but their minds were dull and closed. She doubted they had any deep awareness of their own thoughts, much less of her probing. One clear impression came through—the officer apparently in charge of the expedition, blond, wide shouldered, narrow hipped, close-cropped beard—handsome by the standards of his people and fully cognizant of the fact, possessed a probing mind, not Greenmind. He looked at people and saw more than he realized. He was prone to boast that he had good instincts when it came to sizing up potential adversaries.

I'd rather we be friends, Millicent thought. The officer shifted on his feet. He hadn't read her probing but it tickled his awareness, left him feeling watched.

"Anything on your scan, Techsergeant?" she heard him say.

The reply came muffled, but she caught it. "No, sir. Nothing but trees between here and the village up ahead."

"What's it called?" asked the officer, although Millicent saw that he knew. The question was a test.

"Shelton Crossing, Sir. Survey says about three hundred people."

"Ever been there?"

"No Sir. This used to be part of an old Republic Containment District. Resisters. Aberrants, the Republicans called them. Crazyweird people. Nobody ever comes up here anymore."

"That's what we're about to change," said Lieutenant Sherman Tecumseh.

Eric, my love, I need you now, Millicent thought to herself as she went out her door. Eric would know how to deal with these technophiles from down river. No answering thought came. Eric was dead. After four years, the wound in her soul still bled grief as often as that wicked day came to mind. Her Eric, so capable in all things, had somehow managed to fall out of a tree, scattering his brains among his beloved lilies. Lucia and Alice had been there five minutes after Wallace found him, but not even Alice's dragonfire had been able to put him together again.

Lisa, Millicent thought. *Are you listening?*

Almost immediately, a response, but not from Lisa Charon.

Yes?

Mother? Is that you?

Your old mom. Lisa's checking out some guests. You seem urgent. Even at a distance, Millicent was transparent to her mother.

Sort of, Millicent thought. *We have incoming from down river. I'd like to send them to the hotel, if I may, until we get them sorted, and not have them wandering around town willynilly, unsettling folk.*

Send them on, Angel. We'll put them in their place.

Thanks, Mom, and Millicent turned her mind back to her side of the river. *Sergeant, where are you?*

Two seconds later, *At the Café, listening to Foragers' complaints. What's up?"*

Visitors headed upriver. Feel official. Can you greet them properly and guide them to the other side?

Charon's?

Yes, I'll meet you there.

Can I take Firehand, in case they need impressing?

Millicent laughed out loud. Alice could impress anybody. *Suit yourself, but we want to keep them away from town until we get to know them.*

She stepped out of the street into the Talking Garden. Nobody was about. She listened to the song of the Queen's Crown for a moment, gazed at the marker advising the traveling public that it had been erected *In Remembrance of Eric Treetalker, the First Gardener*, then closed her eyes and gathered herself into the music, the singularity where all places touch, and opened her eyes on the veranda at the Long Broad Hotel.

"Nice of you to pop in," said Lisa Charon. "Amelia tells me we have company coming."

———

The three women stood together in the shadows and watched the interactions out on the water. Just as the lead hummercraft began turning toward the village landing, Sergeant and Alice put out in his johnboat. Sergeant signaled to the pilot to head across the river to the opposite dock at the hotel. The hummer slowed but didn't change direction. Alice raised her arms and the johnboat lifted out of the water to meet the craft nose to nose. This display persuaded its pilot to veer around toward the hotel. Still airborne, the johnboat led the flotilla toward the hotel dock and the Tennesseans obediently followed.

"Bubble, bubble, toil and trouble," murmured Lisa.

Millicent, who had read the exchanges over the water, smiled and waited. When all the vessels were settled on the river again and made fast to the dock, five uniforms exited the lead hummer and Sergeant gestured them toward the hotel. Alice fell in at the rear of the party as they climbed the hill toward their reception. Millicent was gratified to note none of the Tennesseans carried weapons, or, as far as she could tell, any sort of electronics. *They've done their homework and they have some manners at least*, she thought to anyone who might want to pick it up.

Lisa eyed the blond officer. *They sent us a Lieutenant. I might have thought we'd at least rate a Captain.*

They wouldn't want us to feel too important, projected Amelia.

Millicent shook her head. *They just don't trust us. Lieutenants are more expendable than captains.*

The delegation halted at the veranda steps, stood looking up at the women as if awaiting permissions. Millicent came down the steps and Sergeant proclaimed introductions. "Millicent Firemother, First Advisor of Shelton Crossing, here befound Lieutenant Sherman Tecumseh, Ranger of the Tennessee Holding."

Millicent held out her hand. "Welcome to Laurel District, Lieutenant Tecumseh. What compels you to Shelton Crossing?"

Tecumseh shook hands, not aggressively, but with polite firmness. "We are grateful for your hospitality, First Advisor. We pledge not to abuse it." He gestured at his comrades. "We are not come to invade your peace, but to invite you to share ours."

"In that case, Lieutenant, have your people come inside and refresh themselves, and share our supper tonight. Then we might converse in comfort about all the things we have in common."

Tecumseh apparently felt it prudent to leave his river craft with crews onboard, but that evening he and three civilian personnel he described as "cultural liaisons" sat at table with Millicent, the two innkeepers, the teacher, Molly Deere, and the healer, Lucia Kirk. Sergeant and his cohort remained outside in the night, surveilling the hummers. One of the liaisons, a woman named Amanda Crow, was particularly inquisitive. "You have electricity," she said, stating the obvious in the well-lit dining hall. "We were not aware the Shaconage are technical people."

"We are not all Shaconage, actually," Lisa corrected.

"Most of us, except for the new generation, were exiled to the Laurel Creek Containment District by the old Republic. It is true we were forbidden technology, but our borders have always been somewhat porous. Traders come and go. The Republic would have called them smugglers, I suppose. We have whatever technology we feel a need for. Most of your toys we've chosen to forego."

Millicent added, "We have several small hydroelectric generators on nearby creeks that keep the lights on for when we have company."

"How do you power your field emitters?" asked one of the two male civilians with Tecumseh.

"We're not familiar with field emitters," said Millicent.

"It's how we power our hovercraft," Tecumseh put in. "We assumed that's how you levitated the little boat that met us on the river."

Lucia laughed. "That wasn't technology. That was my assistant. Or more accurately, it was Greenmind."

"What is Greenmind?" asked Amanda Crow, her words too quick, her tone too loud, eliciting a frown from Tecumseh.

"Greenmind is us," said the doctor patiently, as if explaining simplicities to a small child, "All of us, all the energy and presence in all the souls of Shaconage, the humans and other-than-human creatures, the falling waters and the uplifted stones, all the trees and plants, all the light and air and scent and sight of here, brought to purposeful manifestation in a common intention."

"So, Doctor," said Tecumseh, "you are saying you are in possession of the accumulated life-force of the entire Shaconage?"

Lucia shook her head. "No, Lieutenant, I'm saying we are possessed by it. And so can you be, if you are willing to be used by a larger purpose than your own will and desire."

"What I will and desire," Tecumseh countered, "is that all the scattered communities of surviving humans can be reunited in some degree of peaceful harmony, that together we can find healing for ourselves and restoration for the Earth we have very nearly destroyed."

"It was not Earth we were destroying," argued Molly Deere, "but merely our place in the world. Earth may have decided she doesn't need our kind anymore. She may determine we are not worth the resources we take to sustain. Ours would not be the first species to disappear from the natural order."

"Surely you don't believe that, Teacher," countered the lieutenant, spreading his hands. "Look how Shaconage has sustained and nurtured you while the whole outer world has been in conflict and turmoil."

"That is because we've learned to behave ourselves," Molly said, her passion flashing in her eyes. "I'm just saying we are not the deciders. Nature is neither merciful nor cruel. She ever seeks a balance. If she weighs us and finds us wanting, we will be gone like the fog over this river when morning brings the sun back."

Perhaps uncomfortable with the debate, or with the direction the discussion had taken, Amanda Crow attempted to change the subject. "Firemother," she said, turning to Millicent, "you have an unusual name. We have heard stories about the Dragons of Shaconage. Are you by any chance one of them?"

Millicent smiled her sweetest smile. "No dear, but my daughter is."

Tecumseh, searching for humor, asked, "Would we recognize a dragon if we saw one?"

Lucia turned on her serious doctor voice when she said, "If ever you did, you might wish you hadn't."

———

Real negotiations began the next morning over breakfast. The First Advisor, the teacher, healer and town Marshall spoke for Shelton Crossing. The Lieutenant and his cultural liaison Amanda Crow represented the Tennesseans. As Tecumseh sipped his chickory, he said, "We have real coffee in the Holding."

"Did you come all this way just to improve our breakfast?" asked Millicent, holding onto her serious face.

"We have solar panels, electric vehicles, communications technology, too," said Amanda Crow.

"Do we appear to be suffering without them?" Millicent asked.

"We have medicine, scientific inquiry, education," Tecumseh said.

Millicent lifted her palms. "And what do we have that would benefit you who appear to have all already?"

"Location," said the Lieutenant. "The Tennessee Holding would like you to grant us free passage along the Long Broad into Carolina."

"We've never hindered anyone's free passage along the river," said Sergeant. "Carolina is Republican territory, though. We don't want to be no-man's land in the middle of a war."

"The Republic has abandoned everything south of Richmond Enclave, as you probably know," Amanda Crow said.

"What happened to Norfolk?" Molly Deere asked.

"It's somewhere out to sea now, "Tecumseh said.

"My point is," Crow said, visibly annoyed at having lost their attention, "there's no civil authority left in Carolina. People are suffering there."

"And you intend to lift them from their misery? That's admirable," Millicent said. "So what else do you need from Shaconage to facilitate this mission of mercy?"

"It would be helpful if we had a base somewhere along the route. Someplace to rest and re-supply," admitted Tecumseh.

"And maybe process all the abandoned tech you glean from Carolina?" said Lucia.

"Your river becomes our river downstream," Crow said. "We'll process our finds in Carolina. Any residue will be left there, where the harm has already been done."

"Shaconage is not a dictatorship," said Millicent. "I can't give you yes or no. The people will have to reach consensus. Come back in three weeks and you can present your case."

"Why not now?" said Crow. "We're here."

Sergeant said, "As you have noted, we don't have hummercraft and electric vehicles. Not all our folk are flyers and dragons. Some will have to walk to Shelton Crossing, and some who might travel faster may prefer to approach this with slow consideration. Three weeks, and we'll be ready to hear you out."

There was little left to say. The food was all gone. Everyone stood, made polite exchanges. The Tennesseans left the table more resigned than satisfied.

Millicent and the town Marshall stood on the dock in front of the hotel, watching the Tennessee party preparing to disappear down the Long Broad.

"I don't trust them," growled Sergeant.

"Neither do I," Millicent agreed. "That's why I'm sending the doctor with them. An ambassador may serve where a spy may not."

"They'll show her what they want us to see," Sergeant observed.

"Yes, but Greenmind will reveal whatever they hide. Lucia has enough sense of their science to know where to probe," Millicent said. "Meanwhile, we have a reprieve to make a little expedition of our own. I'd like for us to know whatever it is in the Republic that they find so worthy of attention."

"They claim to be salvaging tech gear."

"You saw their equipment. They wouldn't go to so much trouble for salvage they don't really need," Millicent said. "And they were also intentionally shielding their thoughts from us. Lucia thinks they were assisted to that end by medication. Pick three of the Foragers to go with us. Make Slide Underhill one of them if he'll consent."

"When do we leave?" asked Sergeant.

"Are you ready yet?" Millicent said, took a deep breath, closed her eyes and opened them in front of the Hungry Dragon. Inside, she found Sharon giving instructions to her cook.

"Sharon, you're in charge of the town until I get back." Millicent informed.

"Where are you going, Firemother?" asked the surprised landlord.

"Hunting," said Millicent.

Sharon didn't inquire about the object of the hunt, and

Millicent didn't have an answer, but walking toward her house to gather her gear, she let her mind range among the fog and clouds east of Shaconage and began to think she might have some idea. Passing the Talking Garden, she saw the boy who had turned up all alone in Shelton Crossing four years before. Without a family of his own, he had taken up with Wallace, the Republican deserter become gardener. Orphan, as everyone in town called the boy, had appointed himself Wallace's apprentice and constant companion. Now in his teens, Orphan seemed to prefer the company of plants to humans. He kept his thoughts to himself, could no more be read than a closed book.

As Millicent approached, Orphan looked up from his weeding, surprised. She wondered what had happened to him to close his mind so thoroughly to his own kind. She also wondered how, as a child, he had found his way alone to Shaconage. She knew then what she would do.

"Orphan, did you have a name before you came to us?"

"Yes, Firemother, I did."

"Would you tell me what it was?"

He stood, stared at his feet as if caught in a crime, then suddenly looked straight into her eyes and said so softly that Millicent wondered for a second if he'd only thought it, "Under the Shadow, I was found Benjamin."

"Well, Ben," she said, "I'm about to go back there and see what's become of the place."

"I'd be curious to know," the boy said, "but I wouldn't care to stay."

"I won't stay long, I promise. Will you come with me?"

"If we go and return together, I will, Firemother."

The First Advisor laughed. "If we're traveling together, you can call me Millicent."

Sergeant, Slide Underhill and two of his forager colleagues, caught a ride to the Republic frontier on Amos's truck. "Go slow and watch for sign of outerworlders. Wait at the border for three days. If I don't join you by then, or if in that time you see any threatening moves from Shadow, come home and alert the town," Millicent had instructed them. In any case, slow was as much go as Amos's conveyance could muster.

She kept her own plans to herself, knowing that Sergeant would not approve. In his place, neither would she, but she saw what the others could not, and that vision made her more ready to trust her back to this boy than to all of them together. Orphan was ready at the Garden when she came for him. As she had told him, he carried no pack or gear beyond the clothes he wore.

"How will we get to Shadow?" he asked.

"We're going to fly," she said. "Give me your hand."

The boy took her hand. She sensed his trust and gathered him into her presence. As she had suspected, once they were meld for flight, his mind became clear and open to her.

It's just like in my dreams, he thought.

My darling boy, her mind answered. *We've had the same dreams, you and I.*

They rose into silence, no wind, no rush of air, only a profound stillness as the Long Broad fell away below them, narrowing into a rippling ribbon of sunbright and greenshade winding among the tree garbed ridges. Amos's truck crawled along the East Road like a bug along a string as they passed overhead and left it in their wake. An indistinct brown smudge on the far horizon swelled steadily into a towering wave of opaque chaos endlessly cresting and breaking in upon itself. Lightning flashed around them, a strobing blue intensity that they neither heard nor felt, for where the lightning was, they were not.

Where are we going? The question surfaced from Orphan's mind.

It pleased Millicent to sense only curiosity, unencumbered by fear or apprehension. *Back to where the world began to unravel,* she answered. *Back to where a silly little girl broke her arm.*

Shaconage behind them, they passed into a dismal that was neither night nor day, only a murky shadow that might have been the beginning or end of either. Overhead, a muddy turmoil of cloud and storm, below, a greenless, lifeless brown desiccation. Nothing alive stirred. The only movement, the dust on the wind. Millicent's aura shielded her boy from the heat and sting of it. The heavy air stank of death and pestilence.

They've killed everything, thought Ben.

Who? queried Millicent. Ben closed his mind around his thought, and she didn't probe. She opened to receive his apprehension, perhaps terror, but found only a calm and implacable will to continuance. Whatever happened to the boy before he came to Shelton Crossing had moved him to a place beyond fear.

They passed low and slow over the High Balsams. Here and there, something green persisted. Not all was dead. Down in the folds of the mountains, life hung on. Something familiar flickered close for an instant and was gone, but Millicent's mind fixed on the maze of ruins in the valley beyond. She detected no human souls at all, and little else that might claim to be alive, but there were strong patterns of movement there. Energy was being expended. Matter was being manipulated.

Ben sensed it, too. She felt his awareness focus with hers as they closed on streets of ruined houses and abandoned commercial structures. Across the river, the hum and clatter of machinery. The sound seemed to come from a range of low buildings, flat roofed and windowless, closed and uninviting as a prison, but amid the gutted and desolate ruins surrounding it, the complex stood solid, square and maintained.

The flyer and her boy settled in the upper story of what may have been an apartment building in an earlier age. They watched through an opening in the broken wall as a trio of incredibly raw and rangy canines as large as ponies angled across the tarmac behind one of the mysterious buildings near the river. Without warning or preamble, beams of brilliant green flashed from the roofline of one of the supposed factories, and all three of the wolfish beasts went to earth without a yelp. Millicent caught the stench of burned flesh even at the distance.

Where there had been only a blank wall, suddenly there was a door, spilling garish orange light across the pavement and a metallic, whirring, spiderish monstrosity the size of an elephant emerged, throwing a tangle of stark shadow before it, as it descended upon the slain animals, gathered up the corpses, then ponderously but with eerie quiet, retreated inside the building. The door irised shut behind it, and the lights went out.

"Replicants," whispered Ben. "They kill everything and put it in their soup. They even ate the people."

You saw them do it? Millicent thought, not daring to speak aloud.

I went in their place, saw where they took my folks. Saw the tanks where they throw anything that lives so they can make the soup they drink. They would have done the same to me but they can't see me for some reason, and I slipped out again when one of them went outside.

They can't see you? Millicent asked.

One of them nearly stepped on me. They acted like they didn't know I was there. I don't know why.

You came to the Crossing all the way from here? How did you manage?

Ben shrugged. In the dim light Millicent caught the gleam of tears on his cheek.

It was a long past. At first there were still some people, all of them trying to go west toward the mountains. A few guards were with us. They had weapons, some of them, and managed to wreck a few of the replicants that came to feed on us, but they kept making more just like them, but faster, and harder to break. By and by I walked by myself. I found food in houses along the way. The replicants didn't eat our food. They hungered for live protein, one of the Guard said. That's what they were programmed for. To kill and eat the enemy, only when all the enemies were gone, there was just us left to feed on. All but me. They can't see me.

Even fliers get weary. Millicent didn't want to sleep in proximity to the replicants, as Ben called them. She gathered him into her presence and they dwindled to a bright spark of singularity that opened into a gap in the High Balsams. A place Millicent remembered. A place where they might even now find some potable water. Food was more than she hoped for, but she had brought along a bit of cheese and a few pecans, wrapped in a kale leaf. The boy would have a few bites to eat before he slept.

In the high gap above the waterfall where she had first seen the dragon, a few scraggly trees persisted. Blighted and half naked, they would yet have presented a bit of green under the sun. In this high stony ground, persistent roots found at least meagre sustenance. She was astounded to see their old cabin still stood. Almost invisible in the gray night, only the peak of a gable against the turgid sky gave it away. Lightning flashed, revealing a glint of glass in one of the windows, and beside the steps, an unblighted sapling of unidentified species, now grown as tall as the chimney. The glossy foliage glittered like otherworldly jewels in the intermittent bursts of heavensfire.

Coming closer, the flyer and her boy could see that the door stood shut and intact. Millicent remembered what her father had said on occasion, referring to his hideout. "If you want to be left in peace, build where nobody ever wants to go."

He hadn't built it, though. Joshua McTeer inherited the place, which included the waterfall about a fifteen-minute walk along the ridge below the cabin, from his grandmother Alice. Before she slept tonight, Millicent meant to walk down to the falls and test the water. She felt thirsty herself, which meant Ben would be dry to suffering.

They stood close as family, still as trees for several minutes while Millicent let her awareness roam through the near night until she was sure the dark concealed no hostile presences. Then she crossed the yard, stepped up onto the porch. The unlatched door swung open with unexpected ease when she pushed against it. She glanced back at the boy, ghostly pale in the dark, waiting for something terrible to happen. Nothing did.

"Shall we go in?" she said with a smile invisible to Ben.

Enough light filtered through the curtains to make sense of the single room. It surprised Millicent that curtains still hung in the windows, that the panes were intact, and that the interior appeared kept and orderly, as if the occupant had just walked out. The beds were neatly made. On a counter by the sink, she found a pot to fetch water. A sense of presence hung in the space, though she could detect no human soul within her mind's reach.

Millicent picked up the pot and said to Ben, who had followed her to the door and stood peering into the shadows inside, "Let's go find us something to drink."

"You've been here already," he whispered.

"Yes," Millicent said. "But it was a long time ago."

Ben's response was unspoken but clear. *Don't feel like long to me.*

The moon, a grim, grimy disk, barely discernable through the clouds, hung low in the treetops, strangled by the bare contorted branches of the dead. Small unseen creatures scurried out of their way as the flyer led her boy down to the waterfall. The farther they descended the ridge, the more the sigh of wind became the song of water.

The path be worn. Some come by here regular, Ben thought. Millicent wasn't sure whether to her or to himself. But she took it to answer, *four leggeds, most likely, but we'll be quiet and watchful.*

The trees parted before the fractured stone upthrust that Millicent recalled from her former life. Water still tumbled down the jagged face to find the dark pool below. Around its verge, some stalwart botanic beings had found purchase and nourishment to sink roots and summon green. Although the ridge above occluded the moon by now, and the clouds roiling overhead blinded the stars, a silvery luminescence in the water itself allowed the seekers some sight. As Ben watched, tasting the air, Millicent knelt on the stone where she had made her first dragon sighting, and scooped up a handful of water. It smelled clean, tasted sweet and clear, and though it glowed warmly in her palm, felt icy on her teeth and tongue.

Drink but slow, she thought at Ben. He was already on his knees beside her, kissing his reflection. When he finished killing his thirst, the boy looked up at her and whispered, "There's something in the water."

"Yes, it's healing," she reassured him, and knelt to fill their pot. Ben was still staring at the luminous cascade when she stood to go.

May I carry the water? from Ben, caution overriding the impulse to speak aloud.

It's all yours, Millicent thought, handing over the filled waterpot. She felt a vague unease that made her reluctant to be overly obvious to the night. As they started walking away from the stream, back up the ridge toward the house, it came to her again, that momentary flickering of the familiar she had sensed when they had crossed over the High Balsams earlier. Like the first time, gone as soon as she caught it.

Away from the shimmery pool, the night and the forest closed in around them again. Most of the trees they passed under appeared dead, yet they stood, like memories stripped by time of all but their naked essence. Some of their roots, hidden in the mountain, yet held potential for becoming, hoarding their life toward some future when the land above might be cleansed of her affliction. Again the scrabbling of lives wee and swift, and a little higher up on the ridge above them, something larger moved, keeping pace. Millicent could not discern what it was but gleaned a sense of something feline from her probings. She wondered what such a large cat would find to eat up here, not thinking to veil her thought from her young companion.

Maybe it's been waiting for us, from Ben's answering mind. In his own ways, he had also been drinking the night.

When the house came in sight, again Millicent caught the scent of kinship. *I know you,* she threw at the impression.

Yes, you do, the voice so real and solid in her head she wondered if Ben had heard it, too.

He pointed toward the house. *In there.*

Millicent put her hand on Ben's shoulder and they stood like two trees until there was nothing left to do except either go into the house or leave. Motioning Ben to stay where he was, Millicent took the pot of water and walked to the house, stepped onto the porch and pushed open the door with her booted foot. Someone had covered the windows during their visit to the waterfall. Except for the faint glow from the water in the pot she held, the inside of the house was pitch black. She held the pot at arm's length in front of her and made out the dim outline of a figure.

The figure stepped closer and a face emerged from the shadows, a man, older, smiling now, "Bring in your boy and close the door, Angel, so we can have some light in here."

His unleashed presence enveloped her in a stunning flash of recognition. Millicent was too shaken to voice her wonder, only the resounding realization, *Dad?*

CHAPTER 2

"Do you remember that night up on the Balsam? What is it, four, nearly five years back now?" Joshua McTeer asked his daughter as they sat over his birthday supper at the Hungry Dragon Café.

Millicent, dismayed at her initial reaction to their reunion, shook her head. "How could I forget? The first words I said to you were, *You're not here. You're dead.*"

Joshua laughed. "You didn't look happy to see me."

Millicent stared at her wineglass. "I was in shock. We'd had enough years to get used to the idea that you'd been killed by the guard. That's what we believed."

Joshua stirred his salad with his fork, as if to hide a recollection among the green. "So did the guard who hauled me out of Hillhaven in a body bag. We were all mightily surprised when I sat up in the transport and began telling them what I thought of them. Fortunately, the Republic was having a labor shortage at the time. Live prisoners could do more work than dead ones. They were starting to assemble the first replicants and people who could read directions were scarce by then."

"And now you are still here, love, and the replicants are all gone." murmured Amelia, reaching to lay her hand atop her husband's.

Joshua gave her a troubled glance, as if he didn't entirely believe her declaration. He said, "Not before they demolished half the East Coast of North America. The builders missed an algorithm somewhere along the line when they did the re-programming on those devils. As soon as they started manufacturing their own kind, humans were just livestock to them. A handy source of protein to add to their culture vats. Once they got started, they learned fast. One lesson was enough."

"So they really had brains, like we hear said?" asked Sharon.

"Not like humans," said Joshua. "Cellular protein, but more like insects than mammals. Replicant brains are dense, folded, half the size of a human brain with twice as many cells. If not for the Earthlight disrupter fields, all of us might all be farm animals now, or culture tissue."

"This is a birthday celebration, not a post-mortem," protested Amelia. "Let's not spoil our dinner with macabre talk."

Alice Firehand stood and raised her glass. "I propose we toast my grandfather, Joshua McTeer, who gave us Earthlight. Happy birthday, Grandfather."

"I gave you nothing," Joshua said, looking more embarrassed than honored by all the praise and attention. "Earthlight was here before us. Sherman's people provided the tech. I simply suggested an application."

"In the nick of time," said Ben Orphan, who had sat silent until now while the elders bantered.

Everyone stood, glasses came together with the chorus, "To Joshua McTeer, who first saw the light."

Alice Firehand sat down. Major Sherman Tecumseh, lately of the Tennessee Rangers reached over and squeezed her mother's hand. Millicent returned his smile. Sergeant spoke to him from across the table and she let the talk flow over her while she culled her own memories, recalling in vivid detail the day when Lucia Kirk came walking up the Long Road with the returning Tennesseans in tow.

Three weeks after Amelia returned from her foray into Carolina, Millicent knew that under Sherman Tecumseh's uniform dwelt a human male more scientist than soldier. Sherman's primary field of endeavor was quantum robotics. That, and not his military prowess, was why he had been chosen for the fishing expedition to the Crossing. Fortunately, the Lieutenant lacked Greenmind, and remained unaware of Millicent's probing to discover what fish the Holding sought among the Shaconage.

The mutual attraction between them complicated both their missions. Tecumseh blatantly contrived opportunities for them to be alone together. Millicent knew that despite his confidences he kept his motives private. Meanwhile, his cohort found his appetite for the Resister's company a fertile ground for humor. In truth, the First Advisor enjoyed his attention, though she neither encouraged nor discouraged it, and she was reluctant to allow tactical realities to intrude into their conversations.

The third night after the Holdings delegation had arrived, the Lieutenant invited her to supper at the Long Broad, and while they communed with their chicken mole and blackberry wine, Millicent sensed his defenses were on stand-by and summoned her attack. "Tell me something, Lieutenant Tecumseh ..."

He interrupted. "Won't you call me Sherman?"

"Okay, Sherman. Will you answer a question for me?"

"If I can. Fire away, Firemother."

"Real friends just call me Millicent. What are SRAN's? Whatever they are, there are none in Shaconage."

Instantly, Tecumseh's inner walls went up. "What do you know about SRAN's?" he snapped.

Millicent tried to project a friendly calm, "Nothing, except that's the real reason you came to the Crossing. You were hoping we had them."

"Then it's true what the doctor told us about your Greenmind. You've been reading me all along?" His face couldn't mask the trouble behind it.

Millicent tried on a smile. "I haven't been stalking you, if that's what you mean. I couldn't reach anything you deliberately wanted to keep from me. But mostly we wear our thoughts on the outside. It's just a matter of learning to listen. That's all Greenmind is, simply paying deep attention to all your connections."

Sherman sat silent for a full minute, gazing at her, taking a couple sips of his wine during the interim. She could feel his focus on her, his desire for connection. He hadn't quite summoned the proper intention yet, but Millicent thought he had potential. *This one will learn.*

When he had weighed their situation to his satisfaction, Sherman put down his wine glass, sighed either in submission or relief, or perhaps a blend of both. "Officially, this is not your information, but since you will glean it from our heads eventually, I'll tell you. Self-Replicating Autonomous Nanobots. They are microscopic robotic devices that can self-replicate more of their kind. They have spontaneously evolving programs based on a prime directive, so they can actually learn, develop new responses and initiatives. The only limiting constant in their behavior is the original programmed directive. Supposedly, they cannot alter that."

"Supposedly?"

"SRANS are artificial intelligences. Since they are self-evolving, their actualization of their directive might alter over time as they respond to changing circumstances. Directives must be termed precisely and exactly to inhibit aberration."

Millicent forked a bit of her mole into her mouth, chewed it thoughtfully, savoring the essence of it, then swallowed and said, "This is delicious. I don't often eat animal flesh, but I was born a carnivore, I guess. So, what do you want to do with your SRAN's if you find any?"

Sherman had shed his hesitancy then, clearly warming to what evidently was a favorite subject. "The basic SRAN unit can be programed for an enormous range of tasks. The ones we are after are FDI's, field disrupter implants.

"And why would you think we would have them?" Millicent queried.

"Because the replicants haven't touched Shaconage. They've gutted Carolina, must be strapped for resources, but have left you people alone."

Her mental replay paused as she heard her name. *Milliccennttt...* Startled, she glanced around the table. Nobody looked to her, their attention all on some other. Sergeant still talked animatedly to Sherman. She'd lost track of their subject. Then again, *Millicent Firemother*.

Yes? She must have also said it aloud because Sherman broke off his conversation and looked at her. "You talking to me?"

"No," she tried to laugh. "I was just thinking aloud. I have to leave."

She had his full attention now. "Everything all right?" he said. "I'll go with you."

"No, I'm fine," she answered, trying to sound calm and pleasant, relieved he couldn't read her thoughts. "You stay and enjoy. I'll be right back." She got up and walked away from the table, sensed her daughter's attention on her back all the way to the door. She felt Alice's question and realized she didn't have an answer.

Millicent stepped down into the cool night and waited. Away over the river to the west, the faint rosy trailing edge of the gone day faded as she watched. Overhead stars sang their silver silences. An owl called her name. A light breeze flowed among the trees, worrying leaves, trying to sound like water. Wrapped in dark and shadow, a fox barked his question to the night and the fox and the flier waited together for their answer.

After a brief forever Millicent felt a tiny tugging at her mind. It wasn't a word or a thought, more of a pressure, a point of vacuum in the fabric of her here-and-now that wanted to pull her in to some place or some time other.

In there. The thought came clear and sharp as any spoken word. She turned her attention inward, past all her thoughts and worries, all her hopes and strivings, all her burdens and attachments, deeper down past fears and loves, beyond all powers and surrenders, inward to the dark core where there was no gravity, no time, no want or will or becoming self. There she saw the door, wide open, all the light in the world shining through.

Not now, what was left of Millicent, the Flier said.

Evernow, said the Door.

"What was that all about?" Sherman asked as Millicent stepped from the shower, wrapped in one of the thick luxurious cotton towels Major Tecumseh had brought to her from his last trip down river to the Holding.

"What was what about?" she asked, hoping to escape the question.

"Please don't game me, Love," he said. "It isn't fair. You can read my mind. You knew what I was asking before I could say it."

"I'm sorry," Millicent said, lying across their bed, feeling deliciously decadent as he began kneading her aching shoulders. "I hardly know how to talk about it."

"You came back into our dinner, pale as death. You looked like you'd seen a ghost. Amelia thought you were ill. She's worried about you. She says you're thin, losing weight."

Millicent rolled onto her back, grabbed Sherman's collar and pulled him down to a kiss, murmured, "Do I feel to you like I'm wasting away?"

She realized he was not liable to be distracted when he pulled away and said, "Is your mother right? Are you sick, Millicent? What's going on?"

She took the towel and began drying her hair, wondering why she wanted to hide her face when she answered, "I don't know what's going on. I've been having a dream lately, almost every night. It's the same thing every time. A voice, breathy and wavering like the wind or water, calling my name. I go outside to see who's calling. It's night, dark. No moon. Just clouds and a few stars. The voice keeps calling and suddenly I see a door. No wall, just a door against the air. The door is open and on the other side it is day. I can see sunlight coming through. The voice wants me to come through and I refuse."

"And last night?" Sherman persisted.

"Last night it happened while I was awake. Right in the middle of dinner, I heard the voice speak my name. I recognized it right away from the dreams."

"What happened when you went out?"

"It was night, of course. Then suddenly there was the door, right in the middle of nothing, and I could feel something pulling at me, dragging my mind toward that light. I was afraid, Sherman. I resisted and the door was gone and I was alone. I don't know what any of it means. I'm not sure I want to know."

"Everybody's unsettled these days," Sherman said. "Not just here. It's as bad down in the Holding. Too many new things coming on too quick. We're all getting unrooted. I've played my part in that and I'm sorry for it."

Millicent cinched her robe tight around her as if girding for war. "If it hadn't been you, Love, somebody else would have come upriver and flashed their tech at us. It's human nature to prefer the clean and easy over rough and real."

Sherman allowed a chuckle to escape under his breath. "I'd rather be clean than easy. That's why I left the Rangers."

Millicent sat down on the bed beside him again. "Do you miss it?"

Sherman laughed. "I miss having people around who are obligated to do whatever I tell them, but I don't miss being under obligation to follow the orders of people who only love the world they've met on a map. No, I don't miss the Rangers at all. I've been born again a Shaconage boy."

Sherman was already gone when Millicent woke from a dream of impenetrable darkness and blinding lights and doors that appeared out of nowhere and opened to radiant oblivions.

She bound her visions and gathered herself into wakefulness and forayed into her kitchen. The red light on the new electric coffeemaker informed that her mate had left her caffeine fix, although closer inspection revealed he had gone off without his breakfast. She knew that oversight would be rectified upon his arrival at the Hungry Dragon.

The sun was throwing long skeins of light down the street when she stepped out her door and began walking toward the library, which also housed the post office and the town hall. She was to meet with Wallace Williams who had been elected Mayor and would taking office at the end of the month. She could have found herself there quicker, but in a town where one could walk from one end to the other in less than ten minutes, flying was an ostentatious expenditure of energy. Besides, she needed time to ponder, and walking facilitated the process.

When she came in sight of the library, about a dozen people were clustered around a vehicle parked out front. It was one of the new solar powered personal transporters lately vaunted on NewScreen casts. *The more things change* . . . she thought to herself. She remembered GO_2's and guessed she might see such things again before she returned to earth. The notion did little to lift her gray mood.

"Hello, Mayor," said Marvin Paige, who still eked out a living of sorts foraging the mountain, even though food could be brought in from the Holding now for less labor than it would take even to grow it in one's garden. Marvin pointed at the car as if it were a stray bear. "Next they'll want us to pave our road for these things."

"Whose buggy?" Millicent queried, not wanting to encourage disparagement even though she was in sympathy with it.

"Some lady in a dress, all shiny and neat to a pain. She's in your office with Wallace," Marvin volunteered.

Millicent looked at the car. *Who wears a dress except to a wedding or a party?* "Did she say what she wants?"

"She said she came up here all the way from Knox just to see you." The idea seemed to strike Marvin as hilarious. "I'm astounded this dainty little contraption would get that far."

"I'm mad at you," Millicent said calmly, as if reporting a newspaper headline.

"What about?" said her father.

"Mattie Stone came to see me today. She offered me a book contract."

"That isn't a good thing?" Joshua answered her scowl with a smile calculated to disarm.

"I gave you my manuscript to read, Dad, not to go bandying it about to your publisher and God knows who else."

"I only showed it to Mattie. You told me you were done with it."

"I think I liked the world better while we didn't have publishers, when people could write books just for themselves."

"If you wrote The Forest Soul just for yourself, you wouldn't have let your old man read it."

"Point taken, but I'm still mad at you. You should have asked me first."

"If I'd asked you first, you would have said no and hidden it away. People need to read this now that the world is finally coming together again. We mustn't forget the things we've learned living close to the ground. We need to keep our connections else it will all go down again one day and we might not come back next time."

"I'm wondering, Dad."

"Wondering what, Angel?"

"I'm wondering if we ought to come back, as you put it. Cars, screens, publishers, using up the world to make more stuff we'll have to build a place to store. Mattie was carrying something called a MeCom, complaining that she couldn't get a signal here. We're going to wind up with a hive mind like the replicants."

"If enough people read your book, we might wind up with Greenmind."

"People don't want Greenmind anymore, Dad. They'd rather have a MeCom or some such. Even here, folk act offended if you try to converse mind-to-mind. They want to talk out-loud, so they can be insincere. Everybody has gotten so loud. It's oppressive."

"Spoken like a true Resister," said Joshua, laughing.

"I am a Resister. I was and I still am. Everything is new and nothing has changed. I need to go someplace and think."

Joshua had a response ready. He opened his mouth to say it but before he could shape a word, a flush of heat filled the room and his daughter dwindled down to a night that swallowed him whole.

Dad? Millicent thought as she turned to find him staring into nothing, eyes vacant, his face contorted into an unnatural mask that might have been grin or grimace. He stood weaving like a pine in a stout wind, gave no sign that he'd registered her question.

"Dad?" aloud this time. Millicent blinked and she was across the room to catch Joshua as he toppled.

"This is one more incident supporting my argument for mandatory physical screenings for any new arrivals from Shadow," said an exasperated Lucia Kirk as she attached an array of medsensors to the figure on her examination table.

"My father is hardly a new arrival," said Millicent. "He's been among us for years now."

"Yes, and that's how long I've been trying to get him to come in for a physical," snapped the doctor.

"I tried to talk him into it," said Alice Firehand. "Grandfather kept saying he'd had enough of medics in the Republic. I couldn't get him to talk about it, though."

The doctor studied the lines and symbols flickering on the screen before her. She had apparently converted to medical technology since her sojourn in the Holding with Tecumseh's first incursion. Her surgery was crowded with imported devices of efficacy dubious to anyone but her and her medtech, Alice Firehand. "This is strange," she murmured, more to herself than to the others.

"What's wrong?" Millicent said. She could catch no thought at all from the unconscious Joshua, not even dream images. "Will Dad be all right?"

"He's in no danger," Lucia said, her tone too brusque to convey much reassurance. "Why don't you go on home and we'll call you when he comes around?"

"I want to stay until he can talk to me," said Millicent,

uncomfortable with her sudden and unaccustomed role of supplicant.

"Then wait outside," Lucia ordered, sounding more like an officious physician than a familiar friend, "and let us work here."

Reluctantly, Millicent obeyed.

"What's up with this?" Alice asked when they were alone with their patient, as puzzled as her mentor by the data flashing before them. "Is the Bioscan malfunctioning? He's oxygenated, circulation's good, pressure steady, but there's no heartbeat registering."

The doctor's voice came calm and dry. "That's because there isn't any. The scanner's fine."

"He's awake now. You can see him," Lucia Kirk said.

"Is he all right? What happened to him?" asked a distraught Millicent.

"We're not sure," confessed the doctor. "We need to persuade Joshua to stay here for some tests. He seems fine for now."

Millicent started for the door but the doctor put a hand on her arm, "Before you go in there, there's something I need to tell you. He isn't quite himself."

"What do you mean?"

"Something happened to him while the Republicans had him. His physiology is all skewed. He doesn't register a heartbeat because he doesn't have a heart."

"That isn't possible," Millicent said, shaking her head.

"It isn't, but it is," said Lucia with a shrug. "Apparently all his arteries oscillate with contractions along their entire length to maintain circulation. At least, that's how it looks to us. His nervous system is strange, too. Diffuse. Impulses seem to originate throughout his body. A brain scan didn't enlighten us much. Alice took a tissue sample that immediately began reproducing itself. Whatever your father is made of isn't human. His cells are like nanobots, more like plant cells or ..."

"SRAN's." Millicent blurted.

The doctor nodded, didn't say more.

"But he seems so like my dad. Talks like him. Moves like him. Feels like him. Smells like him. How can he not be my father? How could he fool us all?"

Lucia reached up, touched Millicent's face until their eyes met. "He hasn't fooled us. Whoever or whatever he's become now, he still believes he is Joshua McTeer."

———

"I thought you were my father," Millicent whispered.

"I am," Joshua said reaching out as she instinctively stepped out of reach. "You read my thoughts, Angel," he went on. "What do you see?"

"Everything I expect to see. Everything you allow me to see. Is there more I should know?"

"There's nothing more to know," Joshua said. "I have Joshua McTeer's memories, his hopes, dreams, loves. I'm human in every essential way. If you cut me, I'll even bleed for you."

"But your flesh isn't human," Millicent said. "You're a replicant."

"And you're a flyer," Joshua countered. "You have Vinia in your veins. Your daughter is a dragon. Is that human?"

Millicent sat beside the bed, hesitated, and took his

hand when Joshua extended it. "Were you dead, then?" she asked, meeting his gaze.

"All but," Joshua said. "Machines kept the body working until the nanobot injections took hold, copying my body cell by cell, eventually modifying and improving them, evolving for survivability."

"What about your mind?"

Joshua allowed himself a sad and rueful smile. "What we call mind resides somewhere within the electrical and chemical relationships that comprise our brain. When the brain goes, so does personality and rationality, and remembrance, and all our deductive powers. How does my mind seem to you?"

"But surely there is more to mind than brain tissue," Millicent said.

There must surely be, for I'm the proof of it, thought Joshua.

"It's too much for me," Millicent murmured, as much to herself as to her father. "I have to go somewhere I can think."

Don't think, just be still until you know, Joshua thought at her as she stood, folded her body into a tiny starpoint and blinked gone. He smiled just for himself. He knew she'd read him on her way out.

CHAPTER 3

Millicent was not awake and she wasn't dreaming. She was flying. When in flight, she wasn't quite anywhere and almost everywhere. Flight was singularity touching any place or time her mind could conceive of going, and an infinite number of destinations he could not imagine. Below, Shelton Crossing, just a glimmer in the mists. Above, the roving planets and the constant flickering stars. Shaconage humped and rolled away north and south. Faint where the Long Broad got lost in the westward horizon, the glow of New Town, and farther, almost beyond her sight, if she stretched her awareness, she could catch the busy rush of Knox. Eastward, under the first pale of coming dawn, the brown shroud over Carolina had dissipated and the lights were on again, and she could see the warm bright Asheton, strung between the hills like a reflection of stars on a river.

For a time unmeasured, that could have been an hour or an instant or an age in the world beyond her present, Millicent raced the inexorable revolving of the Earth, searching the night for the Door she had so often refused. If the Door meant to extend another invitation, it was evidently to be at some point in the future. When she could see the outline of the High Balsams against the rush of the coming day, blue and undulating like the wave of a distant sea, she fastened her mind on Asheton.

A breath and she hung low over the town, watched it shake itself loose from night and grapple with its new day. Threading the glances of self-subsumed pedestrians, she settled undetected to the pavement on Main Street, unseen until she willed herself fully there, walking along like any other of a hundred souls in sight. *A few years and the Crossing will look just like this.* The thought only contributed to her unmooring.

Asheton was Asheton again, brash and busy, not quite the Asheton of her childhood, but neither the ruin of her more recent memory. The only GO2's she saw were a pile of rusted and flame-blasted hulks lashed to the bed of a truck grumbling past. Vehicles aplenty, though, of all shapes and usages, many of them small personal transports, but all of them duly piloted by functioning humans. Among the cultural morays instilled by the Upheaval was a passionate stewardship of individual autonomy and responsibility. *How long will that last?*

Millicent walked slowly along the street. *Like a tourist.* These weren't tourists, though. Most of them refugees, displaced or unhomed in one way or another, coming back in hopes they might still find a place in the Carolina of their memories, or perhaps their parents' memories. In this Asheton, though, raw and new and rootless, severed from her past, old memories would find no soil to sustain them.

Some of the actors in this new play were easy to spot among the crowds, like the entrepreneurs from the Holding, and from all over the Continental Confederation, what used to be called the Middle States, eager to make quick and substantial profit from the ruined corpse of the Atlantic Republic. *Like plucking coin from a dead man's eyes.* Where had she heard that? Probably something she'd read in one of the old books in the Shelton Crossing Library. The library was packed with new books now, thanks to Sherman Tecumseh and Amanda Crow. Millicent hoped they hadn't thrown out the old.

She didn't know what she sought here, certainly nothing from her old life. The soul she thought she'd known best there, the one who had always bound her lives together, was nothing she could conceive. As for this place, she had no involvements here at all. She'd become the penultimate observer, seeing everything for what it was, drawing no conclusions, making no judgements, venturing no interventions or participations.

All sorts of humankind brushed past her, intent on business that was none of hers. All manner of garb, costume and uniform, several languages she knew to some degree, or at least recognized, and some she didn't. Light everywhere. Night here had been rendered a myth, folklore from the Upheaval, no longer a practical reality. More light on this one block than in all of Shelton Crossing, lights flashing and shifting colors, demanding possession, wheedling consumption, exciting appetites for all manner of things unnourishing and burdensome.

Millicent stepped aside for a uniformed trio engrossed in their celebration of temporary unattachment to imposed duty. She noted the double-C on their shoulders, echoed on the side of the huge water tanker that moaned passed. It had not taken long for the emblem of the Continental Confederation to supplant the serifed block T of the

Tennessee Holding, now just one more state among the many. The tanker passed, revealing a glowing rectangle across the street. Startled, for a split second, Millicent thought she beheld the Door of her visions. Not a door, this, but the window of a café, people at tables beyond the glass, drinking and eating in the light. Above the window, in glowing red characters of a strategically dated font, *Other Side Diner*.

She was hungry. When she heard her name in her head, tentative, like a question, but clear and sharp from a mind barely eluding recognition, yet tantalizingly familiar, she felt no need to ponder or interrogate it. Millicent watched for a break in traffic and dashed across the street, like a deer through a clearing when hunters might be watching.

She stepped through the door. A bell chimed somewhere above her head. A crisp young woman looked up from behind an old-fashioned cash register that would have been an antique when Millicent was a girl. Something like vertigo swept over her, a nowthennever wave of disorientation. Either she or this place where she found herself was a total fraud and fiction. She was not sure which.

The cash register, it turned out, was just for show. "Do you have your chip yet?" asked the sharp-edged young female with bright green hair.

"No, but I have my card." Millicent fumbled in her tunic and pulled out the still-virgin CCard Sherman had acquired for her just a couple of weeks before she had left Shelton Crossing. She hadn't been found in the Shaconage since.

The young woman waved her scanner over the card and said, "Get your palm implant. It'll be faster and more secure."

A real human cooked Millicent's vegipat while she sat down and got acquainted with her coffee, an unconvincing approximation of the real thing. A young man at the next table, engrossed in his reader, looked familiar though camouflaged by a new-grown beard he fingered compulsively as he read. She felt his attention, knew he was faking his concentration.

He looked up suddenly and met her eyes and smiled. "Millicent McTeer. I thought it was you I saw across the street, but you are the last person I expected to see in Carolina. What are you doing in Asheton?"

"I don't really know, Ben Orphan. Maybe I've come looking for you. Have you uncovered any sign of your kin?"

Ben got up and came across to sit at her table as a waiter who was likely a machine delivered her vegipat and scurried away. "Not a trace. Everyone I knew here growing up seems either dead or fled. I'm an orphan all over again." He said it like a joke, as if his disconnections were more a release than a burden.

"You can always come home to the Crossing," Millicent suggested.

"If I were at home in the Crossing, I wouldn't be here," Ben answered.

"And are you at home here, my young friend?"

"Look around you," Ben said, with a rolling glance, "and you needn't ask."

Ben advised her not to revisit scenes of her past. "Everything's changed," he said. "You won't like what you see." Well intentioned advice notwithstanding, after she left him at The Other Side, glued to his reader, Millicent carried Ben's promise to meet at breakfast off to McTeer Street. As he had forewarned her, nothing remained of Millicent's childhood. She found the part across the street graded to bare red clay, apparently in preparation for a parking lot. Where her parents' inn had sheltered generations of travelers and tourists, and at the end, refugees and outcasts, a maze of steel and concrete now thrust into the lurid night, surrounded by fences and barriers and sleeping machinery. A sign out front promised, *Future Site of Hillhaven Family Hospital,* and in a line of smaller characters below, *Continental Confederation Health Authority Serving Your Community.*

Welcome to the future, she thought, not without irony, although Millicent found some comfort in the knowledge that her childhood home was still a place where broken souls might come to find healing and be restored.

She was so tightly wrapped in her own head that the woman walking her tiny dog that was almost real startled her when she spoke. "It's free, you know."

"I'm sorry," Millicent said. "I was lost in my yesterdays. What were you telling me?"

"It's free," repeated the woman who looked about her own age, picking up her robotic pet and cuddling it as if it were sentient, "The hospital. It's Health Authority. We won't have to be rich to go there, just sick."

"That's a good thing," said Millicent sincerely.

"As long as they don't let the worker importees take all the beds before us," said the woman, her voice rising. "We stayed and survived the Upheaval. Asheton is our place. We deserve to be first."

"Workers get sick, too." Millicent said.

"You're one of the newbies, aren't you?" The question was delivered like an accusation.

"I grew up here," Millicent said.

"In Asheton?"

"Right here. This was my home. Hillhaven."

"Not so," said the woman, returning her AI familiar to the ground, "All the McTeers be dead."

Not this one. Not yet. Millicent didn't bother to say it aloud, she just turned her back on the living and walked away into the night. She wasn't dead, but she was dead tired. She closed her eyes against the garish city lights and opened them on the porch of Joshua's old cabin up on the High Balsams. The weathered boards gave slightly beneath her feet but held her. The door opened when she pushed against it, sagging slightly, grating an arc across the floor inside.

You're showing your age, she thought at it, but as for that, the interior looked much as she had left it on her last visit. Dusty, but unmolested, as if charmed against time and depredation. There had been human presence here since her departure, Millicent sensed, but it had been respectful, and not recent, faded now to the faintest echo of being. She lay on the bed without even taking off her boots, pulled the quilt folded at the foot up over her clothes, and while she was trying to sort some identities from the dim past, she slept.

Near morning, owls in conversation woke her. Through the window she saw a single star, brilliant and unfamiliar. She watched it slowly, slowly move across the cracked pane until she realized it was not a star, nor even a planet, but a comsat. Humans were junking up their sky all over again.

She got up, took the quilt and walked down to the place she thought of as the dragon falls. She spread her quilt over the same flat stone where she sat as a child, stripped off her constricting clothing, and wrapping the quilt around her like a second skin, curled up puppy fashion into a compact ball. The stone still kept some of the heat of yesterday's sun and shared it with her. It didn't feel hard at all. Millicent thought that if she lay still until morning, she might sink into it out of sight, a babe again, hidden in the mother's womb.

"We never learn," she said aloud to the comforting dark, and fell into a dream about Simon Ryder, who kept shifting his shape, morphing into his dragon form and then becoming her father's likeness.

"I've lost you both," Millicent dreamed herself saying. Simon/Joshua dreamed back. *None of us are lost though all of us be changed.*

When she woke, night had evolved into morning. Everything looked the same and everything looked different. Millicent couldn't tell if the world was changed, or if her sight had somehow been altered, but she felt genuine hunger and thought perhaps hope was not entirely beyond her reach after all.

———

Ben Orphan gave good directions. Millicent had no trouble finding the address he'd given her and arrived on-time for breakfast at a "place where they serve real food," as Ben described it. His promise turned out to be valid. Jimmy's Diner crouched on a tiny lot between two heaps of rubble in process of being disappeared to make way for mightier gaudiosities. Across the street persisted an erstwhile bus station converted into a hostel occupied mostly by the construction workers recruited by the Confederation Restoration Authority. Ben Orphan shared a room there with an electrician from the North Georgia Autonomy and a steel worker from the Richmond Enclave. Jimmy, at least he answered to the name, presided over a solo operation, serving as chef, dishwasher and sweeper of the tiny establishment that couldn't seat more than a dozen souls at a time. The eggs came from live chickens. Blooded beasts had died for the sausages. The pancakes, so Jimmy claimed with some pride, might float off the plate if not promptly pinned with a fork and drenched with his weighty sorghum molasses, which he guaranteed to be local and authentic. The taste vindicated his assertion.

Under Jimmy's approving eye, Ben and Millicent savored their food in relative silence. He filled their coffee mugs without asking, basking in their appreciation of his culinary offerings. Millicent, for her part, was carried away again to her childhood and the breakfasts Cora had concocted for her in the kitchen at Hillhaven. She wondered if Cora were against all odds still out there somewhere under the morning, or if, as was most probable, that lovely and benevolent soul had been brought to earth by age or war.

Ben hauled her back to the present. "How did you find things up on the High Balsams, at your father's old place last night," he asked, peering at her through the steam over his coffee cup.

Millicent put down her fork, which had been dangling unwielded in mid-air, glanced at Jimmy, who leaned on his counter smiling, obviously considering that his having fed them made him party to their conversation. "It was pretty much as we left it last time we were up there, but years of dust layered everything. Weather is getting to it, bit by bit. Depressing to see it like that, so unlived in and abandoned. It was a clear night, so I went down to the waterfall and slept on a stone still warm from the day. The water sang me to sleep and woke me in the dawn. I count it a good night's rest. Maybe the best I've had in a long while."

Ben looked thoughtful. Something held his mind. "Do

you remember when we were up there years ago? The first time we flew together, when we found your father?"

"How could I forget?"

"Do you recall what I said, when we walked down to the waterfall?"

"You said there was something in the water. I thought you were talking about the fluorescence."

"That, too. But there was something I couldn't see. Down deep. I couldn't understand why you didn't feel it, too."

"I was distracted at the time," Millicent said. "That isn't an excuse, mind you."

"I still have dreams about it," Ben continued. "I was hoping that while you're in town you might have time for us to go up there and take a closer look."

"What sort of dreams, Ben?" asked Jimmy.

"Always the same dream," he answered. "I fall into the pool, sink down among the stones, surrounded by shadows or fish or something that moves and watches. I think I'm drowning and then I see at the very bottom, an opening like a door, with light shining through. I start swimming toward it, but I always wake before I get there."

Millicent stared at him for a moment before she spoke. "How about we go now?"

Ben set down his coffee and stood. "I'm good for that if you are."

Millicent shoved her card across the counter toward Jimmy. "You're Joshua McTeer's daughter?" he asked. "The one he called his winged child?"

"I'm Millicent," she said.

Jimmy pushed her card back to her. "You don't owe me anything. Your daddy saved my life."

"Well, thanks for your hospitality, Jimmy. I'll tell Dad

we've met when I get back to Shaconage. Close your eyes, please."

Through his closed eyelids, Jimmy saw a flash of sun, heard a resonant ping like a coin dropped into a metal bowl. When he opened his eyes again, he stood alone at his counter.

———

Millicent and Ben returned to earth under a bright blue-eyed morning in the yard before Joshua's old cabin in the mountains above Asheton. The air no longer reeked of the metallic burn that assaulted them when they discovered a resurrected Joshua here. As Millicent had noted the night before, this part of the world had begun to breathe again. In the woods surrounding the cabin, they still saw as many dead trees as live ones, but a rich and vigorous green burgeoned from wherever new life could take hold.

A faint human presence hung in the air. Somebody had been here since Millicent's departure earlier that morning. An official admonition posted on the cabin door greeted them. Still crisp and unsunned, left within the past hour, she judged.

Ben read it aloud, CONSERVATION NOTICE: *This unoccupied property has been designated by the Continental Natural Resources Authority to be included in the High Balsams Wilderness Area. For compensation, proof of previous ownership must be presented to the CNRA registrar in Asheton within 90 days of this date.* "Posted today, it says," Ben informed her as if she couldn't read over his shoulder. "Are you going to prove Joshua's claim?"

"Nobody has proof from before, and they know it down there, Ben. Besides, wilderness suits it best." She stood for a long moment, gazing up through the sun-jeweled leaves of the tree beside the porch. "Wendl was right," she whispered.

With that, Millicent turned her back on her father's house and began walking down the ridge into the trees toward the water. Whoever had been to the house before them hadn't taken the path.

"As long as there's any living, there'll be a trail to water," Ben pronounced. "Although looks to me this one's been kept of late more by four legged than two."

Millicent didn't voice her agreement. She was listening for birds, but they were being selfish with their song. She put her finger to her lips and Ben lost the tune he'd started humming to himself. They walked on, unspeaking, watchful, their awareness wandering among the trees along the ridge above, finding no soul resembling themselves.

They heard the wind until they heard the water. When they reached the falls, the sun was already above the trees and its fiery ghost in the pool blinded them. But in the shadow at the very foot of the falls, the water lay as clear as air, rocks tumbling down and down into formless shadow, dapples of reflected sunlight swimming like fish over their surfaces and on the fish themselves, small ones, snaring insectoid snacks from the surface, and large fish, circling slow and silent farther down, waiting for spent lives to sink to their level.

"I'd love to get a hook into one of those," mused Ben. "It would be breakfast, dinner and supper."

"You lured me up here to chase trout?" Millicent asked.

"Fish don't keep me awake at night," Ben said. "What calls is down deep, down where the light can't get to it."

"But you said the light shines through it."

"I see the light yonder of it, but none of it comes

through to touch anything on this side. The closer I come to it in my dream, the darker I'm in. It's like there's nothing here but me and everything real is through the door somewhere on the other side."

"Maybe your dream is all there is to it." Millicent didn't believe her own words because standing here in the broad day she could feel the subtle pull of whatever resided in those dim and murky depths. It was the same sort of compulsion she had felt as a child when she saw the dragon on her twelfth birthday. If there had been one, there were likely to be two, and if there were two, more were certain.

Ben kicked free of his shoes and began pulling his shirt over his head. "If it's just a dream, you can wake me before I drown," he said, and dove into the pool. The water took him without a ripple, closed behind his feet smooth as glass. Millicent watched the little fish scatter as he kicked and pulled himself down and down, an occasional bubble breaking past his head and rolling up toward the light to be reunited with the sky.

The big fish widened their circle and closed tight again when Ben passed below. Millicent could barely make out his shape now, a shadow among shadows. *Like a sponge diver. Where did he learn that?* Obviously, there was a side to Ben Orphan that had never surfaced in Shelton Crossing. *Come back now*, she thought at him. *You're not a fish, you have to breathe.*

She caught a vague, momentary flicker of drowned sunlight on his face, looking up at her, as he paused, pointed at something hidden from her view. A flash of green limned for an instant rocks and long-drowned tree trunks and Ben wasn't there.

Ben? It didn't bother Millicent that she couldn't see the swimmer, but it terrified her that she couldn't touch him

with her mind. He wasn't hidden, just gone. Ben Orphan
had departed the world.

———

Water. Millicent didn't jump into the pool. She thought
water and felt water on all her skin. She sank like a stone,
following Ben Orphan's trajectory into oblivion. The sun-
dappled surface soared away above. Curious fish passed by,
barely glimpsed before they rose swift and soundless out of
sight. Stone closed in around her like the walls of a
narrowing well and where she'd expected bottom, only
deeper black. She resisted the impulse to rise, let the
descending current carry her deeper into what she could
not see. Ben had come this way, willing or not. She could
taste his passage in the aqueous dark.

The current accelerated as it pulled her down and
down. She could feel the rush in her ears, hear the flow in
her mind. Faster and faster yet. Quicker than thought.
Speedier than time. A brilliant point of light blossomed in
the void, hurtled at her until it assumed a shape and she saw
the door of her dreams.

Now? Millicent begged.

Evernow, said the Door.

She didn't go through the door so much as it passed
through her. An instant before Millicent reached it, the
door was behind her and she stood beneath a sky too bright
to allow color. The sand under her feet stretched flat and
red for an undefinable distance. Perspective truncated.
Footprints ahead of her led away toward a rippling horizon
that might have been near hills or far mountains. She
recognized the tracks as human. Ben Orphan's? She thought
it most likely but could not identify them with any

certainty. A glance over her shoulder informed that the door had vanished. There seemed nothing to do but follow the unknown trekker across nowhere. She walked all day. She dreamed the heat and the dry, but neither hunger nor thirst. She was not tired even when the sky dimmed to a deep purple where something like stars flickered and flared. When not enough light remained to shadow the tracks, she lay down and drifted into a sleep more waiting than rest. She dreamed that a wind rose in the night and swept the sand across her, tickling her face and arms. For some reason it did not bother her that she might be buried in her sleep.

Morning came slow and gray. Low clouds scudded across the sky offering no rain but cooling the day almost to a chill. Although the wind had blown steadily all night, shifting and altering the drifted sand, the tracks she had followed the day before yet lay clear before her. As she studied the horizon ahead, Millicent thought she glimpsed a tiny shape, vaguely humanoid, disappear over a ridge.

She sighed, and then she walked, following the footprints down barren miles and empty hours until the day, that never brightened much, began to dim toward dusk. Tired now, hungry and thirsty, Millicent had forgotten how to fly. She plodded on into the twilight, following the elusive footprints, not out of any particular hope or purpose, but because they were the only evidence of her own reality in the unhomed landscape of her dream.

Inevitably, night either fell from the sky or rose up out of the ground, obliviating the footprints. Millicent was preparing to spread her jacket for another night of sleeping in the sand when she saw away at a distance the flare of flame. A campfire, apparently, small and contained. She studied the flickering shadows around the fire, could see no sign of living moving beings, human or otherwise. She watched until curiosity, or perhaps mere loneliness outweighed caution. Then she got up, and made for the fire.

Slipping and stumbling across low dunes, Millicent floundered her way toward the light. When she finally reached the little bivouac, the fire burned hot and bright, as if made just for her arrival. A small clutch of wood piled next to the fire, enough to see her through to morning. On a clean folded blanket within range of firelight, she found a clay bottle full of clear clean water, cold as if just dipped from a Shaconage spring. A small pot, warm to touch, revealed a savory stew of unidentified roots and flesh. Beside it, wrapped in a woven cloth that might have been a shawl, Millicent found bread, brown and dense. She broke off a piece. It tasted of oats and coffee. With no further questionings or examinations, she began to spoon up her stew with pieces of the bread, stopping midway through her meal to shout, "Thank you," to the dark.

When Millicent was full, she drank from the clay bottle. The water inside was as cold as her first taste. It seemed just as full when she finally set it aside. Fed and watered, Millicent added some wood to her fire, watched the sparks rise and swirl away toward unseen clouds, then she folded her shawl for a pillow, wrapped her blanket around her and was asleep. Once, far into the night, she woke briefly. The fire was still bright. The night was still dark, but the sky had cleared, she realized when she saw stars, close and brilliant, like the campfires of a multitude.

Millicent woke to her third day in the desert, unable to say if she'd slept for seconds or centuries, but the sky was blue and right and the light that fell upon her was emitted by the same sun that had warmed all her days, or if not the same, so like it that she couldn't discern a difference. She still had her blanket and shawl, but found no trace of her bottle and pot, nor the fire that had lit her to sleep. The tracks she had followed the day before had been swept clean, but behind she saw her own tracks remained clearly visible. Far off, at the limits of her vision she saw a tiny figure, apparently tracing the path she took the day before. Millicent pulled her blanket around against the still cool morning, sat and watched the figure gradually close the gap between them. Step by step, their separation diminished until Millicent realized the walker was wrapped in a blanket much like her own, the face and head swathed in a shawl to ward against the sand and the dust. As the solitary walker came closer, Millicent thought it moved like a woman and when they were near enough to speak, the woman looked up from the tracks she followed, threw back her shawl and Millicent gazed into her own face. She smiled at herself and reached out her hand. Millicent took it and she and the world she was in burst into a million tiny sparks.

Nothing. No light and no dark. No time. No movement. No sound. No thought. No will. Awareness, yes. And a voice. A man's voice calling her name and the sun in her eyes blinding her and unyielding stone at her back and a shadow between her and the sun and the shadow congealing into a face as it spoke her name again.

"Millicent? Millicent, do you know me?"

"Of course, I do, Ben," she said, her voice sounding to herself oddly weak. She felt fit enough, although a bit disoriented, as one does when awakened too suddenly by a loud noise.

She reached up toward him, unable to control the tremor in her fingers. Her hands too heavy to reach his face, she gave up the effort and felt her own. She was real. Millicent wanted to say something else to Ben but she couldn't remember what she had done with the words. She closed her eyes, took a deep breath, and felt the world lock into place.

"What happened?" she said when she opened her eyes again.

"I was hoping you could tell me," Ben said. "I jumped into the water. I could feel something pulling me down. I swam with it. It was dark down there. I thought I saw a flash of light and suddenly, like an instant replay, I was back here alone, standing on this rock, dry as if I'd never jumped in. I looked into the pool and I could see you way deep among the stones, swimming on down. I jumped in after you and when I got to the bottom, you'd vanished. I looked up and saw somebody swimming down behind me. When he got close, I realized he looked just like me. He reached out and I grabbed his hand and there was that flash of green light again and I was standing on this rock like I'd never left the first time, and you were lying here totally out of it, still as death. I wanted to check for a pulse, but when I touched you, I got a shock like I'd been struck by lightning. When my head cleared, your eyes were open, and here we are."

"Time stands still," Millicent said, wonderment in her voice, as she sat up and stared at a hawk circling the high blue above them.

"Time flies is more my experience," murmured Ben.

"Time doesn't fly," insisted Millicent. "But we do."

Far and silent, the hawk continued her circling against the sky. A bird called from deep in the canopy of trees above the waterfall. A single golden note, heard and remembered at the same instant. *Light is shaped by shadow, sound by silence.* Millicent didn't know if the thought was her own or came from somewhere deeper in or beyond herself entirely. She reached up and took Ben's hand, pulled him down to sit beside her. Close together, shoulders touching, they waited and listened. Both felt the current flowing between them, a mutual belonging, not eros, but a joining deeper than word or thought, two bodies contained in a single soul.

Ben listened for some word from his future. Millicent waited for a stone to shift, become a face, for some wind or water to whisper her name. The lengthening shadows brought no dragons. No unbodied voices called to her, inviting her into herself. Just as she released her introspection, Ben started, as if he'd picked up a stick that turned out to be a snake.

"Evernow," he said. "That's what the swimmer told me down under the water, then set me back at the beginning."

They parted company in the resurrected Asheton, which seemed now to Millicent nothing resembling the old one, although this world where everything had changed, seemed everyday more the same as the one they had known before the Upheaval. As Millicent shifted out of place and set her mind on Shaconage and the Crossing, she thought the boundaries between self and other, here and there, then and now, if they existed at all, were exceeding permeable. She wasn't sure whether her experience on the High Balsams had transported her to another dimension, slipped her into another time, perhaps gifted her a vision, or if she had merely hallucinated. She didn't know what to make of Ben's experience, either, and apparently, neither did he.

"Let's share a meal before you go," Ben said when they

got back to town that evening. He led Millicent to a little restaurant he knew. Millicent thought he knew a lot of them, wondered if he had ever learned to cook for himself. The Green Lantern was small, dim, clean, on a relatively quiet side street, and devoid of screens. The food was simple, tasty, light and nourishing.

Over dinner, they talked round and round, circling the day's experiences like hounds about a treed bear. In the end, they agreed that they had encountered a mystery too deep for explanation. When the restaurant where they'd taken refuge was closing around them, their thoughts inevitably turned to what came next.

"Will you stay here, then?" Millicent asked Ben, as he pressed his thumb to the waiter's Payscan.

"Here suits as well as any place," he said. "I have a job of sorts. I can cast around and try to locate any family I might have left, although if any survived, they probably fled west. Still, there's a lot happening in Asheton right now. It's exciting, seeing the new world come together. I might want to be a part of all that."

"Send for me, if you need me," Millicent said. She saw nothing in this new Asheton she wanted to be a part of. There was no peace to rest in or place to fly for anyone in this dense tumult of competition and acquisition.

They barely stepped away from their seats before a bustling cleaner who may have been human but as likely a replicant, upended their chair atop the table behind them. Millicent found it moderately upsetting that for all her covert probing, she could not tell the difference with any certainty. *I couldn't tell my father from a machine, either.* Even at this late hour, when they came out on Main Street, they met frantic traffic. While they waited for a light to cross, Ben asked, "You going back to the Crossing?"

"I don't know," Millicent said, opting for the honest answer over the simple one. "I'm homesick for some place I've never seen."

"How will I find you to get in touch?" Ben asked.

"Just call my name," said Millicent, "and I'll be there already."

They shook hands. Millicent felt Ben's longing for her to stay, turned and walked away into the crowd. She sensed his gaze on her back, and in an instant when no eyes but his were on her, she became a spark and went out.

Asheton swirled away below and behind, like a bed of dying coals, until swallowed by a moonless dark where the only light came from a swarm of angry stars. The world was passing too fast and aimless, Millicent thought, like the hunter who jumps on his horse and rides off in all directions. She needed space and stillness to take some measure and count some cost. This trip had done nothing to make sense of the maze of contradictions her life had become. If she had come back to Carolina to clarify the mystery of herself, the trip had been a waste. To Millicent, though, no trip was wasted if she could walk home. As soon as she sensed the forested up and down of Shaconage beneath her in the night, she sought a dim glimmer of road under the rising and beclouded moon and settled to earth. *Welcome to the real world, McTeer*, when her feet planted her firm and solid on familiar ground.

Millicent walked alone but not lonely. The close hills and the closer dark were filled with voices and scurryings of beings whose belonging in this place surpassed hers or any human's. They were kin and company enough.

She was not entirely human herself, she guessed. Maybe more a replicant's child than she wanted to acknowledge. But she was still Millicent McTeer and she could walk as well as she could fly, and some miles ahead along this benighted road were people she knew and loved with a mutual affection. Wherever she had been, she was going home. She didn't know if the prospect made her happy or sad, but upon reflection, it satisfied her longing soul.

As miles walked away behind her, Millicent thought about the strange new world she had glimpsed in Asheton, a world rushing frantically into a future without history. Unrooted, unstoried, likely to repeat all the forgotten mistakes that had gone before. She could not accept that this was the only reality Creation afforded the tired world.

A profound weariness settled upon her, not of body but of soul. She could close her eyes now and set her mind on it and be in Shelton Crossing in an instant, but she was not ready for people. She was not yet able to abide more of their continual striving and jostling to be something other than they were. She stopped, looked up and stared at the moon finally winning out over the thinning clouds.

Millicent McTeer sighed, took a deep breath and shifted just shy of the moment. She drifted up to the top of an old pine, anchored her presence to the topmost branch and let herself spread out onto the night like an unfurled leaf before the light, a skein of fog visible only by its faint reflective glow answering the moon. Moonlight fed her, nourished her, restored her substance. She felt the silver gleam pulsing in her veins, flowing across her limits like a calm sea caressing a beach. She breathed in the light and there was no shadow left in her at all, there in the clearing night, under the waxing moon.

CHAPTER 4

Visions. A river, a flood, an ocean of flight and sight. Whether she saw in dreams or in the outer world, Millicent could not tell, but she saw humans and their machines teeming like bees in Asheton. She saw Shelton Crossing flaunting her unaccustomed glare in the face of night. In the gleaming towers at Knox, greedy men and ruthless women plotted empire. She saw humanity scheming to repeat itself one more time, and as she tasted the air and weighed the dawnserly light, she knew there was not time enough for their broken world to rebuild itself in its own image. The unbecoming of the Anthropocene now had surpassed any creaturely power to prevent or control.

After dreams, an unknowing stillness until shadows paled, became trees and hills and a road as mists twined away into morning. Millicent gathered her being into a sigh and the sigh settled to earth and assumed womanly form. She weighed flight in her mind, but the road still invited and she could summon no hurry. She was hungry, and somewhere up ahead, not far, food awaited. She could not discern its form, but it was there in company of beings like herself. She began walking toward her intuition. The morning brightened, though high clouds still obscured the sun. Birds offered praise to the new day and squirrels gossiped about the stranger passing by. If this were all that remained of her world, Millicent decided, it was quite enough.

A quarter mile of easy walking and she smelled the smoke before she saw it. A campfire, all dry wood. There were two of them, humans, female, feeding the fire. Their fecund presence drifted like the breath of an invocation on the morning air. One of the women was very old and the other was as much resident in another world as this one.

The road took a sharp right turn skirting a looming outcrop of mossy boulders and between the trunks and branches of the woods, Millicent glimpsed the slate-hued column of smoke rising straight in the windless glade until it flattened in the cooler layer of air above. She stepped out of the road and among the trees, following the sound of women's voices singing. As she drew closer, the words came clear:

> *Now let us take the morning road*
> *that leads far from the town,*
> *With hopeful hearts and lightened load,*
> *Go walking up and down;*
> *By field and wood and singing stream*
> *We'll seek that holy ground*
> *Where spirits speak and mortals dream*
> *Until we all are found.*

Finally, the woods parted to show Millicent the pale of a small clearing and the glint of a fire. Two figures, one shrouded in a black ruana, only a pair of legs visible, long, thin, would have been at home on a water bird. The other figure, swathed all in white, hovered near the fire, reached out a pale attenuated hand to fling some yellow powdery substance toward the flames, inciting flare and color. Millicent couldn't see their faces. The singing stopped as she approached.

"Here she be," said an old voice, pleasant enough.

"Now we're three," said a young voice as the white figure turned and pointed in Millicent's directions, revealing a face not much beyond childhood.

Millicent stepped clear of the trees as the pair stretched out their arms to her in a gesture that bespoke both summons and welcome. Emerging from the black shroud, a face, aged and weathered, marked by time and hardship, wrinkled around a habitual smile. The unmarked face of the young woman in white, young and fresh, seemed unnervingly familiar. So did the old woman, Millicent decided on second glance.

"Do I know you?" she asked, feeling somehow that she should.

"Oh, you've quite forgotten us by now, I think," said the young face.

"But over time, you will know us well enough," said the old face.

"I feel like you've been waiting for me," Millicent said.

"We came as soon as you could," said the young woman in white.

"We've been with you the whole way," said the old woman in black.

"Sit with us and have some breakfast," said the young

woman, bending over their campfire to stir a pot filled with something that exuded a warm and earthy pungence.

"Yes, eat up. We have a long way to go yet," the old woman said, speaking with the young woman's voice.

"This is just the beginning," said the young woman, speaking with the old woman's voice.

Millicent knelt by the fire, ladled some stew into the bowl the young woman handed her. There was just enough for her and she ate it all. It tasted herbal and meaty and held the heat of spice, blended like past and future into a nourishing present. When the bowl was empty, she stood, filled and grounded and restored to hope.

"Thank you," she said to the fire and the trees and the air and to herself. There remained no one else to hear her. She stood a long time, how long she didn't know, waiting and watching and listening for what had gone and would not come again.

Millicent stirred the ashes at her feet. There had been fires lit here, but the last one had been a long time past. The two women were gone from sight, but she still felt their presence. They were with her. Had always been. They were her. Their past and future touched her present. Their times were her time. Their moments as real and eternal as her moment.

It began to dawn on her that there was no need to walk or fly to get to Shelton Crossing or anywhere. If she had been there, if she would be there, she was there now and already. All she needed to be in her proper place was to pay attention, not be swept away in the flow of becoming and unbecoming, but to be entirely and wholly herself.

She fastened her mind on Shelton Crossing. There were an infinite number of them, apparently, on innumerable worlds, in all seasons and times and weathers, all the same place and each one different. She reached out her mind as far as she could and touched a place with the tip of an outstretched thought and found herself walking into town on a foggy morning in what appeared to be early autumn.

The air held an edge, crisp and sharp with chill. She anticipated the scent of chimney smoke on the breeze, but smelled only the piney tang of evergreens and the sour hint of tannins from the leaves littering the road underfoot. A clutch of houses ranked the street ahead. The windows, gaping dark squares against the pale walls. Some doors stood half-open to the morning, most were just vacant frames, like the windows. The grasses in the yards lay matted and frost-burnt against the cold soil. Gardens, wild and overgrown, had obviously gone unkept for numbers of seasons. Saplings of maple and poplar, some higher than the houses, populated abandoned lawns. Millicent could see no sign of humans nor any of their four-legged familiars.

A rusted personal transport resembling the GO2 she remembered from her university years crouched silent and abandoned in front of her house. As she came closer, she saw there was no glass in the vehicle's windows. The wheels had been removed, the interior stripped to the frame. Her own house stood wrecked. A tree fallen across it during some storm past had caved the roof. The front door was just an empty frame. She could see through the ruin to the trees beyond.

For a moment, she thought it strange that none of this troubled her at all. She felt at most a mild nostalgia as she assessed the remains of her former life. One of the three who were Millicent McTeer now remembered all this from a distance. It wasn't an ending she saw around her now, but the tracks left behind by some new beginning.

She resisted the impulse to look inside her desecrated house. She knew it would be empty of anything that had meaning to her. Something crunched underfoot. Nuts scattered over the street. Another fell at her feet with a resounding pop. Millicent reached down and picked up a couple. Chestnuts. *There are no chestnuts, anymore, not here, not in a hundred years and more.* But she held two in her hand. She was certain. Millicent looked up into the three trees beside the street, still holding a few leaves. *Castanea dentata.* Wendl had taught her that.

"Hello, Sisters," she said aloud to the trio, large, on their way to being larger, already older than her. She looked away into the woods beyond the houses, thought she glimpsed a scattering of more chestnuts among the crowns of trees familiar and some she didn't know at all. "Nothing is lost, though all be changed," she repeated aloud to herself. How long had she slept? How much time had passed since she last left Shelton Crossing?

Except, she knew now, nothing had passed. It was all here, sometime. Time now and forever. Only her point of presence changed and shifted. Humans habitually lived toward the future, like a compass needle swings to north. She knew now that her life could flow in any direction she willed once she found the stillpoint at the center of all becoming.

Millicent laid the chestnuts gently to earth and walked on, expecting any moment to see beyond the broken houses and liberated trees the roof of the Hungry Dragon. She was halfway there when she realized it had vanished into her past.

Nothing remained of Sharon's café but the stone front steps and a scattering of old ashes on their way to becoming good soil. A metal sign painted in Shaconage colors stood beside the steps. Millicent read it through tears.

HUNGRY DRAGON CAFÉ

On this site stood the Hungry Dragon Café, de-facto capitol of the Laurel Creek Containment District, self-declared as the Free Laurel State following the collapse of the Atlantic Republic in 2096. The FLS incorporated into the Tennessee Holding in 3033. The following year, Tennessee became the 36th state to join the Continental Confederation.

Separatist vandals burned the building in 3043 to protest the establishment of the Shaconage Federal Park.

This marker erected by Friends of Shaconage.

"It didn't happen so clean and easy as that," Millicent said but the sign stuck to its story. No names of people who had lived and died. No recitation of loves and sufferings. Just dates and events. Without the lives, the happenings meant nothing. Just facts for children to memorize in school instead of learning things that might save their souls.

Millicent turned and walked away, unforgotten names swirling in her brain. Sharon. She was the Hungry Dragon. Sergeant, Eric, Molly Deere. Shelton Crossing hadn't just been a town. It was people, alive, loving, gifted every and each. Where had their times gone? But it wasn't time that had gone, Millicent knew. Time remains while worlds fly away. She had flown away and now landed home again and far from home.

A building stood ahead on the ruined street, out-of-place in its pristine newness. She recognized it all the same, stopped in front and read the sign.

SHELTON CROSSING LIBRARY

The original building on this spot served as public school and library for the village of Shelton Crossing, the largest settlement in the Laurel Creek Containment, and designated as their Principal Town by the Free Laurel State. The Declaration of Union with the Tennessee Holding was signed here on May 2, 3033.

The original Library building was destroyed in the Separatist Uprising of 3043. This replica reconstruction is erected and donated to the Shaconage Federal Park by Friends of Shaconage.

An edgy wind set up a rattle of leaves around her feet. The library door stood open in spite of the chill. Millicent walked up the gravel path, climbed the three steps and looked inside. Shelves of books ranged around the walls as she remembered them, but in the center of the room, a video screen that would have been unimagined during her tenue as First Advisor offered some scene reenacting an imagined past that would have gone unrecognized by anyone living the real history. Flanking the screen, racks and tables displaying leaflets, maps vid-disks and even real books on paper, describing the lives of the Gifted, as the former inhabitants of this place were popularly known now.

Behind a counter trying to be more rustic than it was, sat a young man in a green uniform. He looked to Millicent barely escaped from his teens. He smiled as she came in. "Welcome to the library," he said with practiced cheer. "You're out early. Our first visitor of the day. We don't have as many this late in the year."

"Good morning, Ranger ..." she said, glancing at his shiny new nametag ... "Sargent. I knew a man here once by that name, although he spelled it different. He looked a little like you. Are you local?"

"Name's Roland," said the cheerful youngster, leaning across his counter to shake her hand. "I grew up in New Town just down the river west of the park. You wouldn't have known my grandfather, surely, but he was town Marshall of Shelton Crossing before the Union. He had been a sergeant in the Republican Guard during the Upheaval, and took his rank as his Shaconage name. All the Gifted took new names for themselves when they arrived in the Containment."

"Well, some of them did," Millicent said. "Your Grandfather's name was Roland, too."

The young ranger looked surprised. "Yup, I was named for him. How did you know that?"

"Because Millicent McTeer was the First Advisor of Shelton Crossing and my name is Millicent McTeer."

Ranger Roland grinned. "Always wanted to meet a genuine Shaconage McTeer. Us mountain apples don't fall far off the tree, do we? Are you staying at the campground or the hotel?"

"I camped along the road," Millicent confessed.

"That isn't allowed. You'll get fined if a ranger catches you, and thrown out of the park," Roland said.

"You're a ranger," Millicent replied meekly. "Am I under arrest?"

Roland laughed. "I'm not a real ranger. They didn't give

me a gun. All the same, if you want to continue your park visit past today, you'd best stay at the hotel."

"Where's the hotel?" Millicent asked.

"Across the river, where it's been since the Containment."

"You mean Lisa's place, The Long Broad?" Millicent couldn't keep her childlike delight out of her voice.

Roland nodded. "The very same, only now we call it Shaconage House. It's been in continuous operation since the collapse of the old Atlantic Republic, except for a brief hiatus during the uprising. It was one of the few major structures in Shelton Crossing that wasn't burned by the Separatists. Legend holds that Lisa Charon and Amelia Montford stood out on the veranda with their laser rifles and promised to burn a hole through any Separatist who set foot on their side of the river."

"Thanks for the history lesson," Millicent said. "I wish I could've been there."

"The park did a complete renovation last year. It looks just like it did during the Containment," said Roland.

"If memory serves, it probably looks a good sight better," Millicent replied dryly. "I'll check it out."

Ranger Roland gave her a map of Shelton Crossing, which she saw immediately wasn't quite exactly the Shelton Crossing she knew. She left him cheerfully at his desk and began walking through the warming morning toward the river. Curiosity drove her. She had no expectation her cash or plastic would be good for anything after all these decades, dissolutions and unions of institutional powers and governmental gulags. Where had she been for so long?

Now, she had come home a stranger to all. She could look and remember and then she would move on, not for having another place to go, but simply because she could not stay. This was her place, but not her time. This was her home, but no belonging was left in it for Millicent McTeer.

From the library, Millicent wandered on through a town now mostly ruined and reclaimed by forest, down to the river where she met a sign declaring *Charon's Crossing*. The text meant to clarify, she found on reading, to be as much fable as history. A gaggle of park visitors had preceded her. Apparently, most of them had come camping or hiking and her rough clothes were not out of place among them.

"Here it comes," a boy eight or nine years old said, pointing out across the river where a small hoverferry blew up a storm that carried it above the shallow water. When it settled at the landing, a young woman in a Ranger's uniform ushered a half-dozen passengers ashore then beckoned for the waiting group to board. Millicent was relieved to see no fare being collected. She went on board with the tourists. The Rangerwoman pressed a button on her tablet and the gangway retracted and folded out of sight as a railing slid into place separating passengers from the river. Rotors hidden in the hull somewhere below decks whirred to life and the craft lifted and moved away from the shore. It was quieter inside the cabin than Millicent expected. She thought of her first hummercraft ride on the Long Broad all those years before when she had floated down to New Town with Lieutenant Sherman Tecumseh. Where was he now? She wondered if he still lived. If he still breathed, he would have improbably survived all the years she slipped past. He might well be a centenarian by now.

Millicent didn't hear the excited chatter of the other passengers. She listened to voices from another life in other years long past as she stared through the glass at the building on the opposite shore. It was the same as the last time she had seen it except it wasn't. The seasons had not made their mark on this one. It was too new. Too perfect, of a whole piece out of the box. Lisa's hotel had grown and altered over years. It was never new all at once.

The ferry released them onto a dock with no resemblance to the hand-crafted structure of logs and found stone she held in her memory. The tourists swirled and flurried up the hill toward the hotel. Millicent turned, looked out over the water toward what remained of Shelton Crossing, resisted an almost overwhelming urge to turn around and join the departing group heading back across the river. She hadn't come this far, she decided, to run away from her future. She sighed, walked up the hill after the rest of the new arrivals. A sign over the front veranda of the hotel declared in a Republican-era font, *Shaconage House.* Lisa Charon's Long Broad had never dared the pretension of a sign.

Millicent climbed the steps onto the veranda, avoiding the ramp for the mobility challenged. The door stood open and she stepped inside. The place was lit like a stadium, the warm shadows and flickering hearthflames she remembered, banished now by clusters and banks of harsh light wherever she looked.

She could smell cooking food and glimpsed people seated at tables in the dining room. The aroma reminded Millicent that she was hungry, but she supposed food required some sort of payment. She turned to leave when a familiar voice behind her spoke.

"Dry McTeer. Will you not share table with us before you go?"

She turned, stunned and unbelieving. In this world where nothing was as it had been, he hadn't changed at all. "Wendl," she said, too full of joy and tears to speak more.

"Tell me about your life, Dry McTeer," said Wendl VonTrier, as they sat at his corner table in the dining room at Shaconage House. Between them, plates of local roots and greens awaited their participation, along with hearty servings of something neither beef nor pork but vaguely meaty that Millicent could not identify. When she saw Wendl prepared to eat it, she assumed it was one of his unique vegetable concoctions disguised as game. Whatever it was tasted rich and delicious, and landed with merciful lightness in her empty stomach.

She had expected to be inundated with memories in this place, but apart from the food and heavily chicoried coffee, nothing rang familiar. The grounding aroma of cooking didn't quite dispel the underlying odors of new-cut wood and fresh paint. Shaconage House was more a facsimile than a restoration. It might fool tourists, but anyone who had lived in the Containment would not recognize it as the same place.

Wendl, though, remained real to her, wearing the same faint and inscrutable smile he had shown her at Wildness Emporium when the world was yet new and discoverable, large enough to contain hopes and alive enough to inspire dreams. Millicent focused on that flicker of a smile as she summoned her answer.

"I don't have a life, anymore, Wendl VonTrier. This isn't my place. I'm out of my time. Everyone I've known and loved is beyond touch in some past removed. I have no more continuance here than a ghost."

Wendl blinked. Millicent knew from experience that this signaled he was about to make one of his summary pronouncements. Wendl, now as ever, defied time and change.

"The past is ever within touch, Dry McTeer," he said. "That was your first lesson. The past is as near as the future and the future is only the becoming of our present unfolding. As there are roads leading us from place to place, so there are ways between times, that are plain to see if we pay attention to our journey."

"I've paid attention," Millicent said quietly, making a statement rather than an argument. "The times, on closer inspection all turned out to look the same."

"Even now?" Wendl said.

"Now, I just feel tired," Millicent confessed. "And more than a little lost."

Wendl VonTrier liberated an unguarded smile, a rarity for him. "Dry McTeer," he rumbled, low in his throat, managing somehow to make his growl sound gentle as his touch, as he reached across the table to lay a feathered and taloned hand on Millicent's. "When one begins to long for home, One is already found there."

Millicent felt the healing flowing in his touch, and when she looked at Wendl's hand again, it would have passed for human. His voice sounded restoration, too. Revived and regrounded, Millicent emptied her mind of all that was troublesome to her and began to enjoy her meal. Halfway to dessert, Millicent realized the trace her mind had been seeking but not found. She looked up from her plate and saw in his face that Wendl already knew her question, but she spoke it aloud all the same. "Where is my daughter?"

"Alice Firehand teaches at the Confederation University at Tecumseh Landing. She's no longer practicing medicine and she frequently visits us when she and her students are in Shaconage doing field research."

"Field research?" Millicent asked, mystified.

"She's leading the university's neurobotany department."

"Simon has a long arm," murmured Millicent, gazing into her wineglass. If Wendl didn't understand the reference, neither did he seek an explanation.

"There's someone here you should see," Wendl said, when they stood from their food and recollection. "Someone who knew Shelton Crossing as you do." He beckoned for her to follow him out of the dining room and across the entrance hall to the great room where visitors gathered before a huge stone fireplace to pass cool and rainy autumn afternoons. This room had survived its times in better condition, thus, escaped the more extreme predations of the renovators. As much as Millicent could recall, it looked the same as when she and Lisa and Sharon had plotted and gossiped together before the hearth. Even the smells were familiar. Millicent felt years slipping away. She felt some shared identity with her younger self just by entering the space.

The large room seemed almost empty, although two youngsters were intent on their chess game before a tall window, and two women, who could have passed for their grandmothers, sat on the opposite side of the room conversing barely above whispers. Either they had retained their natural hearing in their old age or possessed good augmenting devices. Near the fireplace, directly in front of the hearth, sat an old man, his head bent to a drowse, his open newspaper folded like a blanket across his chest.

Crossing the room in Wendl's wake, Millicent felt she should know the aged male asleep in his chair. He was shrouded in a heavy green coat that looked to be some left-over uniform from past military service. A name almost rose to her mind before they were there and Wendl bent over the chair and touched the occupant gently on the arm.

"Colonel, pardon me for disturbing you."

Pale blue eyes opened in the wasted and weathered face. Surprise and annoyance flashed across it before Wendl spoke again and the blue eyes focused on him.

"Colonel, there's someone here I thought you would want to see." He gestured, and the ancient visage turned to Millicent.

Neither saw Wendl's satisfied smirk as they stared at one another for a full minute in dead silence.

"Check," said a boy's voice from the game table by the door. The two women continued their whispering contest, sounding like a pair of poplars in a gentle October breeze. The fire crackled and spat contentedly until the old man's eyes, like a rain-washed sky after an autumn rain, lit with recognition and disbelief.

"It can't be you," he said at last. Age had not wrecked the voice past recognition. Millicent felt her heart breaking as she remembered all. The old soldier went on, "You must be McTeer's daughter. You look so like she did then, in Shelton Crossing. I never knew she had another child. What became of your mother?"

Standing suddenly required more effort than Millicent wanted to expend. Wendl pulled a chair over and she sat down gratefully. The old Colonel reached out a hand to her and she took it, felt the tremor in it not so much from age as sheer emotion.

"There were none but Alice, Sherman." She said, bending close to be heard, "I am what became of her mother. I'm your same old Millicent."

"Impossible," Sherman snapped. He squeezed her hand. "But you are. I can feel you here." Millicent nodded, wiped gathering tears as he released a tumble of words to her, "But how? You haven't aged a day. Where were you hiding as the years went by? I thought we were lovers. You disappeared without even a goodbye. We looked for you. All of us, Alice, your mother, Joshua, everybody. Where did you go?"

"I hardly know, Love," Millicent whispered when she found her voice. "But I'm here now."

They talked and talked, until the old soldier's voice faded to a raspy breath and his mind began to lose track of his thoughts. Times and changes lost substance. Shaconage House almost became the Long Broad Hotel. They were together as if they had never been parted. Wendl, who had been forgotten along with the rest of the present world, leaned into their conversation, addressing Millicent by her Shaconage name. "Firemother, your room is ready. Let me show you."

Tecumseh raised a hand in protest. "We're not done talking," he rasped irritably.

"You can talk more over breakfast, Colonel," Wendl said amiably. "In the morning, we'll set your table for two."

Millicent, herself utterly spent and disoriented by her displacements, meekly allowed herself to be led away by her old friend and mentor. Tecumseh dreamed again beneath his newspaper before they passed the door.

"I can't stay here, Wendl," Millicent said as they stepped into a lift. "I don't have any means to pay."

Wendl's face assumed an avian aspect for a second, his equivalent of a smile. "You're home here, Dry McTeer. You needn't pay to play. You can share my hideyhole for as long as you need."

Millicent's stomach informed her the lift had stopped, the door sighed open, and they stepped out into a hallway enough like one she remembered that she felt awakened from a bad dream. At the far end of the hall a door with a placard above it, *Private*, and a palm scanner mounted in the wall right of the jamb. The LED sconces they passed looked for all the world like the old gas lamps from Containment days. For some reason she couldn't fathom, Millicent fought back tears. As if he sensed her discomfited spirit, Wendl, walking beside her, lay a hand against her shoulders. His touch was light and warm and motherly, and Millicent glancing at his face, saw it softened and rounded, almost a reflection of her younger self. Suddenly the presence beside her felt feminine and intimately knowing. Awash in the rush of empathy, Millicent wanted only to lie down and sleep, but Wendl's steady arm kept her upright while he lifted her hand to the scanner. Something like a bell sounded in her head and the door opened.

"Here you are, Dry McTeer," Wendl said softly in her ear. "Rest well, Little Sister." She stepped through the door, heard it close behind her, and looked out into the trees.

———

"What happened to the day?" Millicent asked herself aloud. On this side of the door, the sun had set maybe an hour ago, leaving a lingering smudge of crimson on the horizon, barely glimpsed through the trunks and branches of the intervening forest. She looked out into the surrounding woods, saw no sign of the town at all. Just trees and more of them, away to the hazy distance where ranging mountains occluded the gone sun. The carpeted floor of the hallway continued this side of the door, about thirty feet above the ground, as near as she could reckon in the dusky dim, suspended there without any visible means of support. No walls, no ceiling, just the floor. A glance behind assured her the door was still in its place, floating, it seemed to be, in the quiet air. She opened it slightly, was reassured to see it still led to the hallway in the hotel. There was no sign of Wendl.

Millicent closed the door again, turned to look out into the gathering dusk. About twenty yards ahead, another door, identical to the one she had just passed, anchored the far end of the walkway. Although darkness rose up out of the forest now, the patterned carpet and paneled door beyond presented bright as afternoon, whether the light came from within or without, she could not tell.

She reached out a foot and took a tentative step. The carpet bore her weight as solidly as if it were the floor of the hotel. That didn't come as a surprise to Millicent. Since Wendl had directed her to this place, it must surely be ready to serve her need. Wendl VonTrier, whoever or whatever he might be, was thorough to a fault. Nothing in Wendl's world came by accident or without purpose. If he had willed it to be night here, it was to enhance her need to rest. If a way opened to her here, however improbable or impractical it might appear, it would support and facilitate her practice. This was nothing she could prove short of actual experience, but she knew it with certainty because she knew Wendl VonTrier.

Millicent began walking toward the far door. She felt the floor meet her boots but her steps elicited no sound at all. She strode silent as flight. The world around her, though quiet, was not without sound of its own. She heard the wind and the trees conversing softly, the whisper of leaves mingling with the sigh of her breath, and the rustle and scurrying of unseen creatures settling down for the night among the boughs and branches of the overarching wood.

Something big crossed beneath her path, concealed by the dark but not attempting stealth. She could hear the footfalls plainly, too heavy and uncadenced for a deer, a bear maybe, though she detected no scent. She stopped, peered down into a dark made darker against the light at her feet, could see no movement, but the steps below didn't pause, continued on and away behind her, as if the bear, or whatever it was, hadn't been aware of her at all.

Approaching the far door, Millicent saw no knob or handle, but as she reached out her hand to push, an instant before her fingers touched wood, the door swung open, smooth and silent as a page turning in a book, to reveal a small room tight and tidy as a well-kept ship's cabin. Millicent stepped inside and felt the door close behind her, too softly to be quite heard.

A large antique styled armoire stood against the wall to her right, flanked by a small plain door on one side and a floor-to-ceiling bookcase on the other, packed neatly full with books and papers, leaving no room to spare. The double doors of the armoire were carved in relief to depict a pair of creatures that, depending on the angle of the light and the viewer's state of mind, might have been birds or elves or dragons.

On the left-hand wall, beneath a large many-paned window opening onto featureless night, Millicent saw a small desk with a straight highbacked chair. Atop the desk, seeming unhomed in this room that looked lifted straight from an eighteenth-century maritime novel, a closed notebook computer. Millicent laughed aloud at the notion of Wendl reading e-mails. Obviously, there were sides to his character she had never glimpsed. This was thoroughly and unmistakably his room. His 'hideyhole' as he called it, could tell her more about her old friend and mentor than she had learned in all the decades they had been acquainted. She wondered if that was precisely why he had consigned his space to her.

A wave of utter weariness overwhelmed her urge to explore and discover. Opposite the door where she entered, loomed a four-poster bed, made up with a quilt of a thousand pieces arranged to image a many-winged creature that would have been at home in some time-shrouded myth or nightmare. A wooden chest, dark and heavy, crouched at the foot, plain and unadorned, although in the uncertain and shifting light, the grain of the wooden sides seemed to mimic the form of fantastic chimera that shifted shape and species while she gazed. Carved likenesses of falcons crowned the bedposts. Their feathers glistened in the light, they seemed alive and aware and watchful and fully capable of both assault and flight.

Millicent sat on the bed, for the moment too tired to stand. She sighed, lay back on the intricately patterned quilt and it received her close and gentle as a mother's arms. She stared up at a ceiling full of stars. Before she could begin to count them, her eyes closed and Millicent slept.

———

She knew it was morning before she opened her eyes. Sunlight lay across the room, warm and weighty as a quilt. Millicent stared through the glass at the new green and crimson of the budding poplars and maples in the woods outside. Irrefutably spring. A winter gone while she slept. Time lost before she ever lived it. Millicent felt her being flowing away like liquid pouring from a pitcher. She lifted her hands before her in the light. The fiery sun limned bone and tendon vivid and distinct in her translucent flesh. She had no more substance than water, she reckoned, no shape at all except as formed by the moment that contained her.

Fresh clothes lay folded on the chest at her feet, chosen and placed for her alone. The door beside the armoire opened to a bath, with hot water and towels and a tub and everything else she needed to gather herself into this new day. She surrendered to her bath as if it were a baptism, pulled her head and body down into the water until there was nothing left of her in the airy world. For a time she couldn't measure, she lay there, curled like an unborn, not breathing nor feeling any need to. Millicent fancied she was dissolving, being carried gently away down creeks and rivers to a far and endless ocean.

When the fragrant water, dense and salted and warm as her own blood, had washed away every thought and fear and regret and sadness within her, she rose into the world again and filled her chest with Shaconage air, lively and scented with the green life of mountains, and reached for a towel, thick and soft and heated by the windowed sun. Millicent McTeer was herself again and something more and new, as well, the gift of all the losses and becomings of her life.

Before she dressed, Millicent stood for a long time studying the woman she saw in the mirror, a human female of indeterminate years, leaned and weathered, but not diminished and wasted by her times. What she saw contented her. She had no desire to be any different or any other. If she had any power to alter her soul or her life, she let it go.

Rain stuttered and sighed against Wendl's big window, loosing to earth the last of the autumn's glory to feed a future spring. Millicent knew then that she had only slept one night, not seasons or years. When she opened the door, she saw no airy bridge, but only the hallway at Shaconage House. She stepped into the morning after and closed the door behind her.

Millicent avoided the lift and took the stairs, passing framed photographs on the walls as she descended. The frames and glazing were new, most of the pictures faded and sepiaed by the passing lights of generations of humans. A few seemed familiar. She stopped and communed with one portrait of an aged woman in particular, she was certain had hung at Hillhaven Inn during her childhood. There was no mistaking the identity of the subject, her great grandmother, Alice McTeer.

When she exited the stairwell onto the main floor of the inn, Millicent found Wendl in solemn conference with three of the staff, his expression serious and stern, even for Wendl. He saw Millicent and came over and took her hand, assuming one of his gentler avian guises.

"The Colonel won't be joining us for breakfast," he said quietly.

"Is Tecumseh all right?

"He went as he slept last night," Wendl said. "There was no sign of any distress or struggle. He must have died peacefully."

"Does he have any family?"

Wendl shook his head, "He never married. He was waiting for you to come back, I think."

The next week was longer than long to Millicent. Alice Firehand flew upriver to Shelton Crossing in a hummercraft as soon as word was sent. Her native powers had waned during her sojourn in the Holding, acculturating to its electronic enhancements and extra-biological intelligences. The years apart had grown a distance between mother and daughter that proximity could not bridge in the few days they had together. Alice belonged to the new world that Millicent had renounced. Shaconage was no longer home to either of them, and Shaconage was all the life they had known together.

"We'll have a memorial service come spring," Alice said over the third breakfast they shared. "Scatter the Colonel's ashes on the Long Broad as he wanted. He loved that river the way he never loved another person, unless it was you."

"I know," Millicent, in a bleak whisper.

"Why did you leave him? What did he do?" Alice almost succeeded in keeping the flint out of her tone.

Millicent sighed. She knew no defense, and the truth wouldn't shield her. "All he did was love me, Daughter. It wasn't him. It was all me. I wasn't who I'd always imagined. I was the child of a machine."

Alice, exasperation and disappointment plain in her voice. "Surely, you couldn't blame Grandfather for what the Republicans did to him?"

"No, I couldn't blame him at all, but I couldn't love a facsimile, Alice. He was not blooded. He was not Joshua any longer. The Republicans rendered me an orphan."

"But he was, Mother," Alice protested. "He was the same in his heart."

"He didn't have a heart. The Republicans fed it to their replicants." Millicent murmured. Alice felt her mother's bitterness wash over her. It stung like sleet or fire.

"You're being cruel, Mother," she said. "You're trying to wound the world with your own hurt. You know what I meant. His love was the same. His mind worked by the same passions and affections that had always ruled him. Your abandonment broke his spirit. He and Grandmother went back to Otherside with Vesuvia Wildness and her people not long after you left."

"Do you hear from them at all now?" Millicent asked softly, repentant and subdued, bruised by her own hardness. She could not bring herself to ask aloud if against all probability, they were still alive.

"Only through Wendl," Alice said. "He's able to navigate the Separation. Time flows differently over there. Wendl says they haven't aged a day. They call their realm The Laurel now, after the old Containment. They don't approve of the way our world is going."

"I'm not qualified to judge it," Millicent confessed. "But I'm no more at home in it than they would be."

Alice was very much at home in it, Millicent conceded the next morning as she watched her daughter board the hummer to skim back to New Town and Tecumseh Landing. Wendl had disappeared himself for the day, and Millicent spent it walking the woods alone, the only place left in the turning world where she felt at peace with herself.

Wendl was back before sundown, and invited her to share his supper. He'd spent the day in Otherside, the Laurel, as Alice had called it.

"Your parents wouldn't come back with me," he said. "But they say you are welcome to visit or stay with them in the Laurel. They think their world would be much more to your need."

"Their world is too good for me," Millicent said wistfully. "And their lives are full without me. They love me. I don't doubt that any longer, but they always had enough in themselves. I was just their winged child, destined time and again to fly away."

"And where will you fly this time, Dry McTeer?" said Wendl, as he spoke, himself shimmering on the verge of soaring away from the moment.

"I'm too tired tonight to fly," Millicent said. "I will sleep on the question and perhaps the morning will tell me."

"What dreams may come ..." quoted the bird/man, as he stood, leaned across the table and kissed her hair, so lightly, she wasn't sure he had done it until she felt his warmth inside her head.

CHAPTER 5

T his might be a dream, Millicent whispered in her mind as Wendl's bed one last time lifted her soft and silent as a thought up beyond the walls of her refuge and aloft among stars and a round buttery moon playing hide and seek with her among silver-rimmed clouds. Below, the room dwindled and turned until it was only a tiny bright square against the formless night. If she was dreaming now, could she say with certainty there had ever been a time in her life when she had been awake to see the world as it really was? All her experience added up to impressions and interpretations and opinions and guesses sometimes educated and sometimes the product of unverifiable intuitions. She rested, and waited. Something was coming, she was sure of it.

Somewhere in the high dark over Shaconage, Millicent found herself apart from the bed, aloft and alone and free as the air. The night around her thronged with the suns of other worlds than hers. The sky grew blacker as the proliferating stars brightened. One of them in particular, brilliant and flame-hued, flared and seemed to rush at her from above, or was it below? She couldn't tell if she were flying or falling. But her star was definitely nearer now, assuming a shape, a square, bright and warm as morning. *Now?* She dreamed. *Evernow*, dreamed the Door.

She closed her eyes and Millicent McTeer was there, felt the familiar soft warmth of pillows and quilts. Barnaby Bear lay cradled in her arms, still missing one button eye, just as she remembered him. Breakfast smells wafted up from the kitchen below. The cleaning staff bustled and bumped in the hall outside her door. Millicent opened her eyes and watched dust motes dancing in the sunlight streaming through her window and pouring thick and gold like new honey across her bed. Through the window, a glimpse of pale green leaves and a snatch of birdsong. It was morning and it was spring and it was her birthday and she was home.

Millicent pushed back the covers and climbed out of bed and stood for a moment rubbing the sleep from her eyes while she listened to the murmur of all the lives in Hillhaven's other rooms. She gazed at the child in her mirror and thought it was a fine thing to be eight years old and know how to fly.

The day was longer than long. Millicent thought her party would never happen in her lifetime. When her friends finally began to arrive, an uncharacteristic timidity overwhelmed her, and she hid in her room, listening through the half-open door to the excited voices down the stairs.

They don't miss me at all, she thought. It was not long, though, before several were asking, "Where's Millicent?"

and Cora came to her room and commanded, "Come down and enjoy your friends."

That broke whatever spell it was that held her. Millicent came out onto the landing, waved, and for lack of anything memorable to say, called out, "Hi!"

A chorus of happy birthday's answered. She turned to go down the stairs when the terrible conviction seized her. Cora had disappeared into the kitchen. There were no grownups in sight. She knew she could still do it.

"Watch!" she shouted, clambered over the stair rail, and launched herself into space.

She heard shrieks of terror from below, felt herself plummeting, then, as soon as she knew she was falling, her imagination upheld her. The shrieks turned into awed sighs and wows, then cheers as she hovered for a moment over their heads before sailing through the open door into the yard, her party running after her, a raucous riot of jubilation. She looked down upon them all, saw their pale faces upturned like flowers to the sun, and she loved them every one.

Everything will be different now. While her friends point and marvel, Millicent McTeer becomes sky and gone to a place she knows in time where an old cabin lies ruined and tumbled in the shade of a strange tree nobody will see for long years to come. Later, the children who came to her party will try to describe to their elders what they saw that day at Hillhaven Inn. They will be interviewed by police officers and news reporters and psychiatrists. Nobody will believe them.

EPILOGUE

Mother Wandalena stirred the coals in her brazier. Insidious chill crept in from the corners of the room. Shadows lurked contagious beneath tables and chairs. Trier Abbey stood apart from the Fallen, though not entirely immune to the predations and dissolutions of that realm. In this thin place, their darkness seeped through from time to time, dimming the joy. But that was the reason the abbey was here. The instability of the region facilitated access to the lesser world. Wandalena sat down again, peered into the seerbowl on her desk, saw her round face reflected on the inky water, like a gibbous moon in a starry night. Almost immediately, Wendl's face flickered beside her own image. The coals in the brazier flared to flame, the room brightened and warmed, and she looked up to see her congregant seated across her desk.

"Brother Wendl, do I see you right?" she queried. With púca like Wendl, one could never be certain.

"Yes, Mother. Would you like me to shift?"

"No, be as you are. I think I prefer you male right now."

Wandalena wrinkled her nose. "Brother, what is that smell?"

Wendl extracted a small white carton from the depths of his voluminous robes, and held it out toward her. "Sausage and biscuits, as the Fallen say. It is delicious, Mother, whatever it is. There were two of them. I saved one for you."

Wandalena opened the carton, removed a redolent something in a waxy papery covering. She unwrapped the artifact, Wendl gestured encouragement, and Wandalena bit into the thing. Bread, dense and oily. A biscuit of sorts, and meat. Real flesh, once alive and blooded.

"Wendl, this is killed food. You know better."

Wendl shrugged. "I could not have resurrected the beast had I gone unfed. Besides, it was given me freely as I shared it with you. Would you have me reject hospitality? Which is the greater rule?"

This stuff is right tasty. Instead, Wandalena said, "Brother Wendl, you have snared me into sin and enjoyment of it. Fortunately for us, our iniquities are trite, while gjrace abounds.

"Nobody's perfect," observed Wendl pleasantly.

"That doesn't excuse us." Wandalena found it difficult to sound convincingly stern while wiping her satisfied chin.

"I make no excuses, Mother Superior," countered Wendl. "It was merely an observation."

"So tell me then, Brother Wendl," said Wandalena, as she carefully folded the bag and wrappers and deposited them in a desk drawer, "what you have you found of our Flyer among the Fallen?"

Wendl reached into his robe again, and brought out a glass jar of coins and currency and set it between them.

"You'll have to take that back." This time, Wandalena's

frown was genuine, "There is no place for greed to rest in Trier Abbey."

"By your leave," said Wendl, unperturbed, "I will. Before my return, I tried to give it away, but folk only gave me more. Whatever the Fallen have lost, generosity is not entirely dead among them. Some few of them still retain at least a remnant of the Rule."

"But they forget more than they learn," said Wandalena. "They feed on other lives, and reverence coin. You were sent to find the Flyer and bring her back into our Stream, not hoard vain riches for yourself."

Wendl retrieved from his robes the hand-lettered sign he'd displayed on the street in Drovers Gap. "As I said, Mother," he answered, unfurling the damp cardboard, by now unreadable, "none saw my invitation, several saw my money jar, but one woman saw my hunger, and I saw the Flyer in her mind."

"And did you find the Flyer?" Wandalena said, her tone impatient.

"Yes, Mother, and she is restored to the Way. It only took one of their lifetimes."

"Don't be proud with me, Brother," snapped Wandalena, striving not to sound pleased. She gestured at Wendl's jar. "Tomorrow, you must go again among the Fallen and restore your filthy lucre to whatever wrongful hands you got it from, but until evensong, you will be out in the apiary assisting Brother Owl with his bees."

"Yes, Superior," Wendl said meekly. He knew this was meant as punishment. He would never tell Wandalena, or Owl, for that matter, that he loved working among the bees, that the bees, infamous for their fierce disposition, knew he loved them and almost never stung. Ignoring Wandalena's severe scowl, Wendl the Fallen, as the other congregants jokingly referred to him behind his back, dwindled and morphed into a shining black crow and flew out the window to find Brother Owl.

———

As he stepped up onto the sidewalk, the loneliness and isolation of these souls washed over him like the cold rush of a mountain stream. Now, as much as the first time he'd entered Shadow, Wendl felt a sad astonishment at how the Fallen lived so confined by ego and self-definition, each one prisoner to themselves. They were everyone seekers, but few among them were finders. They seldom knew in their questing that they were already found.

It was worse farther in, Wendl knew. Drovers Gap lay in a thin place, which rendered it some degree of proximity. Earthlight glimmered here, faintly, like the sun in eclipse, but it was not entirely dark.

A couple of people actually spoke to him as they passed, as if they knew him. It was a town accustomed to welcoming strangers of all station. That was how this town had survived, and that made Wendl hopeful for them.

He paused in front of a foodshop. The flaked letters painted on the glass read *Wardlow's Lunch*. It didn't appear a prosperous enterprise, but three old men sat drinking coffee at the counter. One of them poured a bit from his mug into a saucer to cool it, then sipped noisily from the saucer. Nobody seemed bothered by this performance, or even to take notice of it. The storefront glass contained the sound of the extended drawn-out slurp, but Wendl could hear it in his mind. It sounded to him like an invitation. He opened the door and went in.

Today, males comprised the entire population of

Wardlow's Lunch. Wendl knew from previous observations that a few women also patronized the place. Unlike the old men who straggled in, shuffling and wheezing, leaning on their canes, flabby and stooped, their muscle long since gone to string and fat, the women carried their years with some measure of grace, lean and weathered, straighter than the males, long since having laid to earth their burden of ailing husbands, or having avoided the ravages of marriage altogether, and so entitled to live as they pleased, a kind of second youth only the aged and unencumbered ever come to know.

"Why do you have to do that, Wallace?" the man behind the counter queried as Wendl sat down beside the old man with the saucer. Everyone looked at Wallace, then, except for the questioner, who concentrated steadfastly on the ham sizzling to a shrivel on his grill. It was a bigger slice than in the biscuits the woman had given Wendl. He wondered if this was the only kind of flesh the local Fallen ate.

Wallace replaced the saucer beneath his cup. "If you didn't make this witch's brew so damned hot, Doug, I wouldn't have to saucer and blow it before I can drink the stuff."

Doug turned and presented Wallace a plate piled with the ham and fried strips of potato and what to Wendl smelled like shredded cabbage. "Then you'd complain that I served you cold coffee. You just like to draw attention to yourself. You don't come in here for lunch, Wallace. We're just a convenient audience."

Wallace picked up the slice of ham with his fingers, put it in his mouth, bit off half of it and chewed around his words. "Well, you didn't think I came in here just for the food, did you now? If you can't learn to cook better than this, you ought to hire somebody."

"I can cook," offered Wendl.

Doug stared at him, as if just realizing that Wendl was there. "I can't afford to hire a cook," gesturing at the other patrons. "Fine dining would be wasted on this bunch if I could. Rough grub and camp rations pushes the limits of their appreciation. As for that, they won't leave enough scrap behind to feed a kitten."

Doug tapped the counter in front of another customer who was totally engrossed in his sandwich, and seemingly unaware of the conversation going on at his elbow. "Connor, tell this man why you eat here every day."

Connor disengaged from his reuben deliberately, taking his time, like a man about to dismount from a horse of uncertain temperament. He looked around at the company, blinking, working his jaws while he digested the question. Doug seemed about to repeat it, when Connor swallowed his bite and wheezed thinly, as if his lungs might be depleted. "I eat here because it's cheaper than the place up the street, but I wouldn't eat bad food if Doug paid me for it." He glared at Wallace. "Wallace Paige is just a complainer. It constitutes his greatest joy. If you told him it was raining soup, he'd run outside with a fork, just so he could gripe that he didn't get his share."

Wallace seemed to take the insult with good humor, waved his fork at Wendl while he nodded toward Connor. "That there's my little brother. He's all the time on my case because our momma always loved me best."

The only other customer, not young, but not as old as the brothers, offered no word at all, shook his head, smiled to himself, stood, paid Doug for his coffee, fumbled briefly for the long walking stick he'd left beside the door, and as soon as he retrieved it, was gone.

"That Catherwood is a man of few words," observed Wallace.

"I suspect he's just saving them for his books," Doug said.

Connor emerged from his sandwich long enough to add. "At least he doesn't say all manner of stuff he don't know, like my brother does."

Doug looked at Wendl, as if he were something that had slipped Doug's mind. "What can I get for you, Friend?"

"Some of that good coffee would be welcome," said Wendl, counting out the appropriate coins from the pocket of his ragged denim jacket and laying them on the counter.

Doug brought the coffee, with a clean spoon, and packets of creamer and sugar and set it before Wendl, leaving the coins where they lay. Then he took his payment from the brothers. Wallace paid, and they left. The door closed behind them and the thick glass of the storefront reduced their continuing argument to pantomime.

"It's their chief entertainment, maybe their onliest one," observed Doug dryly. He looked Wendl up and down, not trying to be sly about it. "You look like you've logged some road time. You get a ride up the mountain?"

"I walked the whole way," said Wendl.

Doug didn't ask where from. Some of the souls passing through Drovers Gap weren't too keen on advertising their points of origin. Instead, "Where you headed from here?"

"Here's far enough for right now," Wendl said.

Doug lifted a brow in surprise. Drovers Gap was a place people passed through on their way to somewhere else, although most of them, sooner or later, came back. If Doug were inclined to wager, which he wasn't, he'd bet that Wendl was not from around here.

"You got family in town?" Doug ventured. It wasn't exactly a polite question, but any stranger in town for more than fifteen minutes was likely to hear it from at least one local.

"Somebody told me there was work here," Wendl said, a more-or-less honest answer, though Doug would not have believed the details.

Doug laughed before it occurred to him it might be cruel. "Not much in Drovers Gap for work or play," he said, as soon as he straightened his face. "There's a notice board at the post office. If there's anybody needing help, that's where you'll see."

"Thanks, Mister Doug," said Wendl, taking the final swallow of his coffee. "I'll check it out."

Wendl set down his cup, and without asking, Doug refilled it. "Want some bacon and eggs? he asked.

Wendl shook his head. "Afraid I've spent about all I'm allowed already," he said.

"No charge," Doug said. "I cooked too much for breakfast and have some left back here. If you don't eat it, I'll have to throw it out." Before Wendl could answer, Doug took a plate of scrambled eggs with two strips of bacon from the warmer and set it on the counter. Then he added a dollop of grits and a biscuit. He did not tell Wendl he had been saving it for himself.

"You'll never make a living like this," said Wendl.

"I've never made a living in this place," Doug answered. "But nobody yet has left it hungry." He pushed Wendl's coins back at him. "You'd better hold on to these, just in case somebody told you wrong."

Wendl's face burst into a radiant smile. He looked like a

saint in a renaissance painting. Doug wasn't sure if he was receiving thanks or a blessing as he turned to carry an armful of dirty crockery to the sink in his back room. As he scrubbed at a pan, he heard coins cascading into the tip jar at the end of the lunch counter.

"I said you didn't have to pay," Doug shouted, charging toward the front, wiping his hands on his apron. The front door was closing as he rounded the counter. Wendl was nowhere in sight. The quart jar, which had held three quarters, two dimes and a dollar bill from the day before was brimming with cash and coins.

ACKNOWLEDGMENTS

I'm ever thankful for the good friends who read it rough, and were brutal as only true friends dare to be, David Longley, Deb Coulter, Scott Derks, and Sharon Claybough. This book wouldn't exist without Jean Lowd and her stalwart team at Creative James Media, who homed and nurtured my Winged Child despite her indeterminate genre. John Paul Krol, through his winter hospitality at Leconte Lodge, gave me the place to write from. Jane Ella Matthews, ever my co-conspirator in my life-long campaign to subvert Western Civilization, badgered me for years to "write something," and having suffered me through seven books, has never once admitted regretting her advice.

ABOUT THE AUTHOR

Henry Mitchell reads and writes in the Blue Ridge Mountains of North Carolina.

He has written five novels and two collections of short stories.